A sparkle caught her eye, and she slid some of the heavier volumes aside. There, as if it had fallen behind the front row of books, a scarlet volume lay hidden, its cover interworked with shimmers of silver. Una brushed off the thin layer of dust that muted the striking color and traced the leafy pattern.

The book sat fat and heavy in her hand, and she paused for a moment before opening the beautiful filigreed cover. All the pages had the same pretty silver lining, and Una turned them with reverent fingers. Then she stopped. She stared hard at the first page. "The Tale of Una Fairchild," it said in a sharp black script. She read the line again, wondering if she was imagining things.

She was Una Fairchild.

MARISSA BURT

STORYBOUND

HARPER

An Imprint of HarperCollinsPublishers

Library of Congress Cataloging-in-Publication Data
Burt, Marissa.
   Storybound / Marissa Burt. — 1st ed.
   p. cm.
   Summary: Shy, twelve-year-old Una Fairchild is suddenly
transported by a mysterious book into the Land of Story, where
characters from books hope to be cast into a tale of their own, and
Una attends the Perrault Academy while trying to discover why she
is there.
   ISBN 978-0-06-202053-6 (pbk.)
   [1. Fantasy. 2. Books and reading—Fiction. 3. Characters from lit-
erature—Fiction. 4. Adventure and adventurers—Fiction.] I. Title.
PZ7.B94558St 2012   2011016619
[Fic]—dc23   CIP
                                                            AC

Typography by Alison Klapthor
20 21 22 BRR 10 9 8 7
❖
First paperback edition, 2013

for the children

Chapter 1

*U*na often told herself that she was invisible. Perhaps that was the reason people passed her in the halls, their eyes skimming over her slight form as if she were part of the scenery: a desk, a book, a classroom, a girl. It could also be the reason why Ms. McDonough, perched on her musty old pink chair, talked to her cats about Una as though Una wasn't there. "The girl sassed me today," she would say, or "The girl is quite selfish and irresponsible." But Una didn't mind too much. The cats couldn't tease Una like the kids in the other foster homes had. There had been five foster families so far, and Ms. McDonough's was the first where Una could actually be alone. Even at dinner, as they sat together at the long mahogany table, the surface polished to such a gleam that Una's big violet eyes looked back up at her, even there Ms. McDonough never acknowledged her, and Una was left to her own imagination.

It became Una's habit, on days that she felt especially invisible, to retire to the basement of the school library. Most students stayed on the main floor, grouped together at sunny tables, giggling over their math problems and English homework. But Una preferred the lower level, where she could sit undisturbed except for the odd student scurrying down to get some reference book needed for a research paper. She would tuck into her favorite desk underneath one of the high basement windows—half daydreaming, half reading—while the minutes flew by and she wondered what it would be like to live a different life.

One autumn day Una made her way down to this spot, humming off-key. She rounded the corner and stopped. There, at her desk, in her particular place, someone sat writing furiously.

It looked like he was wearing the sort of costume she read about in her favorite fantasy novels. The hood of his cloak was pulled up, and it made a little point at the top. Una didn't mind that some other kid had decided to claim a spot in the library basement. *Except that it's my desk.* She glanced at her watch. There was only half an hour left before her next class. She marched up to him and cleared her throat.

The boy didn't even look up.

She coughed louder. Either the boy couldn't hear or he was purposely ignoring her. "You're in my spot," she said pointedly.

The boy kept writing. Una sighed. *It's not like I can lift him up and* make *him move.* For a minute, she imagined what that would look like. Her hoisting the cloaked boy and tossing him to the side, a chorus of cheers applauding her. With one more glance at the occupied desk, she turned and left the row. She'd have to find a different spot for today. After all, there were plenty to choose from.

But she was wrong. She peered down the next row. An identical brown hood bent low over the next desk. And the same across the aisle.

Una threaded her way through the center rows of abandoned old periodicals. She passed musty shelf after musty shelf, and finally settled on a friendly-looking chair in a forgotten corner. Una fitted herself into the small space and scanned the nearby shelves. She knew the books in her old spot well, their Dewey decimal numbers reassuring in their sameness: 372.642

Pho—402.3 Gri. These books were strangers, standing proudly with their battered covers stiff and thick. Una ran her fingers over the faded leather and cloth bindings.

A sparkle caught her eye, and she slid some of the heavier volumes aside. There, as if it had fallen behind the front row of books, a scarlet volume lay hidden, its cover interworked with shimmers of silver. Una brushed off the thin layer of dust that muted the striking color and traced the leafy pattern. She followed the brightness of the silver over to the spine. There was no title, no numbers to mark the book's place in the ordered library catalog.

"Curious," Una murmured. She flipped the book every which way but found no inscription. It sat fat and heavy in her hand, and she paused for a moment before opening the beautiful filigreed cover. All the pages had the same pretty silver lining, and Una turned them with reverent fingers. Then she stopped. She stared hard at the first page. "The Tale of Una Fairchild," it said in a sharp black script. She read the line again, wondering if she was imagining things. *She* was Una Fairchild.

How many Una Fairchilds could there be? She supposed

there could have been a real Oliver Twist who eagerly read of the little boy in Dickens's tale. Was there an actual Harry Potter who, on his eleventh birthday, wondered if something fabulous was about to happen? An Anne Shirley, perhaps, with big starry eyes, who laughed over the misadventures of the girl who shared her name? *It's got to be a coincidence.* Even so, Una's stomach was unsettled with a queer twisty feeling as she flipped the page and began to read:

Lord Peter had been riding for a very long time. The sun was just rising when he left camp that morning, and now he could see it sinking lower and lower on the horizon.

"Lord Peter!" a voice called, and Lord Peter looked back over his shoulder at his companion. She was clad in a pure white riding gown, her skirts trailing over her white mare.

"Yes, Milady Snow?" He sighed and rolled his eyes. "What does the Lady require?"

The Lady slowed her horse down to a walk. She gasped a little, as fair maidens are wont to do. "I pray thee, kind sir," she said, flashing him a brilliant smile, "mayhap we could rest awhile?"

Peter gritted his teeth. "Like we've done every fifteen minutes?" he muttered under his breath.

Lady Snow made a face at him.

He glared back at her. "As you wish," he said formally, half bowing in his saddle and pointing off into the distance. "I know of a cave a little farther on where we could shelter. Would a cave meet the Lady's needs?"

"I suppose so." She frowned at him. "But don't you think it would be better if—"

Lord Peter left his Lady making suggestions to the air and urged his stallion onward. They had entered the forest around midday, the overarching shade a welcome change from the hot sun. Now, the trees loomed in the growing twilight, and small bugs whined in Lord Peter's ears. He waved them off and dug his heels into the stallion's flanks.

"Come, Milady Snow," he called back to her. "The final test must lie ahead."

After a short while they arrived in a small clearing, and Lord Peter dismounted, offering his hand to help his companion down. She took it, but Lord Peter's grip wavered, and Lady Snow ended up in a heap on her hands and knees. She stood and brushed off

her skirts. When she looked up, her brilliant grin was
plastered back in place.

Lord Peter bared his teeth in what passed for a
smile. "Are you well, milady?" he asked.

"Quite," was all she said. Lord Peter lit a dead
branch and held it aloft as he made his way into the
cave. Lady Snow joined him, swatting gracelessly at
the bugs around her head. As her gaze followed the
flickering torchlight, it landed on the cave's far wall.
She grabbed Lord Peter's arm.

"What—?"

"What are you reading?"

Una blinked, disoriented, and looked up to see the
hooded figure who had stolen her spot. He was standing
at the end of the row, a tall shadow that blocked the
aisle.

Una frowned. He wasn't going to take this desk,
too. "*I'm* working here," she said in as frosty a tone as
possible. "You'll have to go somewhere else."

"No," the boy said, moving toward her, and his
voice set the hairs on the back of her neck crawling.
"You will."

Chapter 2

Una's heart pounded. Her corner suddenly felt very small, and the walls of books leaned in, threatening to trap her. The boy's face seemed to shift—a trick of the light perhaps—and his features were more angled than before. His pupils changed, widened like a cat's, until they were two black orbs that locked on to Una's face. Una couldn't look away. She stared into his awful eyes, and she saw images: a starry sky, the ocean, a tiny baby. They flickered faster: a giant tree, a pile of ash, a black dragon rimmed in blue, a forest. She lost track of time as faces she didn't recognize spun together with lights and colors . . . and, then, it all stopped.

She was on her knees. The boy in the cloak reached out a hand and raised her up. The air around him was icy cold.

"It is time," he said. He bent and retrieved the scarlet book from where it lay on the floor and handed it to her. A current of wintry air swirled around them, and Una stared at the now sinister-looking book. Before she could say anything, the boy clapped his hands together. The basement echoed with a resounding crash. Una stumbled and fell back onto the library shelf. There was a blinding flash of white, followed by darkness. The fluorescent bulbs flickered, then they were back on, filling the basement with harsh light.

"Time for what?" Una whispered, but the boy was gone. She peeked around the edge of the library row. The boy was nowhere to be seen. How had he done that? She tightened her hold on the book, and its hard edges pressed into her palms. Had she imagined the whole thing? She glanced at the book. It felt warm in her hands, like it had been left out in the sun. She settled down onto the worn carpet and once more opened the cover.

The Tale of Una Fairchild. She studied the title again. It made no sense. Was the girl with Lord Peter, Lady Snow, also called Una Fairchild? She wiped her fingers on her plaid uniform skirt and opened the book halfway through. She slammed it shut. Counting to three, she opened it again, this time near the end.

All the pages were blank. She flipped backward and forward through the book. Blank. Blank. Blank. She found the pages she had read earlier. She skimmed through them and turned the page. Still blank.

Una found the very spot at which she had been interrupted and read through the paragraph. As she finished, she saw something shimmer just below the last line. But when she looked closely, it was just a matte page. Una loosened the blue tie that now felt tight around her white blouse collar. She continued to read. There was Lord Peter lighting the torch. There was Lady Snow looking across the cave. The paper was hot against her fingers, like it was a living, active thing. Una's stomach twisted again. Suddenly the world was spinning, rows of old library books whirling in a cloud around her head. Una's last thought was that at least she could get out of her next class because she was sick, when everything went black.

Some time later Una awoke with a pounding headache. The ground felt cold beneath her. She was sitting on a circular stone dais. It was smooth, worn, and looked very old. At its edges four arches stretched up to meet at the center of a domed ceiling. There were no lamps, yet everything was bathed in a faint, glowing light. The air smelled spicy, like cinnamon and ginger.

Una sat very still. Where was she?

She rubbed her bottom and winced as her muscles protested. Everything ached. She felt the smooth fabric beneath her hand and glanced down. She didn't remember trading her school uniform for a gray woolen dress and silver cloak. Neither had she strapped the little jeweled dagger to her waist.

She peered around the room. She knew she wasn't crazy, and she was sure she wasn't dreaming. She must have found some sort of secret passageway out of the library. Una stood up and made her way to the edge of the dais. Her eyes adjusted to the dimness, and she could see a door in the shadows off to her left. Approaching it, Una saw thick beams running every which way over its weathered surface.

Taking a deep breath, Una tried the handle. It was unlocked. She pushed the door open slowly and crept through, thankful for the soft glowing light behind her. She found herself in what looked like an underground tunnel. The air smelled earthy and wet. As she moved farther from the door, the cave grew darker until she could hardly see at all. Una felt her way past several openings that seemed to be smaller tunnels off the one she was stumbling down. In the distance, she could see a flickering light and moved toward it. As she got closer, she heard voices.

"I told you to stick with me," someone was saying. "I can't always be looking over my shoulder for you. You've got to keep up." He sounded angry.

Una ducked into a side passage as whoever was speaking drew near. She could hear a different voice respond, starting as a hiss and building to a grating whine. Una realized that the pair must be very close to her now, and she held her breath, listening.

". . . like you're supposed to," the whiny voice said. "I'm a *Lady*, you imbecile, and you have to treat me like one!" The whiner cleared her throat and said loudly, "I do appreciate your valor, Sir Knight, but fear I do not have your alacrity. I beg of you to slow down." Una snorted—*Who talks like that anyway?*—then covered her mouth with one hand, but she wasn't quick enough.

"Shut up!" the first voice said. "Someone's there."

Chapter 3

$\mathcal{P}$eter swung the torch from side to side. If someone else was in the passageway with them, he wanted to know about it. He could tell that the final test was coming but had no idea what it would be. *And Snow's going on about being a Lady.* He inched forward, thrusting the torch into a side passageway. *Why did I have to get paired up with her?* He heard Snow start to laugh as the torchlight illuminated the tunnel.

Peter stepped back. In front of him stood not some threatening creature or dark wizard, but a girl. He guessed that she must be about his own age, though she was shorter than him, and her silvery cloak looked too big for her slight form. Her long dark hair was drawn back into a thick braid, which hung over one shoulder. She locked her big violet eyes on his face, darted a panicky look over to Snow, and opened and closed her mouth like a gaping fish. Then, before Peter could say a word, she turned and ran.

Peter snarled over at Snow, "We need to catch her! Keep up this time, or I'm leaving you behind." He heard Snow's answering sigh as he took off after the girl. Peter sprinted down the corridor. *Why would the examiners send in a* girl *for the final test?* That made no sense. Maybe she had some sort of special powers. Breathing heavily, he burst into a large opening with three tunnels leading off in different directions.

Snow arrived in the same space less than a minute later. Peter stood for a moment, his torch's light casting the corners into shadow. Which path had the girl taken? "Any ideas?" he asked Snow.

She shrugged and examined a broken fingernail.

"Trying to figure out a ladylike way to catch your breath?" Peter snapped. Before Snow could respond, a scream pierced the cave's stillness.

"After you," Snow said, and Peter tore off toward the passage on the right.

Holding his torch high in one hand, Peter sped down the path and shot out into an open cavern. Off to his left, the girl had pressed herself against the cavern's wall. She stood frozen, a wavering dagger held shakily in front of her. And he could see why.

Between Peter and the girl, blocking any hope of escape, crouched a large, scaly dragon. On one side of the girl, the floor dropped sharply into the rushing underground river that ran the entire length of the cavern. She couldn't go that way. On the other was a huge boulder, which, unless she could climb it, effectively pinned her up against the wall.

This had to be the final test. He'd never heard of the examiners sending *two* Ladies for the Hero to rescue, but it didn't matter now. As he crept up behind the dragon, it swiveled its head, opened one lazy eye, and rose to its full height. Red scales layered over black, and the dragon stretched up and up, hissing and snorting fiery breaths in Peter's direction. Then it reared up, roaring, and began pacing back and forth, its talons clicking ominously as it moved. He could hear Snow grumbling behind him, and he glanced over his shoulder at her.

"I am *so* ready to be done," she muttered. "Well?" She picked at a fingernail. "Hadn't you better get on with it?"

"Some help you are." Peter squared his shoulders and turned to face the beast.

"Watch out!" the other girl cried. She flailed her dagger at the dragon with one hand and tried to shoo them back down the passage with the other. "Run! Go! You can still escape!"

The dragon hissed. Its leathery mouth spread wide over yellowed fangs and filled the cavern with an awful stench. *Surely the girl isn't going to . . . ?*

"Stop, fair maiden! I will save you from this foul beast!" Peter yelled. He knew that sounded fake, but the examiners would just have to deal with it. They weren't the ones who had to put up with two Ladies. He looked back at Snow and sighed. She was filing her nails in the corner. *No doubt I'll lose points for that too.*

The dragon hissed once more, spraying the room with an awful-smelling green mist. Peter gagged. *Time to get this over with.* Just then, the beast opened its mouth, and shiny, smaller dragons began pouring out, mewling angrily.

"Gross!" the new girl said, and pressed backward, but Peter could see there was nowhere for her to go. The smaller dragons began to creep about, and a few fluttered toward Peter on uncoordinated wings.

"Back, foul fiends!" Peter cried as he crept closer. Nothing happened. He tried again, louder this time.

"Halt, I say!" The big dragon belched and lay back down.

"Are you kidding me?" the girl shouted. "I don't think dragons speak English!" She slashed the air in front of her, trying to fend off one of the little dragons that was piloting toward her with teeth bared and claws out.

"And I didn't think Ladies fought dragons," Peter said under his breath. He edged closer. *Rescue the Lady first. Then take care of the dragon.* That boulder looked climbable. If he put his hands just there . . . He pulled himself up and felt with one booted foot along the rock face until he caught a toehold. The stone dug into his palms. His arms shook under the strain. He heard another dragon belch, and the air grew hot around him. Fire, this time. Slowly, painfully, he made his way higher. One more reach, and he would be there.

"Hey, where'd you go?" the girl's voice asked from the other side of the boulder, breaking his concentration. "Do you have a sword or something?" He slipped, the rock shredding his fingertips as he scrabbled for any hold. A jagged edge scraped his cheek. He kicked his feet, and then one hand caught. His body swung out to the side until he could get his balance back. His fingers burned. He hung there for a moment and began the painstaking climb again. One hand, then the other. *Just a little farther.* He pulled up over the top of the boulder and peered down. The girl was slashing madly now, striking at any dragon that came close. This time, her voice didn't catch him off guard.

"Are you still there? If you're not going to run," she yelled out into the cave, "get your butt over here and help me out!"

Peter scowled down at the top of her head. "Your wish is my command, fair lady."

She jumped and looked straight up at him. "How did you get up there?" She didn't see the vicious little beast creep up to her foot and sink its teeth into one ankle. "Ow!" she yelled.

Peter pulled out his smallest throwing knife. The tiny dragon never had a chance.

"Here! Take my hand," Peter ordered. The girl wasted no time. She sheathed her dagger and clambered over the dead little dragon and up the bottom of the rock. Bracing one leg against the cavern wall, she reached up to grab hold. He pulled hard, and the next minute she was beside him, gasping for breath.

"Thanks," she managed, and wiped a grubby palm across her forehead.

"Wait here," Peter said. He slid over the side of the

boulder. This was taking too long. They had to move faster.

"Jump!" he called up to the girl once he reached the bottom. She slowly got to her feet and peered down at him. *Why isn't she just doing what I say? Everyone knows the damsel in distress is supposed to . . .* Peter gritted his teeth. *Maybe she's picky about her dialogue.* "I mean, won't you descend, fair lady?"

The girl's mouth dropped open. "Whatever," she said as she inched out toward the edge. She hesitated for a moment, and a blast of dragon air propelled her from behind. Peter was ready to catch her, but he had no idea a small girl would feel so heavy. She landed in his arms and knocked him to the ground.

He could hear Snow's laughter from somewhere behind him. "Very nice," she said. "Very graceful." This was punctuated by polite applause.

Peter helped the girl up and pointed her toward Snow, who was now emitting periodic ladylike gasps of terror over by the cavern's entrance. But the girl didn't move.

By this time, the little dragons had regrouped. Some flew crookedly up and over the boulder in their general direction. The others were rolling and somersaulting toward them.

The girl pulled out her dagger. "This is so weird."

"Your dialogue," Peter whispered meaningfully. He drew his sword. The girl pointed her dagger at him.

"Did you just say *dialogue*?" She turned to knife another little dragon, which curled up, making sad, hurt sounds. The large dragon roared, and spurts of hot, fiery flame shot around the cavern.

"You *are* a Lady?" Peter asked.

The girl shifted her dagger to the other hand. "Look, if you're just going to stand around gaping and blathering about ladies . . . give me that." Before he could protest, she grabbed his sword and whirled away, cutting a small dragon in half as she ran across the cavern. The big dragon now stood in front of Snow, who looked unfazed by the flames that ended inches from her face. She was filing her nails again.

"Good Sir Knight," Snow called in a singsong voice without even looking up, "your assistance is required!"

Suddenly, the dragon spun around more quickly than seemed possible for such a large beast. The girl froze, Peter's sword now hanging loosely by her side. The dragon darted forward, spurting alternate blasts of hot flame and green slime as it moved. It was nearly upon her. *Why isn't she moving?*

Quick as a wink, Peter ran by, snatching his sword out of her unresisting hand. He passed the boulder and scooped up the forgotten torch. Holding the sword high in one hand, he swung the torch back and forth in front of the dragon with the other. The beast reared back to roar again, and Peter threw the torch at its feet, sending slimy little dragons scuttling for cover. The huge dragon looked down at this new nuisance and, in that moment, Peter darted up with the sword and slammed it with all his might in between the dragon's front legs.

Chapter 4

*E*verything froze. And then began to flicker and fade away. The sound of mewling little dragons grew tinny and disappeared. The moist cave air grew warmer. The stalactites overhead turned to stone arches and smoothed out. The torch sputtered and died, replaced by the strange glowing light.

Una looked around, speechless. *I must be going mad after all!* First, there was the giant dragon to come to terms with. And then, the disappearing cave. But what sent chills all over her was the pair standing across the way, arguing in loud voices. She knew that it was Lord Peter who had saved her in the cavern, and the girl with him must be Lady Snow. But knowing didn't make it any clearer. *You don't meet people from books! It just can't happen!*

Lady Snow jabbed a very pale finger at Lord Peter's face. "Enough already," she said. "I don't give a squirrel's behind who she is. The point is we've already failed. Don't you see that? It's over!" She shot Una an icy look before flouncing off through a stone doorway.

Peter screwed up his face at Snow's retreating figure and turned to look at Una. "Thanks a lot," he said. "What were you doing back there? Why couldn't you just be normal?"

Una stared at him. *Didn't we just escape dying a horrible death? Didn't we just fight a disgusting dragon? Didn't I just kill a bunch of little dragons with my own two hands? Didn't I nearly die, because you and your idiot girlfriend stood there saying "Sir" and "Lady" until the dragon had multiplied—no* spawned—*more dragons?*

"Normal?" Una said, her voice rising. "You think *anything* about this is *normal*? You do nothing . . . I . . . the dragons . . . with my dagger . . . the cave . . . your story."

"Slow down," Peter said. "You're not making any sense."

"We almost died back there!" she finally yelled.

Peter's voice was very soft. "Is this your first practical?"

"What?" Una could hear herself screech.

"I figured as much." He gave her a little pat on the shoulder. "You can't die in a practical," he said. "The professors wouldn't really let anything bad happen to you. You're just overreacting." He continued with the patting, not noticing that Una had stiffened her arm beneath his hand.

"You'll be all right," he said. "Though you might have to retake the whole level because of your rule breaking. Come to think of it, I might have to as well." He stopped patting and gave her a stony glare. "Why did you have to go and fight the dragons anyway? That's the Hero's job!"

Una stared right back. "Overreacting?" she said in a deadly calm voice. "*Overreacting?* You're the one talking about examinations! Look who's not making any sense now, *Lord* Peter!" Una almost never swore, and now she had to clamp her mouth down tight to keep from letting out a string of the most horrible words. Her jaw ached with the effort.

"How do you know my name?" Peter asked. His unfriendly stare had given way to a slightly less hostile look of curiosity.

Should she tell him? *Oh, well. Here goes nothing.*

"You . . . are in a story," she finally said in the kindest and gentlest way she knew how.

Peter yawned. "And?"

"No. No! Don't you see?" Una waved her hands in a big circle all around the cave. "A *story*!"

Peter looked at her hands until Una slowly lowered them. "Of course we're in Story," he said. "This *is* the practical examination." His forehead creased in concern. "Are you all right? Did you study too much? Maybe you should sit down." He looked at Una as if she was very fragile.

Somehow the fact that Peter wasn't surprised worried Una more than anything else. *He knows he's in a story, and he doesn't* care. "The story," Una began. "I was reading it at my study desk—no, wait, that weird boy was there. I was in a new spot at the library, and that's when I read about you and Lady Snow, and the lights flashed, and then the pages were blank. None of this makes any sense. Maybe I'm sick or something." She trailed off when she saw Peter furrow his brow. "What?" she said.

"Come here." Peter walked over to an archway tucked off to one side. In the small room that lay beyond was an engraved pedestal. As they moved closer, Una could see a stack of papers.

Peter ran his fingers down the first few lines of text. "Well, I don't see anything about a library or flashing lights."

"What?" Una nudged him out of the way and began to read. "This is the same story I was reading in the library!" she said. "Look, it's just as I told you. Here you are in the forest, talking to Lady Snow." Una paused, rifling through the pages. "You know, the odd thing was that further along, the pages were—" She gave a sharp gasp, bending closer to the paper. "Wait, that's *my* name!"

Una rubbed her eyes and reread the script in front of her. There was her name, no mistake about it, right on the page. The description of the book Una sounded just like her. There she was creeping down the passageway in her silver cloak. Hearing voices and hiding out of sight. Meeting Peter and Snow in the torchlight. Una stared at the words in horror.

"But I was reading this story at school! How can I actually be *in* it?" She didn't want to look at Peter, because she didn't know what she might see on his face. Pity? Shock? She read on and found an account of the events that had just happened. Or almost as they had happened. "I did *not* look like a gaping fish!" she exclaimed.

Peter stepped up beside her. He had none of the expressions she expected. Instead, he was attempting to hide a smile. "You know, the record is pretty accurate," he said. "Really. If it says you looked like a fish—well, you looked like a fish. Una. Is that your name?" He ran his hand over the open page and smiled at her.

Una looked carefully at him. He was about a head taller than her. His floppy brown hair was now streaked with dirt and ash. The blood from the cut on his cheek had dried, tracing a dark line across his face. His brown eyes looked kind, but there was a suspicious twinkle in them as he continued to talk.

"Don't worry," Peter went on. "I don't think they'll mark off for acting frightened. It's only when you hide away because of it that it affects your score."

"Why are you pretending that everything is okay?" she said in a near whisper. She swatted at his hand, which had returned to patting her on the shoulder. "We just missed being eaten by a dragon, if you remember, and your Lady friend went off and ditched us." Her voice went up a notch. "My name is appearing in some random story, not to mention the fact that I'm with you in this, well, wherever I am, and *you are talking about some stupid test?*"

Peter snatched back the offending hand and stared at her. The muscles in his jaw clenched, but he said in a very polite voice, "Do you really not know where you are?"

"Right. I've just been pretending this whole time." She smoothed down her hair, which was sticking out every which way from the now messy braid, and took a deep breath. *After all, Peter is just trying to help.* She began again. "I'm sorry. No. I don't know where I am. I don't know what I'm doing here. Like I said, I was reading a story about two travelers." She turned back to him and took up the papers from the stand. "This story. But I had it in the library at my school. And the next thing I know, I'm in the room out there. Fighting dragons." The tears stung the backs of her eyes, but she willed herself not to cry. It was very quiet. "And now, the story is changing."

"Curiouser and curiouser," said Peter. "And you've never been in this room before?"

"No." Una sat down next to the pedestal, clutching the papers to her chest. *This must be what crazy feels like.* She tried to breathe in and out slowly but could only manage shallow gasps. "Do you know what's happening to me?" she finally asked in a small voice.

Peter was running out of ideas. "I think it must be all the stress of the practical," he said again in what he hoped was a reassuring voice. "Please say something, Una." She hadn't moved from her spot on the floor, where she now sat staring at the exam record. He hated it when girls were upset. He only had one sister, Rosemary. She was the youngest, barely toddling around, and he couldn't stand it when she cried. He took a deep breath. With Rosemary it always helped to distract her, get her thinking about something else.

"Last year, for my first practical, I was so nervous I couldn't sleep the night before." He eyed Una. She seemed to be listening. "My roommate had to get up and help me recite the Table of Fairy Tale Elements." He smiled, remembering. "And it wasn't until we reached Witch's Lair that I could finally fall asleep." He looked over at Una, who had set the papers aside, and kept talking. "Good thing, too! The final test in that one *was* a Witch's Lair. And see, it all turned out right. I passed and everything."

Una frowned. "Table of Fairy Tale Elements? Like

chemistry? I hate chemistry."

"Chemistry! Not likely." Now to keep her distracted. "Though if I knew some potion making, it might've helped with the witch. No, that exam was for Beginning Heroics. We just finished the one for Advanced Heroics. I didn't see you in class this term," he said, hoping she wouldn't start yelling again.

Una looked up. "You're a student?"

He nodded.

"At Saint Anselm's?" she asked.

Peter crossed his arms over his chest. *So that's it! She's from another school!* "This is the Perrault exam wing," Peter said. "There must have been some mix-up with the exam." *Now I'm getting somewhere.* "And you're sure you've never been here?" He waved one hand around the little room.

Una scanned the area. "I'm sure."

"Let's go through it step by step." Peter paced back and forth. "If you haven't been to this Tale station before, you're definitely not from our school," he reasoned. "What kind of Tale were you in before?"

"Um . . . ," Una said.

Peter tried a different tactic. "Well, what do we know? You're a . . ." He hesitated. He was about to ask if she was a Lady, but earlier Una hadn't responded so well to that vein of questioning.

He stopped and frowned at his boots, which were spotted with dried dragon blood. He knew from her dress that she was from the Fantasy District. That was easy enough to tell. But the type of character she was training for was more difficult. If she wasn't a Lady, could she be a Princess? He thought of her dialogue. *Not likely.* He mentally ran down the list of official character types he had memorized last year and examined her. *Village Girl?* He shrugged. *Maybe, but she seems too bright for that.* It was possible she was a Fairy Godmother, although those girls were usually plumper. He squinted at her face, but he didn't see any warts or moles under all the dragon soot. *Most likely not an Ugly Stepsister.* He paused. *What if she's a Villain? An Enchantress?*

"Why are you looking at me like that?" Una snapped.

"I give up," Peter said, spreading his hands wide. "What type are you? You said you weren't a Lady, but I can't come up with anything else."

Una frowned at him. "Type?" She stood up, and it was her turn to pace across the little room. "Look, Peter, I don't know what you're talking about. I don't know anything about heroics or Tale stations or types. I'm just an ordinary seventh grader who got up and went to her school this morning and, instead of sitting by myself eating my lunch, I'm here listening to you talk about witches and fairy tales and exams."

Something clicked for Peter in the middle of Una's speech. "Of course!" he exclaimed. "Chemistry! The library! You're a Modern!" That would explain her refusal to speak in proper Fantasy dialogue. "But why are you wearing those clothes?" he asked. "If you're not in the Fantasy District, I mean, how did you end up in our practical?"

Una rubbed her temples. "I don't know what you're talking about! I'm not a modern! I'm not in any district, whatever that is. I'm just Una!" She tucked her arms in tight across her chest, eyes cast down to the floor. "I wish I'd never found that stupid book."

Peter paused, digesting the weight of her words. "A *book*? You were reading the story in a book?"

"That's what I've been saying!"

Peter took a step back from her. "You never said anything about a book." His voice sounded funny, like he was hearing someone else talk. He swallowed. "You mean you're *not* training to be a character?" he asked in a near whisper. If she wasn't a character, if she didn't know about types, if she wasn't at Perrault, if she had never been to a Tale station before . . .

He moved closer to her and laid a hand on her shoulder. "Don't worry, Una," he said softly. "It's going to be all right." But even as he spoke the reassuring words, he knew that they were lies. He had heard the stories before, of course, but . . .

Una uncrossed her arms and looked up at him. "You believe me?" she asked.

Peter nodded. "Una," he said in a very serious voice. "I think you've been Written In."

Chapter 5

What is *that* supposed to mean?" Una said. She stared hard at Peter. "Why are you talking about writing? I told you I read about you in a book. The same story as this one." She held up the sheaf of papers she had taken from the pedestal.

"No," Peter said. "Not the same. That isn't a book. It's just an exam. Don't you see? You've been Written In to our world!" He ran his hands through his brown hair. "Professor Perregrin talked about it once in Backstory class. Something about how WIs had a special purpose. The Muses were the only ones who could Write people In. And I know they brought WIs here to help them, but he never said—"

Una seized on his words. "Brought here? Where is here?"

Peter rubbed his forehead. "This is the land of Story. I guess you must be from the land of the Readers. That's where the old WIs used to come from, I know that for sure. What I can't remember is what happened to them after the Muses broke their—"

"What do you mean you can't remember? This is important!"

"It's not like anyone wants to talk about how the Muses ran Story, Una. And no one's been Written In since then." He shook his head. "I mean, if someone has been Written In again after all this time . . ." He frowned down at her. "You *are* telling the truth, aren't you?"

"Why would I lie?" she asked in a quiet voice.

Peter took up his irritating pacing again, this time behind her. "If you're not lying, then I wonder what's going on." Peter was talking very fast now. "*No one* will believe me. I can hardly believe I'm actually talking to a WI. I wonder how—"

"*Peter,*" Una interrupted him. She didn't care what Peter wondered or who would believe him. She gripped the stack of papers tighter. "If you're right, and I've actually been Written In to a book—"

"Exam."

"Whatever." Una waved the top page in front of his face. "What I need to know is *who* wrote this?"

"The Talekeepers, and I don't think . . ." Peter stopped pacing, a look of horror on his face. "Oh no!" He snatched the papers from her hand and nearly dragged her to the door. "I need to go get my grades. They'll take off if I'm late! Come on!"

Peter wiped his hands on his tunic. The sweat smeared in with the dragon blood and made his palms feel grimy. He had left Una in the Tale station and sprinted over to the review panel. Now he was standing in a large room in front of an imposing table. A Talekeeper and two professors loomed behind it and looked down at him with disapproving faces. And it wasn't just any Talekeeper, it was Mr. Elton, the Tale Master himself.

"*And* you neglected to slay the smaller dragons and protect the Lady." Mr. Elton spoke in a grating voice that always seemed too loud. He had combed his stringy gray hair back from a very straight part that ran down the middle of his scalp. Round spectacles perched on his stubby nose, and he seemed to be peering down at everything. Because he was so short this had the odd effect of making him tilt his head back and squint at

people. His breath puffed his oversized mustache as he
ticked off a list in front of him. "Improper use of genre
dialogue. Unheroic attitude toward the Lady. Use of
sarcasm. Lateness to review panel. The list goes on and
on."

Peter clenched his jaw. If only he could defend
himself properly. The Tale Master's disapproval surely
meant a failing grade.

"And then there's the matter of the girl," a professor
Peter had only seen once before said. She had the exam
spread out in front of her, and her beady eyes looked
piercingly at Peter, who shifted from one foot to the
other.

"Is she a classmate of yours?" Beady Eyes asked.

Little drops of sweat formed on Peter's forehead.
Think. You can't just tell them that Una's been Written In.
Peter had told Una it hadn't happened in a long time.
He hadn't told her that back before the Unbinding, all
the WIs had been killed when the Muses broke their
oaths. Even though Story was safe from the Muses
now, Peter knew the Talekeepers wouldn't welcome a
WI after everything that had happened.

Of the three, Elton alone was a Talekeeper. But who
was to say the other examiners weren't his friends? And

it wasn't just the Talekeepers. There had been a near riot after it came out that Professor Perregrin had spent that one class teaching the Perrault students about the old ways of the Muses, and he had been dismissed soon after. If people could get that upset over the mention of the old ways, what would they do if they met a WI? Peter just needed to convince the examiners that there had been some sort of mix-up, and they might leave Una alone. Maybe then he'd be able to find out what was really going on. He swallowed and tried to smile at them, but he had waited too long.

Beady Eyes' expression grew sterner. "Well?" she pressed. "This is not a difficult question. Is she a classmate of yours or not?"

Peter nodded slowly, then shook his head.

Beady Eyes clicked her tongue reprovingly.

Peter knew they could check the school records and see at once that Una didn't belong. "She's a friend," he finally said. "Um . . . visiting. And she wanted to see a . . . I mean my . . . exam." He was no good at making things up in the moment. Surely they would see through such a flimsy lie. Peter looked appealingly at the stick-thin man with a shock of white hair who was sitting at the other end of the table. Professor

Edenberry was his Outdoor Experiential Questing instructor. The corners of Professor Edenberry's mouth barely turned up. But he didn't say anything.

Then, Mr. Elton surprised him. He gave Peter a knowing smile. "Ah. Young love," he said in his loud, unpleasant voice. "Wanted to impress the girl, eh? Wanted to be *her* Hero?" He laughed. "I guess she wasn't so . . . impressed." His laugh turned into a guffaw.

Peter glared at Mr. Elton. Like he would sneak a girl in to show off! He began to protest and might even have told them the truth, but the beady-eyed examiner interrupted him.

"Childish pranks," she said. "In *my* day we didn't do such things. In *my* day, I wouldn't have risked my potential career on such a foolish idea. Sneaking someone into an examination indeed!"

Peter balled his hands into fists. *I bet in* your *day you weren't planning on a glorious career as a practical examiner.*

"You fail this examination." Mr. Elton sat back and rested his chubby hands on his stomach contentedly. "With no possibility for a retake."

Peter kept his face neutral. He would not give them the satisfaction of seeing his disappointment. For Una's sake, he guessed it was a good thing that the examiners hadn't pressed him further—that they seemed to buy the idea that he *liked* her. *But failing a practical? In Heroics?* He didn't want to think about what his parents would say. He scowled.

Mr. Elton saw Peter's expression. "And . . . detention with me, I think. For the rest of the term." Apparently, things could get worse after all. No doubt Elton would spend the whole detention prattling on about Peter's family connections like he always did. Just the other day, Elton had caught him in the hall to ask after his parents. Maybe next time Peter could tell Elton how happy his parents were that he'd failed their son. Elton's face looked as though he expected Peter to thank him for such a delightful present. Peter said nothing.

"My office. Tomorrow morning. Six o'clock sharp." Elton smiled. "That will be all."

Una tried to look in every direction at once. Peter had explained that she would have to stay at the Tale station while he went to get the results of his examination and had left her on a bench in the middle of a huge hallway that was lined with doors of all sorts. There were arched doors and studded spiked doors, doors reaching high out of sight and tiny mouseholes. The door she and Peter had exited some time before was made of weathered wood, and, after they had passed through, iron bars had clattered down and locked into the floor.

A constant stream of people passed by her: some entering doors, some exiting, and some waiting outside, calling across the great hallway in loud voices. A woman in a pink ruffled ball gown waved to a sailor. A mummy was asking an old grizzled cowboy for directions. A whole troop of girls in starched blue uniforms giggled as they passed her. Una looked in the opposite direction and saw a small dog barking at a wizard wearing long purple robes with stars all over them.

Peter had made it sound like he was studying to be a character in a book. *Are all of these people characters in stories?* She turned it over in her mind, trying to make it fit. When she read a book, she did sort of see the characters. And when she reached the end of the book, she always felt that their stories must go on. Could it be that whenever she read a book, characters in this world had actually played out the story?

She thought about the papers from the pedestal.

Peter had said the examiners would need to review them. Would he bring the packet of papers back? Una wasn't sure what she would find if she read them. Would there be more about how she had fought the dragons in the cave? Or would reading it somehow take her back to the library? She ran her fingers along the cuff of her sleeve and looked around the wide hall again. Whatever was happening to her now, whatever awaited her in those pages, Una knew she wasn't ready to go back to her old life. *At least not yet.*

A willowy woman dressed all in green walked over and sat down uncomfortably close to Una on the bench. The stranger combed her fingers through long narrow braids that fell to her waist. "Have you seen a tree?" she asked Una in a whispery voice. "It's small, about so high"—she held up an unimaginably long hand with bony fingers—"with twelve branches that have green buds."

"Um," Una said, staring at the woman's fingers.

The woman pulled out a small parcel. "Care for some mulch?" she asked, poking the package toward Una.

Una wrinkled her nose at the earthy smell. "No, thanks."

The woman began to eat. She looked at Una with gold-speckled green eyes.

"I'm sorry you can't find your tree." Una avoided her gaze.

"That's okay," the woman whispered. "I was only trying to transplant it. It would do so much better in a moonlight garden, you see."

"Ah." Una wished that Peter would return. She watched a soldier in fatigues stop and talk to a vampire.

"I'd only just begun working in a new Tale." The green woman chewed slowly, and her teeth grated on the grainy dirt. "I had to leave in the first chapter. My tree was dying. And no one would do anything about it. What was I to do, I ask you?"

Una hoped she didn't expect a response. What if she said the wrong thing? Would the woman know that she didn't belong here? Instead of answering, she stared hard at the pair of characters in front of her.

"I first went to the canteen, if you can believe it. . . ." The soldier laughed and nudged the vampire with a camouflaged arm. The vampire flashed two very long teeth, and his laugh came out more like a spooky moan.

"And then the Talekeeper fired me, all because I

couldn't find my tree. . . ." The woman was prattling on. Una perked her ears up at that, but she heard nothing more about the Talekeepers. While the woman talked rapturously about her tree, Una glanced behind her at a man clad all in black. He was running hard toward a door with red dragons carved on it. He somersaulted twice, flipped his way to the door, and threw a metal star at the keyhole. The door clicked, and he tumbled through.

That was so *cool.*

The tree woman's whispery voice kept right on going. ". . . reliable character work, it's so hard to find these days, especially for a dryad," she said.

The vampire's laughter drowned out her words. Una had missed the punch line. She sighed. Peter was taking an awfully long time, and there was so much to see, and it wasn't like listening to the merits of a lost tree would help her in this new world anyway. Perhaps it wouldn't be too bad if she wandered around a bit. She stood up. "Er . . . I have to go," she mumbled to the willowy woman. "I hope you find your tree."

"That's very kind of you." The woman's eyes welled up with tears.

Una gave her a halfhearted wave. She looked at the

doors around her bench, made a mental note of them, and stood, brushing off her silvery cloak. She ducked under a group of fairies who were giggling and calling out riddles to a handsome elf and made her way up to what appeared to be the center of the building. In the middle of a wide-open space, a formidable statue towered over all the characters, who passed by it without a glance. Una counted seven halls, just like the one she had come from, which sprouted off the circular crossroads like spokes on some giant wheel.

She went over and peered at the plaque beneath the statue. THE TALE MASTER SAVES STORY, it read. And underneath that: ARCHIMAGO MORES RETURNS AFTER DEFEATING THE MUSES. She looked up at the stone figure. He was dressed for battle, and his mouth was open in a fierce battle cry. With both hands he was driving the point of his sword into a pile of thick books. Una studied it for some time and came to the same conclusion she had at first: Archimago did not look like someone she hoped to meet.

After a while, she walked around the perimeter of the area. Between each of the door-lined hallways was a piece of a painted mural that made up one unified scene. After the third panel she found the title:

The Muses Break Their Oaths. Each image was more horrific than the last. They showed a great battle, with characters running and screaming in terror. Tall figures that looked like the gods she had once read about in a mythology book towered over the helpless masses. From their hands, shreds of lightning tore down through the dark sky and pierced their victims. One part showed several families hiding in the mountains, and they looked like they must be sick or starving or something. Another had a whole village engulfed in flames. Una felt sick to her stomach by the end. *Why on earth would anyone paint that?*

She circled back around to the statue of the man in the center and looked at it with fresh eyes. This Archimago had saved Story from the awful Muses. He was a Hero. She wondered how he had done it. Just then, a cluster of pirates who were staggering along and singing about the high seas bumped into her, and one of them hooked his elbow into hers and swept her along with them. She was halfway down the next corridor before he let her go, with a courtly bow and a wink of the one eye that wasn't covered by a patch. Una watched them twirl along other unsuspecting characters until they were out of sight. That was when she noticed a crowd of kids gathered in a circle near a low door, pointing at something. She edged her way forward.

A group of boys her age were flicking burning sticks at a gray, striped tomcat. The cat ran in circles, his eyes dilated with fear. Every time the cat ran, another boy would hiss and throw a flaming missile at his face.

"Stop it!" she cried. "Don't! It's just a cat."

A tall boy with spiky black hair and a pale face stepped forward. "And who's going to stop us?"

"I am." Una frowned at the other boys. "I told you to stop."

"And who are you?" the tall boy asked.

"I'm Una."

"I'm Una," the tall boy whined. "And I want to save my itsy-bitsy weeny-ums puddy tat. Stop it." He put his hands on his hips and notched his voice up an octave. "Stop it." The group around him laughed, and Una felt her face burn.

"I mean it," she said as she fingered the small dagger at her waist. Just the thought of it gave her courage. The tall boy laughed again, but Una saw his gaze shift nervously toward the dagger.

"You're not supposed to have weapons outside of

class." His voice wasn't so whiny anymore.

Una gave him what she hoped was a menacing look. "And you're so worried about me following the rules, are you?" The group around him snickered.

The boy backed away. "Are you going to cry if we don't give you back your ickle sweetest kittyums? Una must love her ittle wittle kittyums." She said nothing, and the boy forced a laugh. "I'm sick of this anyway. Come on, guys."

After the group had left, Una bent down and held her fingers out to call the cat.

"Back off, kid," the cat snarled, coiling to spring at her. One ear was torn a bit, and blood had caked onto the corner.

Una froze. "You can talk."

"Enough with the chitchat," said the cat. "What do you want?" He sat back and licked himself with jerky little movements.

"Want?" echoed Una. "Nothing—er—I mean. You can talk?"

The cat looked her over with slits of green eyes. "Hmmm," he said. "A Lady, I'd wager. And a quick one at that. Head of your class, are you? All right, then—Una, was it?"

Una nodded as though carrying on a conversation with an animal was the most normal thing in the world.

"I'm Sam," said the cat. His licking became less frantic and more methodical. "Where'd those kids go, anyway? I'm telling you, I'd had enough. Just two more minutes and I'd a . . ." He swiped the air with one paw and then another, baring his teeth and growling.

"I see." Una resisted the urge to rumple his ears. "I guess I shouldn't have interfered then. We can go and find those guys, if you like, so you can show them a thing or two."

The cat stopped swiping. "That's okay." He paused. "Er . . . thanks for your help . . . I guess . . . I—"

Una cut him off. "You're welcome."

"You coming or going?" Sam asked.

"Um," said Una intelligently. "Waiting, I think. You?"

"Same. You a first-year?" the cat asked.

"I think I'm a Lady," Una said.

"Okay." Sam gave her a strange look.

"What are you waiting for?" Una asked. Maybe if she kept him talking, he wouldn't ask any more questions.

"My friend had his practical today—the Fantasy District, you know—and we're going to find the way to dinner after." Sam sat up very straight. "I just passed mine with flying colors."

Una smiled. "That's great." Her stomach rumbled. What did he mean "find the way to dinner"?

"My practical was really hard," Sam said. "I had to fight this other cat." He eyed Una. "I mean, lion. It was huge, I mean we're talking king-of-the-jungle size. He was coming at me from the right, and I went left, and . . ." Sam was swiping the air again.

"Una!" Una spun around and saw Peter running across the station toward them. "I told you to wait by the door." He panted, bending over to catch his breath. "You . . ." Peter stopped and swiveled his head back and forth between Sam and her.

Una raised an eyebrow. *Told me to wait?*

"Una and I have just met," Sam said. "Friend of yours? Right. Let's find dinner. I'm starved. Peter, did you pass the examination?" Sam took off, bobbing and weaving through the crowd, so he couldn't have seen Peter's face. But Una did. *Uh-oh.*

Sam kept talking. "I was just telling ol' Una here about the lion. He looks worse than me, I'm telling you."

Chapter 6

It was already dark when they left the station. Peter produced a small lantern from his knapsack. "Travel-size," he said as he lit it. The tiny flame cast just enough glow to illuminate the path ahead of them. Shadows moved on either side as the light swung to and fro.

Una could hear whispered rustling and strange night noises all around. The air smelled of woodsmoke, and the wind was noisy in the branches overhead. When was the last time that she had been in a forest at night? Maybe never.

With a great crushing of dried leaves, Sam darted into the forest. Every so often he ran farther up the path and accomplished some catlike mission before returning to join them. In the beginning, Una had jumped every time the cat appeared, but the longer they walked, the more she got used to it.

"We'll have to visit the Museum soon." Peter broke into Una's thoughts. "It's the only place I can think of where we can find out about WIs without anyone getting suspicious." He kicked at a pinecone in the path. "Students aren't allowed into the restricted areas there, so we'll have to find a way to sneak in." Peter glanced over his shoulder nervously.

They were not alone on the wide path. Up ahead, dots of light swung back and forth, and bits of laughter drifted back to them on the autumn air. Una tried not to stare too openly as two girls in hoop skirts passed them.

Peter dropped his voice to a near whisper. "I've been thinking about it ever since my exam review. We've got to figure out why you've been Written In before the Talekeepers find out about you."

"But why does it matter?" Una asked. "If they're in charge, shouldn't we just tell them what happened? I mean, if no one's been Written In in ages, won't they be interested?"

Sam poked his head out from a bush. "Written In?" He crouched down and sniffed in Una's direction. "Are you kidding me?"

Peter grabbed Sam by the scruff of the neck. "You can't say anything, Sam. We've got to keep her safe."

Sam shook his head free and went back to scrutinizing Una. "And if the Talekeepers catch you? They don't even like us to *talk* about stuff from before the Unbinding. What do you think they'll do with an actual WI?" He sniffed attentively at a speck on her boot.

"It doesn't matter. A Hero never deserts a Lady in need." Peter said this last as though he was reciting a rule from class. He brushed Sam's fur off his fingertips. "And they won't catch me."

"What aren't you saying?" Una demanded. When Peter didn't answer, she planted her feet. "Tell me why I'm in danger." She folded her arms across her chest. "I won't go a step farther until you do."

Peter gave a great sigh and walked over to where she was standing. "I don't know what the Talekeepers would do if they found you, but it probably would be bad. No one's been Written In since before the Unbinding, and back then, it was the Muses who Wrote people In. Since the Muses were Story's greatest enemies, you can see why people would be less than thrilled to meet one of their WI helpers."

Sam coughed. "That's the understatement of the age."

Una thought of the murals she had seen in the Tale station. "You mean the horrible creatures who killed all those people?" Una took a step back. "How could you think I'm connected with them? I'm not anyone's enemy! Before today, I'd never even heard of your Muses."

Peter put out his hands to reassure her. "I believe you," he said in a quiet voice. "But I'm not so sure anyone else will."

Una's heart sank. "Why not?"

"WIs came to Story by the old ways of the Muses." Sam licked a forepaw and squinted his eyes at Una. "And characters are afraid of anything to do with those Oathbreakers."

"What oaths? What happened?" Una asked, but from the way Peter and Sam were acting, she wasn't sure she wanted to know.

"We'd better go somewhere private if we're going to talk about all this." Peter looked back down the path, but no one was near them.

"I saw a good spot earlier," Sam said, and led them through a thick bramble hedge to a cozy clearing under a low maple. The three crouched around the travel light as Peter began the story. "It all happened a long,

long time ago. Back before the Unbinding, the Muses used to create Tales for all the characters."

"What do you mean, 'create Tales for all the characters'?" Una interrupted.

Peter fidgeted with the lantern, and the shadows shifted around them into the blackness of the woods. "They would decide on the setting and a few plot points to sketch out the story. Then, characters would enter the Tale, and what they did there—how they lived out the story—would make the Tale. After the Tale was finished, the Muses would bind the books."

Una frowned. "But I thought you said there were no books. How can you be characters in Tales if you don't have any books?"

"There aren't any books now. Not since the Unbinding. But the Tales were written in bound books back then. Will you just let me tell you what happened?" Peter sounded annoyed.

Una bit back her questions and nodded as sweetly as possible.

Peter leaned back on his heels. "So the Muses, even though they had all these magical powers, promised to be the protectors of Story and to do no harm. For a long time they wrote the Tales and bound them and everyone was happy." He folded his hands over his knees and stared down at the ground. "But the Muses broke their oaths. They attacked the characters they were supposed to protect. The mural you saw? That really happened." Peter hurried on. "Everything went crazy for a while there. People were terrified that the Muses would come for them. There was a lot of fighting. Whole families ran away from home, and some people just disappeared. Bad things happened."

Una's spine tingled, and a little shiver ran over her. No wonder nobody liked to talk about the Muses. She thought about the statue she had seen earlier. "But what about Archimago? The plaque in the Tale station said he defeated them."

"He did," Peter said. "Archimago was a great Hero, and because he had traveled through the Enchanted Forest, he knew how to destroy the Muses. He was the first Tale Master."

"Why does the statue show him stabbing a stack of books?"

"It's symbolic," Sam said, and his eyes glowed in the flickering light. "One book for each of the Muses." He blinked slowly. "And Archimago also began the Unbinding."

The night air was seeping through Una's cloak. She rubbed briskly at her arms. "You keep talking about the Unbinding, but what does it mean?"

Peter stood and stretched. "The secret of Tale writing disappeared with the Muses, and there was no one who could write any new Tales. Which was fine because Archimago said that it was better not to have any new Tales at all than to have wicked Muses around. Writing Tales gave too much power. So he gathered up all the old Tales that the Muses had written and put them in the Vault. Then, he chose Talekeepers from every district to oversee how Story is run. That was the great Unbinding of Story, and there haven't been any bound books since then, no new Tales or anything to do with the Muses." He scuffed the dirt with one toe. "And there haven't been any other WIs either."

Una tried to keep her face neutral, but a knot of worry appeared instantly in her stomach. Who could have Written her In to Story?

Sam blinked owlish eyes up at Una. "A genuine WI. I never would have imagined I'd actually see one."

"It's pretty incredible, isn't it?" Peter said in a hushed voice. "And to think that I found her." He smiled down at Una. "And it's up to me to keep her safe."

"*Found* me?" Una stood and put her hands on her hips. "*Keep* me *safe*? I don't need you to be my Hero, Peter. And in case you hadn't noticed, I didn't need a Hero in the exam, either. I was doing just fine killing the dragons by myself."

"The baby dragons, sure." Peter crossed his arms. "But if I hadn't slain the mother dragon, you'd be in her belly right now."

"I thought you said the exam wasn't real," Una snapped. "That we weren't in any danger."

"I basically saved your life." Peter looked very pleased with himself. "Like it or not, I'm your Hero."

Una bristled. "I didn't need saving, and—"

"Enough already," Sam yowled. "Whether you were in danger in the exam isn't important. What matters is that you are in danger now."

Peter uncrossed his arms. "Sam's right. And I know you don't need saving, but I like to help my friends. After all, it's the Hero's—"

Sam darted over and swiped at Peter's ankle. "Drop the Hero bit," he hissed.

Una bit back a laugh as Sam scampered off into the woods. She felt warm inside all of a sudden. She couldn't remember the last time someone had called her their friend.

Peter rubbed at his ankle and looked ruefully after the cat. "Right. No heroics."

"So what do we do now?" Una asked. "If Sam's right, we're both in danger: me for being Written In, and you for helping me."

"Well, if no one else knows you've been Written In, then maybe both of us are safe."

Una shivered. "If the Muses are all gone, who do you think brought me here?"

"I don't know," Peter said carefully, and started walking again. "I thought that no one else knew how to Write anybody In. But I could be wrong. That's why we have to look in the Museum. I don't know how else to find out what really happened. I mean, the Talekeepers keep track of everything in Story. They would know, but . . ." Peter's voice wavered. "I'm afraid of what they might do if they thought you were somehow connected with the old ways."

They walked on in silence. If anything, knowing more made Una feel worse. If the Talekeepers kept track of everything, surely they'd find out she didn't belong in Story soon enough. She belonged back in her library reading a book about Peter instead of talking to him. She stopped walking. Something Peter had said didn't make any sense.

"You said there aren't any new Tales, but what about the one we were in—the one with the dragon?"

Peter turned but kept walking backward as he talked. "That was just an examination. It wasn't a real Tale." His forehead furrowed. "The Talekeepers know all the old Tales and write copies of them for the characters. So, they decided the setting and the dragons and all that. But how we acted in the exam? That's what made the Tale. That's what shows up in the record."

"So *we* wrote the Tale," Una said. Maybe she could reread the part where she first found the cave. It might have some clues about who Wrote her In. "Do you still have the exam papers?"

Peter shook his head. "The record is erased after the students get their marks. It's not a real Tale, you see. Nothing permanent."

Una hurried to catch up with him. "But without the papers, how will I get home?"

Her words stopped Peter in his tracks. Una stared at his back for a minute until Peter slowly turned around and came toward her. "Get home?" His voice sounded forced. "Well, I'm not sure. Professor Perregrin got fired before he could tell us much about WIs. But we'll find out. If you've been Written In, you can probably be Written Out again."

Una followed Peter around a bend in the path. Her heart quickened. *Maybe there is no going back.* She thought of her room at Ms. McDonough's house, her little desk where she sat doing her homework in front of the window that overlooked the park. The grandfather clock ticking away the hours in the hall. The musty quiet that filled every room. It wasn't that she wished she were there right now. But she would have liked to know she *could* be there if she wanted. She squared her shoulders. Peter had to be right. *If I've been Written In, I can be Written Out again, too. And when I'm ready, I'll find a way back home.*

Just then Sam's furry head popped back into view. His eyes looked wild. "Any hints about finding dinner? I'm starved!"

"You keep talking about finding dinner," Una said. "What does that mean?"

Peter's stomach growled so loud she could hear it. "It's sort of a tradition," he said. "After every practical, the dorm leaders think it's a fun prank to make us find our dinner. Usually they use enchantment to make us solve a riddle or something like that. This time it's

Basic Questing. Everyone knows you're just supposed to keep walking on a quest until you see the lights ahead, but that's just too simple. . . ."

Sam stopped abruptly and sat back on his haunches. "Hmmm. How to find dinner using Basic Questing?" he said. "What a Questing question. A true query for Questing questers."

Peter rolled his eyes.

Sam didn't seem to notice and scampered along in front of them. "Usually you can't go another step and are thinking of your own home fires and a hot bed and a warm meal. Mmmm, fried fish and heavy cream and . . ."

"And what, Sam?" Una asked, but Sam had disappeared again. She tried hard to peer into the darkness around her. The lantern wasn't helping. Just as her eyes got used to the dark, Peter would swing it in her direction, half blinding her. She thought of the peanut butter toast she had eaten for breakfast. Could that have happened today? It felt lifetimes away. She began to think about her favorite foods: big plates of macaroni and cheese, creamy pumpkin pie, baked potatoes piled high with onions and sour cream. Her mouth watered. She whispered, "Grilled cheese, mmmm, and some hot tomato soup." Just then, a warm glow of light burst out up ahead on the path. She blinked her eyes and stared.

Directly in front of her a big redwood tree stretched up out of sight. Its trunk was as round as a dining room table.

"Pretty impressive, huh?" Sam's voice spoke from somewhere around Una's shoulders. He was perched on the lowest branch of the tree. His green eyes glowed in the candlelight, for there were candles everywhere— some nestled in tree branches, others tucked away in birds' nests. Una even saw one on a tulip growing near the roots.

"It's going to catch fire!" she gasped, and blew a puff of air at the red flower.

Sam twitched his whiskers. "Fairy magic," he said. "Same as Birchwood Hall. Where's Peter?" He stretched his mouth into a luxurious yawn. "I give him ten seconds to figure it out. Ten . . . nine . . ." He reached seven when there was a puff of glittering smoke, and a breathless Peter appeared next to them.

"Of course. How stupid of me!" Peter said. "Basic Questing. You arrive at your destination at just the right time—when you need it most. You know, travelers are always bedraggled and footsore and dreaming of home and food, and then they arrive somewhere wonderful."

The three made their way toward the largest of the red trees. It had a great wooden post out front with crooked letters that read: YOU HAVE ARRIVED. CONGRATULATIONS ON COMPLETING YOUR EXAMINATION. BIRCHWOOD HALL THROUGH HERE.

"Yeah," Peter said. "That's right. But it should say, 'Congratulations on *failing* your examination.'" Una followed Peter inside a door in the tree trunk and down a round hallway. Everywhere she looked, twigs and branches crisscrossed the walls. Roots sprawled over the cleanly swept dirt floor, which muffled their footsteps as they walked. The air smelled earthy, but Una didn't mind. Up ahead, she could see the light from Peter's lantern bobbing along.

Presently, they came into a round room with a low desk planted in the middle. An empty chair sat behind it. "Good," Peter whispered. "The dorm leader is on his rounds. That's one set of questions we won't have to answer."

"What about the other students?" Una asked. "Won't they notice me?"

"About seven hundred students live at Birchwood," Peter said. "The tree's surrounded by dorms, and that's only for the Fantasy District. They'll just think you're a student they don't recognize." He led the way to a dark, low-ceilinged room off the hallway.

Shadowy booths lined the wood-paneled walls. Twisted vines interwoven with small white flowers covered the paneling and gave the whole place the effect of being outdoors. There were tables scattered in the middle of the room and a set of comfortable-looking chairs grouped around a large stone fireplace, where Una saw two dwarves busily arguing.

"This is the Woodland Room," Peter whispered. A faun sat in a huge leather chair with a mug of tea. Across from him a boy in jeans and a sweatshirt was talking earnestly to a girl in a woolen dress.

"What about him?" Una asked, and nodded toward the boy. "Why is he wearing normal clothes?"

Peter glanced over. "Normal to you, I guess. He's a Modern. Fantasy folk live here, but some other students come here, too. We all have classes together, and anyway, it's not like your character type is determined until you graduate."

"Have you ever been anything else?" Una asked.

"Nope," Peter said, leading the way to a corner table. "I've always known I was going to be a Hero in a fantasy Tale. Just like my father and all the Merriweather men."

They slid into the booth. "Let's get some food here, and then we can figure out somewhere to stow you away for the night." Sam perched on the edge of one of the chairs and told Peter that he wanted a dish of cream.

"Anything's fine," Una answered when Peter asked what she felt like eating. He headed off to a counter on the other side of the room, and after a short while returned with a tray of food. Una sipped the hot onion soup. "Thank you," she told Peter, and dipped a crusty heel of bread into the warm broth. She sniffed tentatively at the wedge of cheese on her plate. It reminded her of Ms. McDonough, who was always eating stinky cheese that made her breath smell sour. But this cheese smelled like cheddar and tasted wonderful.

What was Ms. McDonough doing now? Had she noticed that Una hadn't returned home from school that afternoon? Did she care? Would she call the police? Una stifled a yawn. Ms. McDonough was probably celebrating, cracking open the special tuna for her cats. No more annoying girl to take care of.

Peter craned his neck and stared intently over Una's shoulder.

"What?" Una set down her mug of cocoa. "What's wrong?"

"Professor Edenberry," Peter said in a low voice. "He was one of my examiners today." He frowned. "Come to think of it, he didn't say anything at all at the review panel."

"But I thought the examiners believed what you said." Una was wide awake now. "Is he watching us?" she asked, and started to turn around.

"Don't look," Peter ordered. "Sometimes professors dine in the dormitories. Maybe it's nothing."

Sam made a sound between a sneeze and a cough.

Una sneaked a peek over her shoulder to see the professor and found herself looking straight into familiar gold-green eyes. "The woman looking for her tree!" she gasped.

Peter's spoon clanked to the side of his bowl. "*You* know a dryad?"

Una whirled back around. "We talked in the station. She sat with me on the bench. I thought she was just some lady who really liked to garden."

"What did you tell her?" Peter demanded.

"Nothing. I'm not stupid, Peter."

Suddenly Peter stood, scraping his chair on the floor. Sam shot straight up into the air and landed on the table, wide-eyed.

Peter grabbed Una's elbow. "We've got to get you out of here." A smile was pasted on his face as he pulled her to her feet. Una glanced back at the other table. The dryad was standing. A skinny man with a cloud of white hair was walking toward their table.

Peter piloted Una toward the door and waved at the examiner. "Nice to see you, Professor Edenberry. Good night!" His voice sounded overly cheerful.

"Mr. Merriweather?" The man said it like he wanted them to stop, but Peter and Una were already halfway across the room. Sam scampered after them, and all three hurried out into the hallway and around a corner.

Peter leaned against the wall. "That was close," he said.

Una joined him. "Do you think he was looking for me?" she asked.

Peter studied a knot on the wooden floor. Finally, he said, "I dunno. Probably just a coincidence." But he wouldn't meet Una's eyes.

She wanted him to say more. "Is the dryad a Talekeeper?"

"No."

"How will I know one? What do they look like?"

Peter shrugged. "You won't know them by looking at them. It's why you just can't go talking to everyone you meet."

"Do you think Edenberry might—" Una began.

"I don't know." Peter straightened up. "I'm just sick of answering questions today. Especially about you, okay?"

Sam made his peculiar sneezing sound, which Una suspected was a laugh. "I think there'll be a few more questions if anyone finds Una in your room, Peter," he said.

"I'm *not* sleeping in your room," Una said.

"Good thing I know of a better place," Peter said. He led them down the narrow hallway past the kitchen, pushed open the last door on the left, and peered in. "Perfect. It's just as I remembered."

Una looked around the tiny room. A stale odor filled the air, and stacks of old blankets were piled haphazardly against the walls. A thin layer of dust covered everything.

"I thought you could make up a bed or something with the blankets. I know it's not great, but . . ."

"Right now I could sleep anywhere." Una bit back another yawn.

"I'll try and borrow some clothes for you, too. I'll bring them to you tomorrow. Let's meet in the Woodland Room for breakfast." Once it was all settled, Una gave Sam a scritch behind the ears and said good night to Peter. She arranged a pile of dusty blankets into what barely passed for a bed and climbed under one of them. After she blew out the lantern, her sleepiness disappeared and she lay awake for a long time.

How could she go to class and not have anyone notice? Something was certain to go wrong. And sneaking around trying to find answers about people who had been Written In? *Sounds like a guaranteed way to get caught.* What would the Talekeepers do if they found out? Take her away? Hurt her? And who had really Written her In? The awful Muses nobody liked? She shivered. Una tried breathing in and out very slowly and thinking of pleasant things. She settled on her last and only visit to the ocean the previous fall. After much pleading and groveling on Una's part, Ms. McDonough had agreed to rent a tiny beach house for the weekend. Una had savored every minute of it. In her mind, she could see the gray sky meeting the cold water that rhythmically lapped against the shore. She imagined standing there, tall and straight, smelling the ocean air and watching the gulls swoop and dive.

"Una," they seemed to cry. "Don't be afraid." She listened to the gulls for a long time, watching the waves and breathing deeply until she finally fell into a restless sleep.

Chapter 7

The Tale Master's study was not a welcoming place. In the middle of the room sat a massive desk, on top of which was a thick stack of papers centered on an old blotter. Two stiff-backed chairs faced the desk, but Peter stood behind them trying not to glare. Mr. Elton leaned back in his chair and squinted at Peter from behind his round spectacles. He held a porcelain teacup, one stubby finger poking through the tiny handle, another daintily extended. A thick gold band encircled the pinky, the flesh puckering around the edges. In the center of the ring a cut red stone protruded, unreadable engravings encircling it. It was a very ugly piece of jewelry.

Elton set his cup down and absentmindedly tugged on the ring. It seemed permanently stuck in the folds of his skin. "So," he said. "You sneaked your little girlfriend into school."

Peter felt the blood rush to his face, and he bit back a nasty retort. After a moment of struggle, he gave a sharp dip of the forehead and cleared his throat.

The corners of Mr. Elton's mouth turned down, and he resituated himself in the squeaky chair. "And you think we should just excuse this kind of misbehavior, do you? You think we should make exceptions for certain students?" Elton's eyes pinched together every time he said the word *you*, and with the effect of his drooping mustache and slickly parted gray hair, he looked like a very distressed walrus. He scooped a large spoonful of white yogurt from a dish on the desk and shoveled it into his mouth.

"No, sir," Peter said, staring at the globs of yogurt left on Elton's mustache. He knew he had to play his part. Anything to keep Elton from asking nosy questions about Una. "Thank you for the opportunity to change," he said in a strangled voice.

"Quite," Elton said, darting his tongue out over wet lips. The dregs of the yogurt made his voice sound thick. "The girl. Who is she?"

Peter took a deep breath. He had been expecting

questions. "She's an exchange student. My second cousin's wife's sister's daughter." That ought to satisfy Elton's obsession with his family tree.

The light reflected off Elton's spectacles as he looked up at Peter.

"No blood relation," Peter said quickly. "Just by marriage. Please, Mr. Elton. You have no idea how much it means to her to study here at Perrault. You have to let her stay."

"*Have* to?" Elton asked.

"I mean, I need the chance to prove myself to her." He managed a sheepish smile, and waited for the chatty Elton who talked about young love to surface.

Elton said nothing. Peter tried one more tactic. "It would mean a lot to my family, Mr. Elton. Please." Peter had no idea why Elton always asked about his family, but maybe his obsession with the Merriweather name would prove useful for once.

"Very well," Elton suddenly said, clapping his hands together. "This girl may have provisional admittance as an exchange student, provided there's no more sneaking around. I'm sure I can think of some way for the Merriweathers to repay me."

There was no way that would go over well with

his father. Peter could see it now. *Oh, hello, Mother and Father. Great to see you. By the way, I failed my examination. Oh, and one more thing. One of the Talekeepers you're always complaining about, the Tale Master actually, helped me, and now he thinks we owe him a special favor.*

Mr. Elton folded a cloth napkin over and over into a tiny square. He handed it to Peter, along with the empty bowl and teacup. "Take those out, and then carry on with today's mail."

Peter gave a little bow and began stacking the dishes on a wooden tray. He set everything down quietly, just as he had learned back in Movement class last term. They had spent a week studying the posture of those in Service, but Peter hadn't anticipated practicing what he had learned quite so soon.

He left the room without a word, closing the door behind him, and set the tray down in the hall. *So far so good.* And if this morning's tasks were any indication, his detention would be mostly spent out of Elton's sight. Getting his breakfast. Opening mail. Running errands.

Peter situated himself at the tiny desk outside Elton's study. With a sigh, he began sorting through the stack of incoming mail. Most were pink complaint slips.

Some mother was unhappy with her son's housing in Horror Hollow. Another character criticized the condition of the horses out on the Ranch. Someone else complained that the historical accuracy of Regency Square needed improving. Interspersed with the pink pages were bills and endless memos. He sifted the bills off to one side, crumpled up an outdated menu for the Talekeeper Club, and aimed at the wastebin. Footsteps sounded in the hallway. Was it already seven? Peter had counted on another half hour before Elton's toadies started showing up to work. He glanced at his pocket watch and frowned. It was only half past six.

The outer door opened, and a figure wearing a bloodred cloak brushed by Peter's desk. The air around Peter suddenly smelled earthy, like a wet day in the forest.

"I am here for Elton," a rough whisper came out of the hood. The stranger didn't wait for a response, and the little pile of papers on Peter's desk fluttered as the cloak swept past. From the folds of the cloak came a pale hand that grasped Elton's doorknob. Nestled on the last finger of the hand was a red-stoned ring, the twin of Elton's.

Peter sat frozen in his chair. The room felt like all the

air had been sucked out of it. The stranger moved into Elton's office. The door shut with a thud that shook the floor under Peter's feet. After that, everything was silent. However much he didn't like Elton, Peter didn't envy him that meeting. But then he thought of the moment when he would have to tell his parents about his failing grade in Heroics and the days of detention stretching out before him. *Maybe Elton will get what's coming to him.*

That, Peter wanted to see. He set the pile of papers he was working on aside and crept over to the door. There was an old-fashioned keyhole, and if Peter knelt down and pressed his face up just right, he could peer into the room. With his head so close to the door, the low murmur of voices became clearer.

". . . it happened last night."

"But who could have Written her In?" Mr. Elton was blotting his forehead with a handkerchief. "I will bring her here at once. I'll question her. Torture her. Do whatever it takes, you have my word."

Peter's mouth fell open. *They know about Una.* He pressed closer, but he could only see the bottom of the stranger's red cloak.

"Do nothing. Leave her be." Peter was surprised to

hear a woman's voice. Her red cloak swished out of sight.

"What do you mean, leave her be?" Elton's voice was riddled with worry. "She can't be a WI! That's impossible!"

"Who are you to say what's impossible?" She gave a throaty laugh. "I have made the impossible possible." Her voice dropped to a near whisper. "And some foolish little girl won't stop me now." Peter's mouth felt very dry. They had to be talking about Una.

"Can one of the Muses be back?" Elton asked. Peter licked his lips. What could Elton mean?

"No, you idiot! Not the Muses. There is one other, a greater threat than any Muse."

Elton's mouth fell open. "After all this time?"

"Time will tell. The girl may lead us to him."

"But is that necessary?" Elton's voice sounded stronger now. "Let me have the girl. A WI could change everything. As Tale Master I'm under tremendous pressure from my Talekeepers, let alone the Perrault professors. They question Archimago's teachings. And there's more. Books are missing from the Vault. Rumors are spreading. The Resistance is growing." He balled the handkerchief up. "They doubt us. Nearly every report tells of some underground meeting questioning the Talekeeper administration. My spies say that—"

"None of them matter. When *he* returns"—her voice rose triumphantly—"they will crumble like the others." The red cloak had swished back into sight. She was standing close to Elton now, but Peter still couldn't make out her features.

Elton bowed his head at this. "We eagerly await that day." He glanced up, a wary look in his eyes. "But, my lady, if I could only have this WI." He twisted his grubby handkerchief greedily. "I can see it now. We could say it was because of the Resistance. That their meddling with the Unbinding brought back a WI, and with her, the evil of the Muses. It would revive all the old fears. And all the problems we've been having in the outer reaches of the realm? We can blame them all on this girl, and everyone in Story will love me when I save them from her. The Talekeepers who aren't with us will welcome my leadership. The Resistance will drop like flies. My colleagues—"

The woman slapped him hard across the face. A handprint blossomed on Elton's cheek, and he held the handkerchief up to it.

The stranger continued. "Do *nothing*. You wanted

to be Tale Master, and I made you Tale Master." There was derision in her voice. "It's not my fault the people of Story don't like you."

Elton's face grew hard, but he said nothing.

"When the time is right, I will dispose of the WI. Until then, let her alone. It is by hunting a wee mouse that you are led to its nest." She laughed. "What can a little mouse do to us? This girl is nothing. The One who Wrote her In is our prey. And this WI will lead us to him. Where is she now?" The woman moved to another part of Elton's office, and Peter couldn't see her anymore.

Elton was scowling down at his desk. "Here at Perrault."

The woman's voice was muffled now, and Peter pressed closer to hear.

"G'morning," a man's voice came from behind, and Peter jumped up. *How long has he been there?*

"Just . . . er . . . tying my shoes," Peter mumbled as he made his way back to his desk. The man didn't question this, and Peter hurried on. "Are you here to see Mr. Elton?"

"Unfortunately so." The man was round, to say it nicely, and his face was sweaty from climbing the stairs to the office. He had no hair to speak of, which emphasized his clear, greenish-gray eyes and the skin around them, which was creased with laugh lines. But no one was laughing when the door to Elton's study opened, and the cloaked figure came out. She said not a word to either the fat man or Peter, and her leaving had the same odd effect of changing the atmosphere in the room.

Peter turned around and stared back into the study. Elton sat slouched in his desk chair. His face looked pasty white. With one hand he dabbed at his damp forehead with the crumpled handkerchief. With the other, he was burning a small slip of bloodred paper over a tapered candle. Elton stared at the small paper curling in the heat, and when only ashes were left, he wiped off his hands on the handkerchief. He glanced up, and Peter cringed. No one, not even Elton, deserved to look that terrified.

But Elton's countenance quickly changed as he scrutinized Peter. "You don't have enough to do, boy?"

"No, sir." Peter studied the desk in front of him. "I mean, yes, sir." He grabbed the nearest pile of papers and began sorting diligently.

Elton turned his attention to the fat man. "George!"

he barked as he stormed into the outer office. "Have you come about the Vault Tales? I told you I wanted each one accounted for."

"We're working on it, Tale Master," the fat man said in a forced voice. Peter sneaked a peek. Neither George nor Elton were looking at him.

"I could have your job for this, George!" Elton said, waving a threatening finger in George's face.

The steely look in George's eyes didn't bode well for Mr. Elton. "Perhaps if you'd let us read the Tales, we could catalog them more efficiently."

"Nonsense," Elton said. "The new copies are good enough. You know that the ink from before the Unbinding is unstable. Archimago said that—"

"Archimago said a lot of things," George said with a frown as he handed several papers over to Elton. "But Archimago is gone. The other Talekeepers want to know why you won't consider any new policies. What harm is there in reading the old Tales?"

"Harm?" Elton snatched the papers from him. "Only the harm of spitting on the graves of the innocents. Have you forgotten what the Muses did? Why would you seek out the old ways when that age ended in such darkness?"

George's face turned red, and he cast his eyes down to the floor. "I don't seek out the old ways, Tale Master. And I honor the memory of the fallen. But you must know that the characters grow weary of the same tired Tales. They are saying that everything is too predictable. They are saying that they would rather not be characters at all than make boring stereotypical Tales."

"I know what they are saying!" Elton banged his hand down on Peter's desk, and Peter flinched in his seat. "And they are fools. Nothing good can come of reading the old Tales. Your time is better spent locating the missing books."

Peter saw George's fists clench at his sides.

"Oh, I heard all about it, George," Elton sneered. "The other Talekeepers told me. Three more books missing from your district?" His voice turned sharp again. "Just focus on your job, George. And if you don't have the accounting to me by the end of the day today, you'll be fired."

Elton swiveled to face him and caught Peter staring. "What are you looking at, Merriweather?" His mouth creased into an unpleasant smile. "You've just earned yourself an extra detention this afternoon. Next time, mind your own business."

Chapter 8

"Won't your parents be worried about you?" Peter asked as he slid a tray of food onto the table. Una had just woken when Peter had knocked on her closet door on his way back from detention, and now they were in the Woodland Room eating breakfast.

Una rubbed at a sooty spot that wouldn't come out of her woolen dress. Peter had brought her a sackful of borrowed clothes, but she hadn't had a chance to change into them yet. "I haven't seen them since I was a little girl." She debated telling the lies that had slipped off her tongue so easily in her old life. *My parents are international diplomats. They're in the Peace Corps. They work for the CIA and have to live at a top secret safe house.* Una avoided Peter's gaze and cut into a stack of pancakes. "The truth is that my parents just left one day. I was too young to remember them, but my social worker said that I woke up one morning and they were . . . gone."

"Oh," said Peter, a forkful of scrambled eggs halfway to his mouth.

"You don't have to say anything," Una said, pouring hot syrup over her plate. "Don't worry about it. I'm fine, really." And she was most of the time. Except on her birthday. And Christmas. Una pushed the memories aside. No matter what had happened to Una's parents, they couldn't help her now.

"Tell me about detention," Una said in a way that ended the discussion about her parents. Sam joined them and settled himself in at the table with a huge stretch. After Una scooted a dish of milk over to him, Peter announced, "Elton knows you're a WI."

"What?" Una's fork clanked onto her plate. "How does he know?"

"He knows?" Sam said as he looked up from his milk. "But we know that he knows." He blinked. "And he doesn't know that we know that he knows."

"Not helpful, Sam." Peter shook his head. He told them about the strange woman and Elton.

Una felt like throwing up. "Someone I've never met wants to *dispose of me*?" She pushed her plate off to the side, and Sam sniffed the leftover pancakes eagerly. "And Elton wants to blame me for all the things going wrong in Story?" She began drumming her fingers on the table. There had to be something she could do. Some way she could fight back. Una tapped her fingers harder. "I can't tell which is worse. Being blamed for everything or being hunted like a mouse. Just great."

Peter swatted at her hands. "Can you stop doing that for one second? This is important!"

Una scowled at him. "Don't you think I know that it's important? The guy in charge of everything is after me. I get it. Just give me a minute, okay?"

Peter didn't say anything for a moment. Then he coughed. "Well, he's not in charge of everything. Just his Talekeepers, and they tell him what's going on in their districts, and then he approves all the copies of the old Tales and does a bunch of other administrative stuff for Perrault and—" Peter looked up then and saw Una's glare. He hurried on. "But the point is, he'll be following you, Una, and—"

"I've got that part," Una said shortly. Like she needed to be reminded that, in a land full of people who hated WIs, the most important character of all was going to be watching her.

"You've just got to find out why you're here before anyone else does," Peter said importantly. "That way he can't connect you with the Muses."

"Great. I'll get right on that." She leaned back in her seat. "Who is this woman, let's call her Red, that she's got the guy in charge of everything"—she looked pointedly at Peter—"oh, sorry, the *Tale Master*, doing whatever she says?"

But no one had an answer, and Peter started stacking the empty breakfast dishes. "Whoever she is, she found out you've been Written In," he finally said. "And she wanted Elton to know. But they can't get to whoever Wrote you In, or they wouldn't be using you as bait for this big threat they're worried about," he reasoned. "That's something, right?"

"That's supposed to make me feel better?" Una snorted. "That someone they're afraid of Wrote me In?"

Peter held his hands up. "I'm just saying we have a little bit of an advantage. Besides, there's more to it than that." He told them about what George had said.

"Maybe he'll be so busy worrying about his Talekeepers that he'll forget about me," Una said hopefully as she placed the stacked dishes on a tray.

"Not likely." Peter wiped his hands on a napkin. "I think he'll do whatever Red says."

Una carried the tray over to the counter and returned to the table with a cloth. "Well, is she a Talekeeper?"

Peter's voice sounded thoughtful. "I don't think so, but I couldn't be sure. She never took off her hood. She looked like she might be from Horror Hollow." He explained how the air had gone all icy cold when Red had entered and left Elton's office. "Maybe we should keep you hidden so they can't find you. The blanket closet—"

"Is not an option," Una said with finality as she wiped the last of the crumbs off the tabletop. "Besides, if I hide away, they'll know that we're on to them." She scratched behind Sam's ears. "After all, they don't know that we know that they know." Una felt a glimmer of hope. She smiled wickedly. "As long as they think I'm their little mouse, I'm safe."

Peter put on his cloak. "For now, Elton's pretending that he buys my lie that you're a transfer student and has agreed to let you attend classes until your paperwork comes through. And"—he brought out a small sheet of folded paper—"you've got a room and a roommate."

Una scanned the campus map he handed her along with a key. She looked at the building circled in red.

"Grimm Dorm? That doesn't sound promising."

"I bet it's nicer than my dorm," Peter said, leading her down a hallway. "Boys aren't allowed in girls' rooms, but I'll take you as far as the gardens."

Sam made an impossibly high arch with his back. "I'm off to Eating," he said, and disappeared into a cluster of cats.

Una laughed. "You've got to be kidding me."

"Eating's a required course every term for all the animals," Peter said as though this was the most normal thing in the world. "We won't take it until next term."

"No way," Una said. "What can you possibly learn in Eating class?"

Peter ducked into a room. "Cooking. Baking. Foraging. You do all those things in a Tale." He skirted a grand piano and a harp resting in its stand next to it. "And the best ones make you want to go rummage through your cupboards for a snack. Do you think that comes easily?"

They had arrived at a pair of glass doors that emptied out into a courtyard. It seemed like everything in Birchwood Hall led out into a courtyard.

"Well, this is where I leave you." Peter turned to go. "I'll meet you back here in an hour, so we can go to class. Good luck."

Una wished so much that she could hole up in her old library desk and escape from the world a little bit. Instead, she squared her shoulders and made her way down the twisty gravel path bordered by a crumbling stone wall. Small trees and shrubs stripped of their spring splendor crouched near the ground. In one corner, an outdoor fireplace crackled. Two students sat bundled up in front of the fire. They waved to Una as she passed.

The whole roommate situation bothered Una. Nothing good had ever come from sharing a room with her foster siblings. *And what kind of girl doesn't have a roommate yet?*

The trees were bigger farther down the path, and their branches were not quite bare. A squirrel scolded her, and a shower of red and gold leaves fell down onto her head. A weathered sign read: GRIMM DORM, FIFTY PACES.

Una followed the path as it wound off to the right. And in forty-nine paces, she climbed a little hill and saw it. The top of a thatch-roofed cottage peeked over a brick wall. Clouds of smoke puffed from the chimneys that were stacked, a little off-kilter, on the roof. The building was not quite level, and some of its edges appeared round while others tilted at funny angles.

Once inside, Una found the stairs and hurried down the long narrow hall to her room. Holding her breath, she knocked. When she didn't hear an answer, she turned her key in the lock and pushed open the heavy door.

Una stood in the doorway for several seconds. She had no words. It was bad enough that the girl lounging on one of the beds looked like a snooty, fairy-tale princess. What was worse was that Una recognized her. *The girl from Peter's exam!*

The Lady Snow ran perfectly manicured fingers through her short dark hair, humming an unrecognizable tune. Small birds twittered to each other as they pulled a garment out of the bureau that lined one wall and folded it into a brown leather satchel.

Snow turned and fixed her shockingly blue eyes on Una. "Ah . . . my new roomie," she said.

Una tripped on a woven rug, fell against the dresser, and with a half turn, dropped onto her bottom at Snow's feet. "Hi," she said in a small voice from her spot on the floor. *Shoot.* She hopped to her feet and stuck out her hand. "I'm Una. I don't think we've been properly introduced."

Snow looked down at Una's hand and went back to finger-combing her hair. "I'm Snow. So glad to see you again. Really." She snapped her fingers at the birds, who had stopped to watch. "I don't have all day," she said. Two small rabbits scurried across the room and rummaged in the satchel.

Una stared at the birds, who had collapsed in a little heap on the dresser, wings spread and tiny chests heaving. Suddenly, it hit her. *Snow.* "Wait—are you *Snow White*?"

Snow laughed. "Didn't they teach you anything at your old school? The real Snow White finished her Tale ages ago." She examined the manicured red nail on her index finger. "Look. Una. Whoever you are, you can drop the dumb and naive act." Snow stood up and glared down at Una. "I don't care why you're here. I don't care why Elton forced me to take you as a roommate. I only know that because of you . . . I failed my practical."

Una took a step back as Snow moved toward her.

Snow punctuated each phrase with her pointing red fingernail. "That's right. Failed. So . . . whoever you are . . . whyever you're here . . . stay out of my way."

Una didn't know what to say. One of the little birds

raised a tiny head and looked sympathetically at her. At least Una thought it was sympathetic. It was hard to tell with birds.

"Are you stupid as well as ugly?" Snow asked. "Hello! Anyone home?"

"I heard what you said." Una forced her mouth into a smile. Maybe she could request a different roommate. But that would probably mean asking for Mr. Elton's help. Her cheeks started to hurt. Better to avoid Elton as much as possible. Una opened her satchel and began to put away the clothes Peter had borrowed for her.

"Uh-uh-uh," Snow interrupted. "The bureau's mine, dear. I'm sure you understand. Princess-in-training and all that." Snow gave an affected little laugh and plopped back down onto the bed.

Una didn't say anything.

After a too-long pause, Snow went on, "I have ever so many garments, you see. My aunt insists I only wear the newest fashions. How very . . . *quaint* . . . your dress is. I always wish I could have such"—Snow paused dramatically—"*simple* tastes, but Auntie makes me shop at Lady Godiva's."

Another affected laugh from Snow. Another short silence. *Quaint. Simple.* Instantly, Una felt frumpy and out of fashion. She folded the rest of the garments Peter had borrowed for her. For each item Snow had a commentary: That one was adorable. Another, darling. Una was a dear for liking such plain things. Una gritted her teeth.

What would happen if she threw all of Snow's pretty dresses out the window? But that would probably mean getting in trouble. *Snow's not worth that.* Una tucked her satchel under the bed and gathered her cloak.

Snow's giggles subsided, and she sat up, cross-legged, on her bed. "I heard Peter Merriweather is in love with you," she said. "Is it true?"

Yeah, right. Una smiled sweetly at Snow. "You can't believe everything you hear."

"What about the things you see?" Snow hopped up and peered into the mirror. She tied a ribbon under her hair and pulled it over her forehead to make a crimson headband. "I could have sworn he was as surprised as me to find you in that cave," Snow went on, tying off the nearly perfect bow. "You know, the examiners were very interested in your appearance in the practical. I rather think they want to know more about you." She paused and studied her reflection. "I told them I didn't know anything, of course, but I suppose soon

I'll know everything about you, what with us being roomies!" Snow snatched her cloak from a peg on the wall and snapped her fingers. A squirrel raced up and leaned against a button that released the dorm room door. She turned to give Una one more fake smile and said over her shoulder, "And if we have any roommate problems, I'm sure the examiners will be glad to help. Right, roomie?"

Chapter 9

Una wrapped her cloak more tightly about her shoulders and readjusted the satchel Peter had loaned her. "She was awful, you guys. I am so not overexaggerating."

"Snow's not that bad," Peter said as he led the way down the wooded path.

"You don't have to live with her," Una said. Snow's threat about the Examiners unnerved her more than she wanted to admit. "Let's just say I'll be spending as little time in my dorm room as possible."

Peter handed Una a red apple. "Rooming with Snow has to be better than the blanket closet."

"I'm not so sure about that," Una said. She twisted the apple stem until it popped off. "I just hope she's not in all of my classes. Does everybody take the same ones?"

"That depends on your District," Peter said. "Take Outdoor Experiential Questing, for example. Fantasy folk have that each term, we just learn different things."

Una took a big bite of apple as Peter listed his other classes. "Heroics and Villainy are both required for everyone at first, but then after three semesters, you get placed in one or the other."

"But everyone can't be a Hero or a Villain," Una said.

Peter pushed an overgrown branch out of the way. "Well, that's not exactly true. Most characters in Story are pretty clear-cut. You either learn how to save the day or how to try and destroy everything."

"But that's not right," Una argued. "In real life, no one is completely good or completely bad. People are mixed-up jumbles of everything." She told Peter about one of the mean girls at Saint Anselm's who made fun of kids for the clothes they wore but always gave money to the homeless man who sat at the bus stop.

"Well, things are different in stories," Peter said.

"You're telling me," Una said.

The path opened up into a grassy square where groups of students bustled down the worn trails that led off in different directions. Most of them wore cloaks of some sort to guard against the chill morning air. It was obvious to Una where some students belonged. She knew that the girl with the magnifying glass was most likely learning to solve a mystery, and the boy in the sleek space suit belonged in a science fiction Tale. But others were more difficult to place. She wished she had explored the library at Saint Anselm's more. Where did the boy in the kilt fit? The girl with a feathered hat? *And what about me?* Where would she get classified if her whole future was decided for her with one stroke of a Talekeeper's pen?

"Do you ever get to learn what you want?" she asked.

Peter considered. "Well, after your first year, you can choose some electives. They pretty much have to fit in with your course of study and your district, though. Since I'm in the Fantasy District, I won't go taking Rodeo Riding class or something."

"Rodeo Riding? Very useful."

"Sure it is," Peter said as he sidestepped a group of clowns practicing their juggling. "If you're training to be a Cowboy. I'd rather take Jousting myself, but I guess I'll have to see. Maybe I'll have to retake the unit on dragons after failing that Heroics practical." He smiled as he said it, but his eyes looked worried.

"Snow said the examiners at her review panel were curious about me." Una ignored the sinking feeling in her stomach and nibbled around her apple core.

"I'm not surprised," Peter said. "Elton can't be the only one who noticed something odd."

Una tossed her apple core into a trash bin. Elton and Red had agreed to leave her alone for now, but who knew what the Talekeepers would do when they found a WI in their midst?

"Just try and keep a low profile," Peter said as they fell into step behind a trickle of students heading across a narrow bridge toward a stone building. "Especially during this next class. Our Villainy professor is pretty sharp." Una's bootlace had come undone, so she knelt to tie it.

"So does a Villain teach Villainy?" Una called after Peter as she knotted the lace.

"That depends on whom you ask," a smooth voice said from behind her shoulder. Una jumped up and whirled around. The owner of the voice had long silver hair that flowed out from under a pointed black hat. A shimmering cloak covered her slender form, and bright green eyes looked out of a flawless face.

"I am the Villainy professor," the woman said. "Welcome to Perrault, Ms. Fairchild."

How does she know my name? Una felt the hairs on the back of her neck rise as she wondered what was considered polite conversation with a Villain. *How very creepy you are looking today, Professor. Your voice makes my insides feel like ice water. And where exactly does one find such a sinister-looking cloak?*

Instead, she took a deep breath and said, "It's nice to meet you, Professor." Which, of course, was a lie. "I've just transferred here, and I'm so excited to study Villains."

The professor studied Una with her piercing green eyes. "We won't exactly be studying Villains, Ms. Fairchild. But why don't you tell me about your classes at—where was it you said you transferred from?"

"Oh, that's not very interesting at all," Una said with what she hoped sounded like a laugh. "I'd much rather hear what I've missed in your class this year."

Professor Thornhill's lips thinned, but she began to talk about the previous weeks' lessons. Una caught a few words here and there, something about villainous motivation and understanding bitterness, but she was much too preoccupied with catching up with Peter to pay careful attention.

Peter had almost reached the classroom by the time Una and the professor crossed the bridge. Una's boots made little clicking sounds, but Professor Thornhill slipped over with whispering footfalls. The trail ran through a gnarled hedge whose thorns made little snags in Una's woolen dress. Professor Thornhill went through unscathed. The path opened onto a desolate plain, where Una's cloak swirled around her in the autumn wind. Professor Thornhill's clothing barely moved at all.

By the time they reached the Villainy classroom, Una felt as shaky as the building itself. The stone tower rose at least two stories high but was so tilted that it looked like it would topple at any moment. Professor Thornhill held the battered wooden door open for her.

"Thanks for filling me in on the class, Professor," Una said, darting past the woman and hurrying over to where Peter was sitting.

"You look as white as a sheet," Peter said around a mouthful of the candy bar he was holding.

Una slid onto the bench. "That could have to do with the fact that I was escorted all the way here by a *Villain*." She glanced toward Professor Thornhill, who now stood at the front of the room. "She was right behind us on the path, and she was asking me questions about where I transferred from."

Peter leaned in. "*Right* behind us? Do you think she overheard us?"

Una paused. *What were we talking about? Classes and something about the examiners being suspicious. Anything about being Written In?*

"I wish I knew. Is she a Talekeeper?"

Peter shook his head. "Professors aren't usually Talekeepers. Too many other responsibilities."

The classroom was warm enough, but Una's whole body felt chilled. She shrank down into her cloak and looked around with interest. Long wooden benches ran alongside the three large tables that were in the center of the room. Above these, low-hung chandeliers cast everything into the yellowed light of many candles. Una felt like she was in a medieval castle. The only windows were tiny slits cut high up into the walls. Curtained-off cabinets and shelves interspersed with shadowed doorways ringed the room. Except for witchy Professor Thornhill, Villainy didn't seem so bad. Then the sound of a girl's laughter floated in through one of the curtains.

Una groaned. Villainy was about to get a whole lot worse.

Snow poked her head into the classroom and slid into the seat on the other side of Una. "Hi, Peter," she said, and reached over Una to wipe a tiny smudge of chocolate off of his chin.

Peter rubbed his sleeve across his mouth. "Hey, thanks, Snow."

Una glared at Peter. They didn't need to encourage Snow. Living with her was bad enough. The last thing she needed was Snow sitting with them in class and following them around.

"Oh, hi, roomie," Snow said, and glanced cattily at a group of girls at the next table. "I didn't see you there. I mean, your dress just kind of blends in." The girls snickered.

Una crossed her arms. "I wonder when the jokes about my clothes will get old. Oh, wait! They already are."

"You're so touchy," Snow said, and snapped her fingers. A tiny squirrel popped out of the curtained room, dragged Snow's satchel over, and deposited it at her feet. "I'm going to sit here today," Snow announced. "It's so nice to be next to my . . . roomie."

Una gave Snow a withering look, but Snow was busy making the squirrel retie her hair ribbon and didn't even notice. Una received much better results when she made a face at Peter. It was quite satisfying to see him nearly choke on his last bite of chocolate. *Maybe he'll throw up, and then Snow can help him wipe the puke off.*

A solemn bell tolled, and the chatter of student voices was instantly stilled by Thornhill's echoing command, "The class will come to order."

Una looked around. The class was already in order. Even Snow's squirrel sat bolt upright on the floor.

"Today will be the evaluation of your Villain's laugh," the professor was saying. "As you know, this is standard Villainy curriculum. So even those of you who are recently joining us should be prepared." She paused, and her gaze lit on Una. Una gulped. Surely a teacher, even a Villainy professor, couldn't really be *villainous*. Elton, horrid as he was, had only given Peter detention. And Una had never even met Professor Thornhill before today, so she must be imagining that accusatory look in Thornhill's eyes. But what if Thornhill had overheard their conversation on the way to class? Did she already hate Una for being a WI?

"I want you to evaluate each other's laughs." While Thornhill proceeded to give the class instructions, Una braved a peek. Thornhill wasn't watching Una anymore. "All right, then. Please stand up and find a partner," she said.

Before Una could get to Peter, Snow grabbed her elbow firmly. "Let's partner up, Una." Peter turned to face the boy sitting behind him, whose laugh sounded like he was choking.

Soon menacing giggles and nerve-racking screeches filled the room. "Well done, Mr. Oddsbody," Thornhill's low voice sounded behind Una. "Now for you, Ms. Fairchild," she said.

Una's throat went dry. She could feel Thornhill's eyes watching her. *You can do this. Just think of the Wicked Witch of the West.*

Una closed her eyes and opened her mouth. Out came a maniacal cackle. Her eyes popped open. *It doesn't even sound like me.* She saw Snow's rosebud mouth gape. The classroom went quiet around her.

"Very good," Thornhill said with a smile that didn't reach her eyes. "And very villainous." She turned to the next pair. "Carry on, class."

Una nodded meekly. Snow's evil laugh was coming out like a nasal chuckle. After Thornhill was out of earshot, Una felt Peter's bony elbow in her ribs.

"Nice going, Una. Now Thornhill's taken special notice of you."

"I couldn't help it," she hissed. "It doesn't matter, anyway. She's been watching me the whole time. I think she suspects." She eyed Thornhill's back. "What's wrong with her, anyway?"

Peter's face went all funny, and he looked over at Snow. Una went on. "I mean, don't you think she's kind of creepy? Our whole walk here I felt like she was going to put a spell on me or something." Una waited for a smile of camaraderie, a chuckle—anything.

"Una—" Peter began, and then bit it off with a smile for Snow. "Oh, Snow, did I mention you looked nice today?"

Snow ignored him. "Why's that?" she asked Una. "Why do you think Professor Thornhill's creepy?"

Peter was slinking back to his seat. Una looked from his back to Snow's unreadable face. "I guess it's because she's so . . . well . . . villainous-looking, and her eyes are too green, and . . ." She shivered, remembering the walk over. "Something's not *natural* about her."

The laugh evaluation was over now, and students were returning to their seats. Snow lifted one perfectly arched eyebrow. "Let me get this straight. *You* think something's not right about *her*?" She gave Una a little chuckle that sounded remarkably close to her villainous laugh and stalked over to join a different table.

Una rolled her eyes at Snow's back and sat down next to Peter, whose attention was fixed on the front of the room, where Professor Thornhill had written *motive* on the blackboard.

"Every Villain has a motive," she was saying. "Often a Villain is purely evil, but he or she has to want something. Let's imagine we are evil Villains, intent on squashing anyone who gets in our way. What are some motives?"

There was a slight pause, and then someone said, "Wealth."

Una expended a great deal of effort trying to copy the words onto her slate. Slates were required for all her character classes, and writing on them was a lot harder than Una had once imagined. Her childish letters looked like something a first grader would write. She saw Peter's neat lettering on his slate and moved her hand to cover her own scrawl.

"What else?" Thornhill asked.

"Power" came from another corner of the room. Students were answering quickly now: "Revenge." "Youth." "Beauty."

"Knowledge," said a boy wearing jeans and a sweatshirt. Una thought he was the same boy she had seen the night before in the Woodland Room.

Professor Thornhill paused at that. "Why knowledge, Mr. Truepenny?"

"Because knowledge is power," he said. His dark hair fell over one eye. "An evil Villain controls knowledge, both what is spread about and what is withheld. That is how he can gain power."

"Very good, Mr. Truepenny," the professor said quietly. She was looking at Una now. "Truth is one of the most powerful weapons against evil. And wisdom, which enables us to discern how to apply the truth. Without truth and wisdom, how would we be able to tell the difference between the evil and the good?"

Una shifted in her seat. There was no way Thornhill could know about all the half-truths that Una and Peter had already told. Una scanned the room. Was anyone else sweating? She fixed her gaze on the Truepenny boy. He had something small tucked into his lap and kept glancing down at it. Under the pretense of scratching her ankle, Una dipped down to get a better peek. It was a book. *What was he doing with one of the old Tales?*

Una jabbed an elbow into Peter's side, but, when

they looked over, the book was gone. The Truepenny boy was writing on his slate, and Peter rubbed his side accusingly. Una watched the boy, but he didn't move for the rest of class. He sat with perfect posture, deep-set eyes fixed directly on Professor Thornhill. It wasn't until he stood that Una realized she had been staring. Class was over, and the other students were packing their slates and scooting the benches back from the tables.

Una shoved her slate into her satchel and hurried to catch up with Peter, who was waiting for her by the door.

Before she could, however, Snow grabbed her arm. "This way, roomie," she said roughly, almost dragging Una to the front. Snow's squirrel chattered ahead of them, glancing back with frightened eyes, until Snow booted it out of her way.

They waited behind a boy who was complaining about the mark he had received for his laugh. "But I did put the extra cackle in, ma'am," he said. Una couldn't imagine what Snow was doing. Was she going to tell Thornhill that Una thought she was creepy?

Thornhill addressed the boy, but she was looking at Snow and Una. "Mr. Boniface, we will discuss this later. You are dismissed." She flicked a finger at the boy, who, with a great sigh, headed toward the door.

Una's heart was pounding. Maybe she could just lie again and say that what she meant was that Thornhill was charming and played the part of the Villain so perfectly and—

Then Snow was speaking. But instead of tattling on Una, she was introducing her. "Una is my new roommate, Professor." She shot Una a challenging look. "Una, meet my mother."

"I can't believe Thornhill is Snow's mom," Una said for the third time. Dinner was over, and they were sitting in a corner booth of the Woodland Room.

Peter was slicing an apple pie. "I tried to warn you, Una."

Sam licked his chops and watched Peter cut the pie into quarters.

"Making funny faces at Snow is not a warning," Una said. "My roommate's mother is a Villain, and to make matters worse, she suspects I'm lying about something." She accepted the plate Peter handed her. "Maybe she wants Snow to spy on me."

Peter slid a cup of hot cocoa across the table. "I don't think Snow and her mother get along all that well," he said. "The rumor is that her mother left her when

Snow was just a baby. Thornhill only came to teach at Perrault this term. Snow lives with her cousin's family."

Sam was mostly interested in the pie's whipped cream topping, but Peter wolfed his entire piece down in three bites.

"Ow. Hot," he said, between mouthfuls.

Una blew on a forkful of pie. "What's the big rush, anyway?"

Peter took a long drink of cocoa from the tankard on the table and stole glances around the room.

"What is it, Peter? You look like Sam does right before he's going to swipe my food," Una said, and swatted at Sam's grasping paw. "You finished yours already, you greedy cat." Sam sat back on his haunches and studied a spot on the table. Then he stood in a very dignified manner and left without a word, his tail arched in a perfect curve.

"Elton left during my detention this afternoon." Peter pulled out a yellowed roll of paper. "His private study was locked, but I snooped around the files in the outer office and found this."

"Oooh, what is it?" Una said. Together, they unknotted a fraying ribbon, carefully unrolled the faded parchment, and weighted the corners down with their dishes.

"It's pretty old," Peter said.

"I can tell." Una squeezed into his side of the table. "Move over." Small bits of paper had flaked off, and some of the lettering was illegible. On one side, tiny spots of mold converged to cover the writing.

It looked like the front page of a newspaper. There were three columns of print under the illuminated title: *The Character Times.* Una scanned the page. There was an opinion piece on the reliability of any character who had ever met the Muses and an editorial criticizing an old couple for wanting to keep their family's Tales, but Una went straight to the article in the center of the page.

"Look at this one."

In the picture, a group of serious-looking men wearing long coats and top hats stood in front of a towering black building. Below the image was the heading MUSE INK TAINTED.

"The Muses' Ink," Peter said. "Maybe there's something in here about the other WIs."

"Sh! I think so too. Let's read it." She bent closer to the page and began to read.

This morning, an emergency council set to oversee the security of Story addressed the characters of Story.

The leader of the movement, Hero Archimago Mores, gave a stirring speech, reprinted here for the edification of all:

> *Dear characters of Story, it is with a heavy heart that I come before you this morning. Many of us have lost loved ones and friends, and none have remained untouched by the recent violence. We stand united in the aftermath of this great evil. I come foremost to grieve with you as a fellow character, as one who has been deeply wronged by the treachery of our Muses. They called themselves the stewards of Story, but I call them nothing but destroyers of Story! Once upon a time they promised to do no harm, to rule benevolently until the return of the King.*

"The King? Who's the King?" Una asked.

"Who knows?" Peter said. "I've never heard of a King of Story. Let's keep reading."

> *And who of us now will believe their words? All that they have told us is lies. I tell you truly—I heard it from the Muses' own lips before I vanquished them—there is no King. There is only ourselves. And*

*so much the better! Together we have overcome our
enemies. The Muses, those vile Oathbreakers, have
been destroyed and will no longer threaten our fair
lands. The Tales they wrote have been secured, and I
promise you this: no longer will anyone in Story wield
such power. Better to have no new stories at all than
to submit to such tyranny as we have seen these many
weeks. Better to bask in the memory of the old Tales
than to risk writing with the Muses' tainted magic.*

"Magic?" Una reread the line. "Their ink was
magic?"

"I don't know anything about their ink," Peter said.
He was frowning down at the page.

*The days of the Muses are over. May those who were
lost to their evil be at peace, and may their sufferings
here be as a dream. May those of us who remain rest
securely in a new era. We have lived through dark days.
But now we emerge stronger, more independent, better
equipped. Look to your right and to your left. See the
strength of Story. It isn't in the magic of a Muse's pen
or in the legend of a King. It is here. In me. In you.
No longer do we need someone else to write our Tales*

*for us. We can script them ourselves. Now is the day of
our salvation. Now is the time for us to take control of
our own destinies.*

"I don't know about that," Una said. "Playing a part
in a Tale, like a Hero or a Villain, doesn't sound like
anybody taking care of their own destinies."

"I'm not that far yet. Just a second," Peter said.

Una scanned the room while she waited for him to
catch up, her eyes pausing on a wolf three tables over
who was napping, his head resting on his paws.

"Well, we get to decide what type we want to be."
Peter frowned. "That's something." He sat back in his
chair.

Una raised one eyebrow and smoothed her hands
over the faded text. "I wonder what was so magic about
their ink." She tapped her finger on the table. "Maybe
that's how they Wrote people In."

Peter furrowed his brow. "I don't think there's really
any way we can know that, Una. Besides, don't you
think it would be all dried up by now?" He broke off
and stared over her shoulder. "Don't look, but that boy
is watching us."

Una looked. A boy with a hooded sweatshirt sat

across the room. It was the Truepenny boy she had seen in Villainy, and he was watching them from under his dark fringe of hair. She turned in her seat so that her back was facing the boy. "I almost forgot!" She told Peter about how she had seen him reading during class.

"You couldn't have seen a book." Peter shook his head. "The Talekeepers have them all locked up in the Vault."

"But didn't you say Elton was talking to George about missing books? Maybe the Truepenny kid took one from the Vault!"

Peter looked doubtful. "That would be pretty risky. Even if that kid had managed to find one, it's forbidden to keep one of the old Tales."

"Forbidden!" Una couldn't wrap her mind around a bookless existence. "You mean you've never read a book?"

"Nope. Haven't you been paying attention, Una?" He thumped the center of the scroll. "*You* think they're just books. But *we* know that all books are the old Tales the Muses wrote. They're probably full of all sorts of awful things. That's why the Talekeepers took them. You must have seen wrong."

Una sneaked another peek over her shoulder. He

had looked away. "I'm sure it was a real book."

Just then, the tall, spiky-haired boy who had tormented Sam at the Tale station appeared at their table. "Oh," he crooned at Una, "where's the little kitty cat? Aren't you having tea with your ickle kittyums?"

"Get lost, Horace. We're busy," Peter said.

Una knocked aside the dishes holding the scroll and it rolled together in an instant.

"Busy doing what?" Horace asked. "Pretending to be a Lady?" He snorted. "I'm not so sure that's possible."

Una gave him a stony glare. "Can't find any tiny creatures to torment? There's no way you could actually bully someone your own size. And it suits you, really."

"What does?" Horace asked.

"Your name," Una said. "Don't you know it means 'horrible'?"

Snow came up behind him just in time to hear Una's words. She held a bright red scarf in one hand. "Let's go, Horace. We're going to be late." A weary-looking bluebird perched on her shoulder.

"What a surprise," Una said. "You two are friends."

"Cousins, actually. Nice work, Fairchild. In one day you've said nasty things about nearly all of my family." Snow glared at Una. "As nice as a little chat with my roomie would be . . ." She snapped her fingers, and the bluebird fluttered up to take the scarf. It wound the fabric once around Snow's neck. "I don't have time for one right now. Horace, come on." As Snow walked away, she flung one end of the scarf over her shoulder. The bluebird went flying, hit the wall opposite, and landed on the far side of the table.

"Oh," gasped Una, but Snow had already left.

Horace leaned in closer. "Do you worry about little birdies, too?" His breath smelled like stale onions. He whispered, "Maybe you should know that a little birdie told me something else about you, something about sneaks and strangers and cheating on examinations."

At that moment, the bluebird, having recovered from its fall to the table, made a break for the door. A second was all it took. A glob of bird dropping splattered onto Horace's head. He froze, the poop trickling down one cheek.

"Maybe you shouldn't be talking to little birdies after all, Horace," Una said. Her laugh came out like a snort at first. Then Peter joined in, and the next table erupted into laughter that followed Horace as he walked stiffly out of the room.

"That bird deserves a round of applause," Peter said

after they had calmed down. "Impeccable timing."

"Hear, hear," Una said, and clanked her mug of cocoa against Peter's. She looked across the room, her smile fading. "The Truepenny boy is gone."

Peter followed her gaze. "Maybe he was just staring off into space. Maybe it had nothing to do with us."

"Or maybe he's one of Red and Elton's spies who's supposed to keep an eye on me."

Peter looked doubtful. "Would they really send a kid after you?"

Una shrugged and spread out the scroll again. She read through Archimago's speech a second time and found a small note under the faded photo.

> *Archimago Mores has assumed duties as the first Tale Master. His new responsibilities will include overseeing the safekeeping of the Tales, advising on character types, and placing . . .*

But this was where the mold now covered the faded text. Una brushed gently at the paper, but she couldn't make out the rest of the article. She began to roll the scroll up again. She had to go slowly so as to keep more of the parchment from flaking off. Which was how another headline caught her eye. PROTESTERS CALL FOR ARCHIMAGO'S RESIGNATION. Most of the article was missing, but Una could read a bit about how a group of characters picketed Archimago's speech, demanding the return of the Tales. They accused the Talekeepers of censorship and called for new leadership that would continue the old ways until the return of the King.

"It looks like some people didn't agree with him," Una said after Peter had read it. She tied the tattered ribbon around the rolled-up paper. "I wonder what happened to them."

"I have no idea." Peter chewed his bottom lip. "Story's never had a King. How could characters be waiting for a King to return?"

Una frowned. "Well, I don't know about any King, but I think those protesters were right about censorship. Archimago called it safekeeping, but I think it's strange that you aren't allowed to read any books."

"Well, the Talekeepers do keep the books safe." Peter finished drinking his cocoa. "We just can't see any of them."

"Come on, Peter," Una said. "You think they're doing you some kind of favor by forbidding books?

Where I come from, censorship always means somebody is hiding something."

Peter sighed. "But what?"

Una thought about what she had learned in history class back at Saint Anselm's. Governments that controlled what people read did it in order to control the people. "Whatever it is, they don't want ordinary characters to find out about it. Without the books, all we have to go on is the word of the Talekeepers." Her heart quickened. "I'd bet anything they aren't telling the whole truth about what really happened back when the Muses were still around. And who knows what else they're lying about."

Peter set his mug down slowly. "I thought the Talekeepers just didn't like people talking about the Muses because what they did was so awful. Do you really think they edited our Backstory?" He had a sick look on his face.

"Well, what the Muses did *was* awful. They tortured characters!" Una tried to imagine what it would feel like if she found out things she had learned in history class were a lie. "But maybe there's more to the story than the Talekeepers are willing to tell. And maybe not all of the Talekeepers are lying. If all this happened such a long time ago, the Talekeepers from today might not know the truth either. All we have to do is find out what really happened." She flicked her finger at the scroll. "I mean, *they* knew, obviously, so—"

"Great," said Peter. "Except they've all been gone for how many years? Or do you think we should just walk up to Mr. Elton or some Talekeeper and ask all about their secret Backstory?"

Una snatched the scroll and tucked it into her cloak. She said in a huffy voice, "No, Peter. *Elton's private study.* If you found this lying around the outer office, just think what he's got locked away inside his own desk. I'd bet you anything there's loads of stuff about the Muses and what the Talekeepers did next and all the rest. We need to find a way to get in there."

"Well, we'll have to do it after the weekend," Peter said. "We're going home tomorrow, remember? Maybe my parents will be able to help us."

"Maybe," Una said. "I suppose Elton's study will have to wait. For now."

Chapter 11

Snow was sitting on a swing in the Wottons' sorry excuse for a backyard. It consisted of a narrow plot of land covered with concrete on one end and badly pruned shrubbery on the other. A bluebird landed on her shoulder, chirping becomingly. Snow brushed it away. She counted it a lucky weekend when she didn't have to return to the Wottons' house. Seeing her cousin in school was bad enough. Living with his family was worse.

She pushed off with one foot as Horace came out the back door, bringing his practice sword with him. Dressed all in black, as usual, he looked like the poster child for Horror Hollow. His hair stuck out in all directions, firmly fixed in place with whatever stuff was giving off that awful smell. He spent most of his time at home running through moves for Weaponry. Badly. Snow watched him swipe at the air. The weight of the sword nearly spun him all the way around. He caught Snow watching him and sauntered over.

"Bet you're wishing you stayed back at school for the weekend," Horace said, and stuck the tip of the sword in the ground. "Oh, no, wait, that's right. Peter Merriweather isn't there, is he? Can't leave if your little boyfriend's still there, can you?"

"He's not my boyfriend."

"Not now. Not ever." Horace leaned against the sword.

Snow stuck out a pointed boot and kicked the sword out from under him. He collapsed onto the ground.

Like I have a choice. About either thing. Peter had taken Una home with him, and the Wottons always told her when she had to go home for the weekend and when she could remain at school. She leaned down to help Horace up. He scowled at her and returned to his poorly executed Weaponry practice.

The bluebird was back. Snow swatted harder this time. *Peter Merriweather.* He was the first student who had talked to her when she came to Perrault. She had been sitting alone in the Woodland Room. A girl

named Harriet had almost sat with her but continued
on when a group of pretty Village Girls called to her.
Which was when Peter had appeared with a cup of
cocoa and introduced himself.

Things had been okay after that. She saw Peter in
class, and twice he had sat with her for lunch. And
then there was the practical. She had asked especially
to be paired up with him. Professor Edenberry said
it was unusual, that official policy frowned on preset
practical teams. But teachers always responded well
to her particular brand of cajoling. A few sad tales of
being afraid, of not wanting to fail, and the well-placed
mention of her mother's name. It had been so easy.

But everything had gone wrong. It was supposed
to be perfect, the experience that would cement their
friendship. Except Peter was in a bad mood that first
day and had teased her about her dress, which of course
meant that she clammed up and barely managed to
form two sentences that night at the campfire. The
journey was hardly better. By the end of the practical,
she half wished the dragon would attack her.

Snow dragged her feet on the ground. She really
didn't care that much about failing the practical. What
bothered her was that there would be no more shared

lunches. No more telling jokes in the quad. No more study breaks in the Woodland Room.

Horace was heading back to the house. "By the way, my mom said to tell you that Mr. Elton's here for tea."

"Elton?" Snow wished she could bring Horace's sword in with her. *Horrible man.* Always lingering in the quad or on the forest path. Asking after her mother. Everyone knew Mr. Elton was in love with her mother. And they all laughed at him behind his back. Sometimes Snow laughed, too, but mostly she just hated him. Hated them both actually. She had managed to evade him most of the term, but now he had her cornered.

Snow hurried around to the front of the house. Maybe she could sneak up to her attic room and climb into bed. If Aunt Becky thought she was ill—

The front door opened. "Where have you been?" her aunt said as she propelled Snow into the parlor. "Mr. Elton has been waiting to see you."

Snow followed her into the cramped room, where her aunt sat down and began pouring tea from her best teapot. "One lump of sugar or two?" Aunt Becky's red skin pulled taut over her angled cheekbones as she smiled coyly at Mr. Elton.

"One will be fine, Becky. I'm much obliged." Mr. Elton patted the sofa cushion next to him. All of a sudden the room felt stuffy and close. Snow sat down on an old rocking chair as far away from Elton as possible.

No one said anything for quite some time. Mr. Elton sat sipping his tea. When he raised his cup, he stuck out his pinky finger, and Snow stared, transfixed by the fat ring that encircled it. It wasn't until her aunt thrust a teacup into her hand that Snow realized she was supposed to talk to Elton. Snow glared into her cup and buttoned up her mouth. Her aunt would just have to be disappointed.

The silence grew. "Are you having a nice weekend, Ms. Wotton?" Elton finally asked Snow.

"Very." Snow took a swallow of scalding tea.

"And your charming mother? Have you seen her lately?"

Snow thought of the excruciating hour of stilted conversation and forced pleasantries that made up teatime spent with her mother. "We had tea together this morning." Snow dropped another cube of sugar into her cup. Whatever Snow felt toward her mother, there was no way she was going to satisfy Elton's nauseating curiosity by talking about her. Snow raised one eyebrow. "We don't exactly get along." It had taken years for Snow to perfect her uninterested drawl, but she had found it well worthwhile. It totally killed a conversation. Which, with some people—with most of them actually—was very desirable. Slowly, slowly, she tapped one fingertip on her teacup. "Was there something else?"

It had the intended effect. Mr. Elton cleared his throat. "What about Una Fairchild? Have you noticed anything unusual about her?"

Besides the way she dressed? *Probably not what Elton's looking for.* "Look," she said. "I already agreed to be Una's roommate. What more do you want from me?"

Elton tucked his free hand into his tiny waistcoat pocket. "Yes. Well, I'd like you to note anything out of the ordinary. We just like to make sure all our . . . *transfer* students are adjusting well." His smile looked painted on. *So Elton didn't buy Peter and Una's story either.* And now he wanted Snow to spy on Una. *Fat chance.* Snow wasn't about to do Mr. Elton any favors.

She set her tea down and smoothed her hair, retying the scarlet ribbon. "I'm sorry, Mr. Elton, I'm awfully busy. Una and I don't see each other very often."

Mr. Elton tilted back his cup to get at the last of his

tea. "Are you sure about that, Snow?" he said in a too-pleasant tone.

"Quite."

Mr. Elton's cup clattered into the saucer. He looked displeased.

Snow's aunt stood. "Snow, please help me with the tea things."

Snow knew that this was code for "I need to talk with you *now*." She followed her aunt's severe form into the cramped kitchen. The tray hit the counter with a slam.

"You ungrateful girl!" Aunt Becky's volume was controlled, but only because Elton was in the next room. Aunt Becky snapped her fingers at the kettle, and Snow took it over to the sink. Her aunt's demands followed her. "After all we've done for you—to insult the Tale Master! To turn down such an opportunity for official favor!"

Snow silently pumped the water into the kettle and placed it on the stove. *Right. Because you've done so much for me.*

Becky Wotton was nothing if not determined. She moved in close to Snow's face, so close that Snow could feel the warmth of her breath. "Who do you think has paid for your bread and butter all these years? Didn't we take you in when you had nowhere else to go? Haven't we cared for you as one of our own?"

Snow schooled her face to impassivity. Sure, they had paid for her food. *And I never hear the end of it.* And they had given her shelter, if the drafty attic could even be called that. The mice and birds who shared the space had been more of a family to her than her uncle and aunt. She hated them both—hated everything about them, from her uncle's stingy ways to her aunt's annoying desire to impress everyone. But she hated her mother even more, for leaving her with these awful people, for abandoning her into their care without a word.

Becky's mouth was moving, but Snow tuned out her voice, waiting for the storm to pass. She wished Horace were there. Despite his bullying, they shared a sort of twisted camaraderie, and he had a way of stopping this sort of thing before it got too out of hand.

"If you don't do this, girl, if you don't give him the information he wants," Becky said in a near whisper, "you'll have seen the last of us. It's off to your mother you'll go, no questions asked."

Snow considered. She knew that her mother

wouldn't put her up in the dorms. She would make her live in the cramped flat. What would that be like? All their time spent in awkward silence like the Saturday teas? She weighed that against the freedom of Grimm Dorm and the occasional weekend at the Wottons'. Snow already had a summer job lined up. She meant to repay every penny they had ever spent on her. Staying here probably meant, what, five weekends with the Wottons? Snow tried to act as if it didn't matter. "Fine. Have it your way," she said. "It's no big deal anyway. It's not like I care what happens to my roommate. But if it's that important . . ."

Becky looked incredibly satisfied, so much so that Snow almost changed her mind. Almost.

"What can I do to help, Mr. Elton?" she asked when she returned to the room.

Mr. Elton clapped his hands, his mustache bouncing with the effort. "Excellent, Snow. Excellent."

Chapter 12

*T*ell me more about your family, Peter," Una said as they made their way through the forest. The autumn air, crisp and clean, weaved through the tops of the tall pines. The leaves on the maples were changing colors, muddy greens turning into brilliant oranges and reds.

"Well, I'm the oldest. Bastian and Rufus are next. They're ten and seven." He rolled his eyes. "Oliver, my youngest brother, is four and just beginning to think he's old enough to be off at school. And then there's Rosemary, the baby." Something rustled around in the underbrush, and the sound carried through the woods. Peter continued. "My parents, of course. And Trix, my favorite of them all." He smiled. "She makes the best cinnamon rolls."

"She's your cook?" Una asked.

"Cook and housekeeper all rolled into one," Peter said. "I've been thinking. Let's wait until after dinner to talk to my parents. That way we can get them alone and tell them everything that's happened. Until then, we'll just go with the transfer-student bit."

Una nodded. If his parents turned out to be weird, she wasn't going to tell them anything, no matter what Peter said.

When they reached the bend in the road, Una stopped and gazed in wonder. Below them, a valley spread out with sheltered houses and patchwork fields dotting the land. "Oh!" she exclaimed. "Which one is yours?"

Peter pointed at a snug house nestled amid a grove of silver and white birches. "We call it Bramble Cottage," he said.

"The name fits," Una said, feeling a smile wipe the worry from her face. If the Merriweathers were anything like their house, Una thought they would get along.

Up close, Bramble Cottage was even better. After turning in at the gate, Peter and Una made their way past an old orchard with its proud rows of bent trees silhouetted in the late afternoon light. Beyond the orchard was a mellow wood fence made up of mossy logs that tottered on each other, and, beyond the fence, a lovely front garden. Broad sandstone steps led the way up to the house itself, and Una had to stop and look at it for a minute before she was ready to go in. The building was shingled with weathered gray wood, and the gables that poked out in just the right places were trimmed in white. Smoke puffed merrily out of two chimneys, filling air with a campfire smell. A lantern with a thick candle hung over the front door, which was painted a willowy blue, but Peter pointed toward the back.

"We never use the front door," he said, and Una followed him around the cottage. She could make out a grassy lawn that stretched off into shadowy woods behind the house. From the open back door delicious smells were seeping out, and her stomach rumbled.

"Welcome home," Peter said, leading the way inside.

Trix, a tiny, wrinkled woman whose white hair was pulled up in a severe knot at the back of her head, shooed Peter and Una in. Before Una knew what had happened, she found herself tucked into an armchair in front of a blazing stone fireplace in one corner of the welcoming kitchen. Herbs that smelled like summers past hung from the rafters of the angled ceiling. Pots bubbled on the old-fashioned cast-iron stove across from her, and a large worktable took up most of the kitchen. A delicious-looking cake sat on one end, and mixing bowls and measuring spoons on the other. Trix wiped her hands on her apron, flour covering her up to her elbows, and went back to kneading her bread.

"And who would this be?" she asked in a reedy voice.

"I'm Una, Ms. Trix. Peter invited me home for the weekend."

"There'll be no *Ms. Trix*ing for me, little one. Just plain Trix is fine, and what do you be thinking of Bramble Cottage?"

The kneading stopped for just a minute as Una said, "Why, it's just lovely. Do you know, it's what I've always imagined home to be?" Trix went back to her vigorous pushing and pulling of the dough. Una took this to mean that she had answered satisfactorily.

At that moment, a side door was flung open, and two breathless boys fell in, pushing in front of each other and clamoring for Trix's attention. "Just a wee bit of cookie before dinner, Trix, that's a nice lady," the one with a curly head of coppery hair said.

The smaller one began to coax too. "Trix, you

know you make the best cookies ever, honest." His blue eyes looked even larger behind a pair of wire-rimmed spectacles. The wheedling stopped as soon as they saw Una and Peter. The two boys exchanged mischievous looks, and the one with glasses hopped over to Peter and Una.

"Let me guess," Una said to the smaller boy with a smile. "You must be Rufus."

The boy scowled, and his curly-haired brother skipped over to poke him in the ribs. "*I'm* Rufus," he said. "This is my big brother Sebastian."

Una hoped that she hadn't embarrassed Sebastian, but before she could apologize, Peter introduced her.

"This is Una, my friend from school. She's here for the weekend, so be nice to her."

"Ooooh," Sebastian crowed, "Peter has a *girlfriend*."

Una opened her mouth to protest.

"Don't bother," Peter said, rolling his eyes. "It'll only make it worse."

The boys began skipping around the room, chanting, "Peter and Una sitting in a tree, K-I-S-S-I-N-G," until Trix gave them each a cookie and told them to be quiet.

Una liked Trix even better after that. Una helped

her set the dining room table, taking pains to make sure the dishes and silverware were all neatly lined up. At the last moment, she stepped out to the back flower bed and picked a little bouquet of yellow roses to set in the middle of the table.

"Just right, my dear," Trix said, carrying in a tray full of good things.

Una liked Mr. Merriweather at once. He gave her a firm handshake and said, "Glad to have you," when Peter introduced them at the table. He was tall, and his dark hair had gray over the ears, and blue eyes peered out through glasses that looked just like Bastian's. But it was his crinkly, deep voice that made her believe they really were happy to have her.

Mrs. Merriweather made Una feel right at home. Her thick auburn hair was piled high on her head, and her brown eyes looked cheerful as she gave Una a big hug. "Welcome to Bramble Cottage, dear," she said as they all sat down to eat. In that moment, all the pretending and trying to fit in, the tiresome efforts to act like she belonged in Story, melted right away.

Una sat between Peter and Oliver, a chubby toddler who tugged on Una's sleeve to whisper little secrets all throughout the meal. "I like your eyes," he told her in his whispery voice, and Una kissed his fat cheek. The only Merriweather she hadn't met, Rosemary, was asleep in the nursery. The food was delicious, and Una polished off two helpings of fried chicken and asked for a third slice of the freshly made bread.

For most of the meal she sat back and watched Mr. and Mrs. Merriweather. They weren't exactly how she had imagined her own parents would have been, but they were close enough to make her look at Peter with fresh eyes. What would it have been like to grow up in a household like this? To have true brothers and sisters and *life* filling and overflowing every room? Rufus and Bastian were sharing the ridiculously unfunny jokes they had made up that afternoon. They kept trying to trump each other, acting out each punch line with abandon, until the entire table had dissolved into tears of laughter.

"They would be funny, dears," Mrs. Merriweather said, gasping, "if they weren't, well, *not*. Funny, that is."

When they had finished eating, they moved into the cozy parlor for dessert. Trix brought in the beautiful apple cake Una had seen earlier. Una took tiny bites, trying to make the treat last. When the younger children were sent to wash up, Peter gave her

a significant look. Una's heart sped up. She liked the
Merriweathers. What if they hated her because she
was a WI? But before Peter could say anything, Mrs.
Merriweather came over to Una and sat next to her on
the couch. "And so you've been Written In, my dear?"

Una and Peter shared looks of amazement.

Mr. Merriweather looked at his wife. The firelight
flickered off his glasses. Both of their faces were very
serious. "Peter," he said. "You should have told us. Una
has been in grave danger."

Peter's mouth hung open. "How did you know?" he
finally managed.

"That's not important," Mr. Merriweather said,
but Una thought otherwise. Had they heard the news
from Red or Mr. Elton? She tried to imagine how the
Merriweathers could possibly be working with the
Tale Master as Mr. Merriweather asked his son, "Have
you told anyone?"

"No one," Peter said. "Well, Sam, of course, but
none of the professors."

Mr. and Mrs. Merriweather exchanged glances.

"But someone else knows," Una said. "And she told
Mr. Elton." She watched the Merriweathers carefully
as Peter described what he had seen in Elton's office,

but they seemed genuinely surprised. Either they were very good actors, or they must have heard about her some other way. Everyone sat in silence for what seemed to Una like a long time. Mr. Merriweather got up and walked over to the mantel. He leaned against it and stared into the fire. *Why won't they say something? Anything?* Una could feel the fear rising up in her, choking the back of her throat. Even the encouraging squeeze of Mrs. Merriweather's soft hands could not make her feel brave again.

Peter said, "But Elton and Red don't know I heard them." He looked from one parent's face to the other. "That's a good thing, right?"

"Of course, dear," Mrs. Merriweather said, but the creases on her forehead gave her away. Una was about to tell them about the scroll Peter had taken from Elton's office when Mr. Merriweather turned and looked at Peter.

"And could someone please tell me how my son came to be serving detention in the Tale Master's office?" he asked.

Una decided to leave out the bit about the scroll. At least for now. Peter started off well enough, telling about meeting Una, but as he got to the part about the exam review panel, his voice grew faint. Apparently, there really was no good way to tell parents about a failed exam and a term's worth of detentions.

At least Mrs. Merriweather seemed sympathetic. "Of course you couldn't have passed given the circumstances, Peter."

Mr. Merriweather wasn't so forgiving. "Don't fail another," he said sternly. "When's your next examination?"

"Wednesday. For Villainy." He fidgeted with his collar. "I'll do better."

Mr. Merriweather spoke to his wife as though Peter and Una were no longer there. "This all seems very suspicious. Why in the world would someone Write Una In through an Advanced Heroics exam? And why is Elton hiding it from his Talekeepers?"

Una didn't think he really expected anyone to answer, so she said, "But who could have Written me In?" She ended her sentence with the question mark she felt was plastered on her forehead. "What's going on? Can you tell me? Please say that you can help me."

Una felt tears well up even as she asked the questions. She hadn't realized how much she had been counting on the Merriweathers' help. Somewhere deep inside she had expected everything to change once someone besides Peter and Sam, someone in charge, someone grown-up, knew. But the tiny shake of Mr. Merriweather's head, the pity in his wife's eyes, and the fear she couldn't shake off—more than anything else, the fear—shattered Una's last hope that everything could be taken care of.

She began to cry.

Mrs. Merriweather handed her a lace handkerchief and said in a soft voice, "We can't tell you why you were Written In, Una, or even how. But we will certainly try to help you."

"You did right to hide her from the Talekeepers, Peter," Mr. Merriweather said as Una dried her eyes. "I can't imagine the uproar finding a WI would cause. All the fearmongering and the new 'protective measures' the Talekeepers would introduce." He snorted. "And then they would whisk Una off to wherever they take those who disagree with them." He walked over to Una and smiled down at her. "But we'll keep you safe."

"You can be sure of that," Mrs. Merriweather added. Una looked from one to the other, and this made the tears come all the more. They were being so kind to her, and here she was a perfect stranger.

Una wiped her nose with the handkerchief and said in a shaky voice, "Do you have any idea why someone would bring *me* to Story? I'm just a girl."

Mr. Merriweather gave his wife a cryptic look. "I don't know, Una. Not for sure. But I have some friends who might be able to help. I'll do my best to find the answers to your questions while you're back at school."

"Can I just stay here with you?" Una asked.

Mrs. Merriweather patted her hand again. "We'd like that very much, but I'm afraid it's impossible. At this point, if we do anything out of the ordinary, it will raise Mr. Elton's and his Talekeepers' suspicions, not to mention this Red person." She stood up and smoothed her skirts. "At any rate, I'm glad to hear you're in the dormitories. You'll be safer in a more conspicuous place. I don't think the Talekeepers would dare kidnap you from there for the outrage it would cause among the other parents."

"Is that what happens to the people the Talekeepers don't like? They get kidnapped?" Una asked.

Mr. Merriweather squeezed Una's shoulder. "Now don't you worry, my dear. Nothing of the sort will happen to you."

Una nodded. *But you didn't answer my question*. Just

then Rufus and Bastian bounded into the room with their littlest brother in tow. "Ollie wants a Tale," Bastian said. "But we're in the middle of a pirate battle."

"'S'okay," Rufus said. "We can stop."

"He's just saying that because he has to walk the plank," Bastian said.

Mrs. Merriweather smiled at her sons. "All right, leave him with us. Come here, darling," she said and gave Oliver's downy head a kiss as she sat him on her lap.

Mr. Merriweather excused himself and followed Bastian and Rufus out of the room as the others settled in for the Tale. Peter sank back into a chair, one ankle crossed over his knee, his foot twitching impatiently. Una drew her legs up under her and settled in. *Finally.* Hearing a story was the next best thing to reading one.

"Once upon a time," Mrs. Merriweather began, "there was a King. He had done many valiant things in his long reign, some of which you know. This is the same King who carried out the Siege of Mysterium Castle, the Rescue of Princess Julian, the Discovery of the Forbidden Lands, the Restoration of the Guardian Books, and the Winning of the Emerald Throne. He was very brave, and, if that wasn't enough, he was good, noble, honest, and true. Under the King's rule, his people had peace, justice, and fruitfulness. In every corner of the land, characters lived in peace and harmony." Bastian and Rufus crept back into the room, their pirate game abandoned, and sat cross-legged on the rug in front of the fire.

"One day the King decided to have an adventure. He prepared for a long journey and placed trusted servants in charge of his kingdom. The day of his departure came, and all his people lined up to bow before him. Their sons and daughters threw flowers on the streets, cheering and laughing as they sang their favorite songs." Una could almost see the dancing children, could feel the sweetness of their farewell.

"This pleased the King," Mrs. Merriweather continued. "And he departed in full confidence, knowing his servants would be careful to rule his land well in his absence. No one knew the King's destination, but all the people, young and old, awaited their King's return. And where do you think the King was all this time?"

Rufus had his chin cupped in both hands, his face fixed on his mother. He shook his head. "Where?"

"Why, the King was traveling the land, living among

his people. Such was the wisdom and kindness of the King. He disguised himself, of course, else the people would have recognized him straightaway. And he didn't want that. Before he decided to leave, he had thrown great feasts at his castle, and everyone who came sat stiffly in their chairs and minded their manners, and wiped their mouths with the corners of their napkins just so. Though the King didn't mind that, his favorite thing to do was to sit around a merry fire with friends, telling stories and eating good food, and he couldn't do that when people were always trying to be on their best behavior around him.

"One day, he arrived in a mountain village, weary and footsore. He looked nothing like the King he was, for his hair was matted, and his clothes were dirty from traveling. He went from house to house, seeking a night's hospitality, but every door was turned against him. One woman said that her rooms were all full for the night. Someone else made excuses about not having enough food. A farmer wouldn't even offer him the loft of his barn. With each refusal, the King went sadly on his way, for he longed to sit at a table and break bread with his people. Finally, on the very last street of the village, he met a little boy. The boy was dressed in rags and hardly had a place of his own to call home. Most nights he made camp on the outskirts of town and curled up next to his dog to sleep. But he offered to share his fire with the King and received in return rich company and delightful Tales. Out of his battered pack, the King pulled all manner of delicious food. The boy had never tasted chocolate before, and to this day he talks about his first bite of it by that fire. And such stories! The boy grew up and traveled around telling the best of the King's Tales, and they are favorites of little boys and girls everywhere. The next morning, the boy's mysterious visitor was nowhere to be found, but he left a sack full of gold coins for the boy." She smiled down at Oliver, who had nodded off in her lap. "And inside the money bag was a note that read, 'Any old fire is fit for a King if kindness be there.'"

"Aw, Mother." Bastian stood up, his owlish eyes peering through his glasses. "That's one of those stories that's supposed to teach you a lesson, isn't it? There wasn't even any fighting."

Rufus stretched. "It made me hungry. Do we have any chocolate?"

"All right, then, boys. That's enough," Mrs. Merriweather said, shooing them out of the room.

"Now. You must need new things, Una. I don't know how you've managed on what Peter's scraped up for you so far." She shifted Oliver onto one hip. "Peter can take you to pick out fabric in the morning, and I'll whip up some new dresses for you by the time you have to go back to Perrault. While I'm gone, why don't you make up a shopping list?"

Chapter 13

*L*ater that night, Mrs. Merriweather tucked Una into one of the spare rooms on the second floor, which had been fixed up just for her. The walls were papered in white, with little daisies scattered about. The ceiling was all angles, and a little cupboard poked out in one corner. Next to it was a squat potbellied stove merrily heating up the little room. Braided mats lay scattered on the wood floors, and one wall had a large bay window, in which a snug window seat was fitted. Even though it was after midnight, Una curled up in one corner of it, looking out into the clear night.

What would it have been like to grow up here? To wake up every day and be surrounded by warmth and love? She thought of Ms. McDonough in her empty apartment and wondered if she was worried about her.

By this time she must have given up on Una. Had there been a search? Una didn't like the thought of being one of those kids whose faces were all over the news. Everyone probably thought she was a runaway. Just another lost orphan. She wished she could send Ms. McDonough a message letting her know that she was fine and not to worry. Maybe then she would feel a little less guilty about enjoying the hominess of Bramble Cottage so much.

She sighed. Sending a message back to her old world was unlikely. Besides, she had a sneaking suspicion that if a message could go back, maybe she would too. And Una didn't want to go back. In fact, just then she was nearly perfectly happy.

From the corner of the garden, under a crooked apple tree, a light flashed. And then another. Una leaned back behind the curtains and watched a carriage turn in at the front of the drive. Mrs. Merriweather emerged from the direction of the flashing light, and the visitor followed her into the black orchard.

Before long, a lone rider on a horse arrived. Mr. Merriweather met him. After they, too, disappeared from view, Una grabbed a wrap, slid her feet into the fuzzy slippers at the foot of the bed, and hurried up the stairs to Peter's room. She crept past the nursery, where Trix sat in a rocker, dozing by a fading fire. Two more doors, and she was next to Peter's bed shaking his shoulder. He woke with a start, and she quickly put a finger to her lips.

"Come with me," she whispered. Together they sneaked downstairs and outside without incident.

"The old potting shed," Peter said when she described the route the strangers had taken. "It has to be."

The night was frosty, and Una tugged her shawl closer as she followed Peter into the woods. He was wearing flannel pajamas that had tiny knights storming miniature castles patterned all over the fabric.

Soon, they reached a crumbling brick structure, overcome by wild vines, with a square glass-paned window in the center wall. Una couldn't see a door, but she could hear voices.

Peter pointed at a broken pane on the far side. Picking their way through a garden, they moved closer to the window. Una had to stand on a rotting board to see inside. Peter, who was tall enough to see on his own, grabbed one of her hands to help her balance. She propped the other against the brick wall and strained up on her tiptoes. The interior glowed with a light that shone faintly through the dirty glass panes. It was a good thing they had come up from behind, as the front of the shed was nearly gone, its bricks having fallen into crumbled heaps, and the little group that was gathered there would have surely seen them.

Una could see Mr. and Mrs. Merriweather standing opposite, but it wasn't their presence that made Una gasp. Leaning in, talking seriously to Mr. Merriweather, was Professor Edenberry. And next to him was the dryad Una had met in the Tale station. Una pressed her face as close to the glass as she dared. Edenberry must be how the Merriweathers knew she was Written In.

"I have no doubt that she entered through Peter's exam," Professor Edenberry said.

"But she looks young. I'd have never thought a WI would be so young. What if she's lying? A Talekeeper spy, perhaps?" That was the dryad.

Una let go of Peter's hand and inched a tiny bit closer. *They don't believe me? Why on earth would I lie about being Written In?*

"I think she's telling the truth, Griselda," Mrs. Merriweather said. The fact that she even had to say it bothered Una.

Especially when Mr. Merriweather said, "Even if she is lying, Elton himself is convinced she's a WI." *Great. The one time I actually tell the truth, and everyone thinks I'm lying.* "And his friend, a woman who cloaks herself in red, knows as well." There was a collective grumble from the group at the mention of Elton's name, but no one knew who Red was.

"But would they really harm a student?" Mrs. Merriweather exclaimed. "Una's just a girl."

Mr. Merriweather patted her arm gently. "Not to worry, Cora," he said softly. "That won't happen." As he turned, the lantern light glimmered off his glasses.

Edenberry crossed his arms. "Elton may have decided to wait, but I don't know what the Talekeepers will do if they find out. We must be careful. If we act too soon, we could risk everything."

There was a crashing noise off in the forest. Una gave a little cry of surprise, but it didn't matter, since everyone in the potting shed had done the same. The crashing grew closer, and the little group clustered together. Una grabbed Peter's hand.

A tall man stumbled into the group. He was out of breath from running, and he cradled a small parcel in his arms.

"Wilfred, you gave us a fright," Mrs. Merriweather said, her hand flat against her collarbone. Two seconds later someone else burst in.

Una clamped down on Peter's hand. He had thrown a cloak over his jeans and sweatshirt, but Una knew him at once. It was the Truepenny boy.

"And Endeavor," Mrs. Merriweather said to him. "I didn't expect to see you tonight."

Endeavor Truepenny looked over at the tall man. "Dad made me come," he said in a low voice.

Endeavor's father shook his head as he tried to catch his breath. He set the parcel down on the potting bench. If possible, the group grew more tense.

Una waited breathlessly.

Finally, the dryad Griselda stepped forward. Her tapered fingers folded back the edges of the rumpled paper. She stood for a moment looking down with wide eyes. She shook her head back and forth. "Another book . . . gone," she breathed.

Una could almost get a good look at the package. She let go of Peter's hand again and stretched as tall as she could, squinting at the charred remains in the center of the parcel. It didn't look like a book; that was certain. Whatever it used to be, all that she could see now was a tiny mound of ashes.

Mrs. Merriweather began to cry.

"How is this happening?" someone asked.

"No one knows," Wilfred answered. "I found it this afternoon. The other Talekeepers at the Vault are all in an uproar."

"Well, whoever is doing it knows," Mr. Merriweather said lightly, but his voice carried an undercurrent of worry. "Someone's figured out a way to erase the old Tales. Isn't it enough to lock them all up and keep us from reading them?"

"This is a new magic," Griselda said. "Erasing a Tale goes against all the laws of Story."

"How many have we rescued?" Professor Edenberry asked.

"I left more in your box in the Vault," Wilfred said to Mr. Merriweather.

"What if it's more than just one of the old Tales," Griselda said, fingering the wrapping. "What if it was a Muse book?"

"But that's impossible!" Mrs. Merriweather pressed both hands over her mouth.

"There were seven Muses." Griselda rubbed her hands together. "Perhaps some of the other Muse books are in the Vault. If we could get our hands on one, we could prove that the Talekeepers are lying about what happened before the Unbinding."

Someone in the little group cleared his throat. Professor Edenberry shuffled his feet and studied his hands. Finally, Mr. Merriweather said in a gentle voice, "Griselda, there's no proof that any of the Muses survived. Quite the contrary. As much as I dislike the Talekeepers, I have to agree with them on this. The Muses would have done something by now if they were still around."

The dryad set her lips in a thin line. "I realize I won't convince you, but I know what I've seen. I've spoken to old characters. I've read some of their accounts." Mr. Merriweather opened his mouth, but Griselda waved her hands at him. "No. Let me finish, for once. Just think. There's no proof the Talekeepers actually destroyed the Muses. If they had really done it, why hide everything to do with the Muses? Anyone who has ever demanded more information from the Talekeepers has disappeared or had a convenient change of heart. What if the Muses really are out there somewhere?"

"Just waiting for us to find them? Nonsense." Mr. Merriweather's voice wasn't gentle anymore. "We all know the Muse books disappeared with them. And that's all the Muse books were: ways for us to visit the

Muses. Looking to the past isn't the way to help Story.
The age of the Muses ended a long time ago. It's the
bad people, evil people even, among the Talekeepers
who have forbidden us our Tales. We know this for
certain, with no room for speculation." He picked up
a fistful of the powdered dust. "What *this* means is that
the Talekeepers aren't just locking up our Tales, they're
systematically erasing them."

Wilfred spoke next. "I don't know about that, Henry.
The Talekeepers seem as surprised as anyone about the
books. And we've been able to smuggle some books out
of the Vault. What's to say other groups aren't doing the
same? Besides, the Talekeepers are hardly organized
enough to do anything systematically. It's such a
bureaucracy over there. Incompetence, inefficiency—"

"Dad," the Truepenny boy said as if to hush his
father.

"Perhaps it's not an organized effort. Maybe it's
just certain Talekeepers." Peter's father examined the
remains of the book. "Maybe they are divided after all."

"Of course they're divided!" Wilfred wrapped up
the little package and tucked it away into a pocket. "I've
been saying it for years. If the characters of Story would
just stand up and call for a vote, we'd have new leaders

in there in the blink of an eye. But does anybody care? They're so afraid, they won't even fight for their rights. 'A big scary Muse, you say? Why, go ahead, take away all our Tales. Tell me what I should learn! Tell me what type of character to be!' It's enraging! What we need is—"

The little group shifted around as Wilfred spoke, and Una thought that they might have heard his ideas before. His son looked embarrassed, until Mr. Merriweather interjected, "I'm all for a good political rally, Wilfred, you know that. And when the time is right, I'll be there standing next to you calling for change. But we don't have enough information yet. If we could prove that the Talekeepers were doing something to harm Story, the characters would rally."

"If we could prove the Talekeepers have been lying all along"—Griselda looked directly at Mr. Merriweather as she said this—"we'd have the beginnings of a revolution."

"Not the kind you'd want." He sounded angry now. "Telling people the Muses might still be around will just make them more afraid than ever, and they'll be begging for more Talekeeper control. It's no use arguing about this now, Griselda. We may disagree about what the Talekeepers are lying about, but we can agree on one thing: it's time for new leadership. What we've got to do is find out what's written in the old Tales, especially the ones the Talekeepers are so keen to keep locked up." He looked at the place where the book had been. "Or the ones that are so dangerous they've found a way to erase them."

Una's first mistake was twisting to look at Peter. Her second was forgetting that she was standing on a board. One minute she was peering in at the little group, the next she had tumbled to a heap in the abandoned garden bed.

She groaned, but the commotion her fall had caused in the little potting shed drowned out the sound.

Peter was by her side in an instant. "Get up!" he hissed. "Quickly. They can't find us here." He tore off into the woods. Una ran blindly behind him, little branches whipping her frozen cheeks. The woods that had seemed so friendly in the afternoon sun were menacing by moonlight.

She soon lost track of where they were going, but Peter forged ahead. Una could hear nothing beyond her own breathing and her slippers crashing through the underbrush. She grabbed at her shawl as she tried to run faster, fighting the piercing stitch in her side. Finally they burst into the yard behind the house and raced up the back steps.

No one was behind them. Whatever the little group in the potting shed thought about being spied on, they didn't think to look in on the children of Bramble Cottage.

"Go!" Peter whispered as they ran up the first flight of the stairs. He pointed to Una's room, "Don't look out the windows. Don't let them see you. Just pretend to be asleep. Meet me in the kitchen in an hour." Una nodded, too out of breath to say anything, fled into her room, and collapsed onto her bed in a shivering heap.

Peter ladled two mugs of cinnamon apple cider from the pot on the stove and set them down on Trix's worktable. A slim tapered candle cast everything into shadow. Una appeared from the dim hallway, slid onto the stool, and took a sip.

Peter sat opposite her, but he pushed his mug away, untouched. "It's just for show. In case anyone comes down," he said. "They'll think we wanted a snack." Peter wasn't sure what else to say. *I guess my parents have been keeping stuff from me all along, what do you think about that? How about that pile of dust that worried everyone?* He didn't want to even think about what they had said about the Muses.

Finally, Una spoke. "So, I don't think your parents are telling us everything, Peter."

"That's the understatement of the age," Peter said. Knowing his parents had been hiding their secret group from him made him feel about three years old.

Una smiled at him. "You see, Peter," she said in a fair imitation of Professor Thornhill, "people aren't always what they seem."

"I just can't believe it," Peter said. "I mean, they're my *parents*. It's like I've been living with strangers my whole life." He looked down at the table's worn surface. He couldn't ignore the Muses any longer. "And that dryad said the Muses are still around."

"I know." Una dropped her voice. "But I agree with your dad. If they were such powerful rulers, why would they stay hidden while the Talekeepers went around proclaiming they had defeated them?"

"Who knows why the Muses did anything back then?" Peter shook his head. *"But what if they come back now?"*

It was quiet for a minute. "Well, they haven't come

back after all this time. That's something, right?" Una
finally said.

"I guess so." Peter snorted. "The Talekeepers really
would have a riot on their hands if the people of Story
thought the Muses were on the loose. I suppose that
could be enough to make the Talekeepers lie about
what happened before the Unbinding."

"Maybe a riot would be good in the end, though."
Una reached over, grabbed an oatmeal-raisin cookie
from the cookie jar, and handed it to him. "Endeavor's
dad seemed to think it was time for new rulers in
Story." She got a cookie for herself. "I almost gave us
away when I saw Endeavor run up. I *knew* there was
something suspicious about him."

"No kidding," Peter said. "His father's a Talekeeper
from the Vault." Obviously his parents trusted some
Talekeepers. At least more than their own son. "I
wonder if George, that Talekeeper from Elton's office,
knows that Mr. Truepenny's behind the missing
books."

"I don't know," Una said, and traced a crack on the
tabletop with her finger. "It's like Endeavor's dad said.
The Talekeepers aren't really unified. Maybe it's only a
few Talekeepers that are trying to hide things or censor

the books or whatever, and some are just, well, trying to do their job." She moved her finger back up to the starting place. "Didn't George ask Elton to let them read the old Tales? Maybe the other Talekeepers are just as upset as your parents."

"Yeah." Peter took a bite of the cookie and said around it, "What do you think about the book? I couldn't believe someone actually erased a Tale!"

Una shrugged. "I didn't get that. Can't you just burn a book?"

"Not in Story." Peter leaned back in his chair. "Or at least not until now."

Una folded her arms on the tabletop and laid her chin down on them. "If the Talekeepers wanted to erase the Tales, why wait so long to do it? Why not do it right after they destroyed the Muses?"

"If they actually did, you mean?" Peter thought for a minute. "I don't know. I've always heard that it was the magic of the Muses that made the Tales indestructible. But who knows if anything we've been told about the Muses is true anymore?"

Una set her mouth in a thin line. "We've got to get into that Vault and see what's in some of those books. Whatever's going on, the book thing was bad," Una said. "Peter, your mom was crying."

Peter ran his fingers through his hair. What worried him more was how tight his father's voice had sounded. Add to that the fact that nobody in the secret group had seemed to know what to do, and things looked grim. How long had these meetings been going on at Bramble Cottage? The entire place felt different now. Peter found himself wishing that he was back at Birchwood Hall.

"Well, we'll just have to find our own answers," he said. "Starting tomorrow."

Chapter 14

*P*eter unfolded the slip of paper his mother had given him. "We start out in Fairy Village. We'll find most things there." He ran his finger down the list and groaned. "It looks like we'll have to visit Heart's Place for fabrics. We need to hurry if we want to make it to the City Hub before lunch."

They set out on a wide lane that ran beside Bramble Cottage and continued past the neighboring houses. It was worn smooth except for two large wagon ruts, which Una tried to avoid as they walked along.

"Are you sure we shouldn't just tell them—"

"No." Peter cut her off. "I know my parents. They'd be upset that we were eavesdropping. And I'd rather not know whether they'd approve of us going to the City Hub. My parents are risking everything to smuggle these books. And I want to see why."

"I get that, Peter." Una found easier footing as the path widened into a clearing. "I'm not saying we shouldn't go to the Vault, but maybe we should ask them more about their secret meeting."

Peter stuck his chin out. "They obviously don't want us to know. That's why it was a *secret* meeting. If they can have their secrets, I can have mine, too."

They had talked long into the night, going round in circles and always ending up back at the books. Una wanted to see one up close. She couldn't remember the last time she had gone this long without reading a book. Besides, Una thought that whatever the Talekeepers were hiding had something to do with what really happened to the Muses. A tingling went through her. And maybe with whoever had Written her In.

In front of her, thatched cottages crowded upon one another, and small alleys twisted off between them. The crooked chimneys puffed sooty clouds into the air and made everything smell a little bit smoky. People bustled around on the streets: vendors pushing carts and calling out to shoppers, women with baskets over their arms, children tugging on their mothers' long skirts. A huge waterwheel stood close to them, creaking merrily next to the largest building in sight.

"That's the Olde Inne," Peter said, following her glance. "It's been around for hundreds of years. It's really famous—Cinderella supposedly stayed there, as well as several Prince Charmings, and a couple of Fairy Godmothers." They pushed their way through the crowded market square. Booths were set up in every available space, and the mixture of smells and sounds had Una trying to look every which way at once. Wherever they turned, it seemed a crowd was going in the opposite direction.

"The weekends are the busiest," Peter said, pushing past an old woman scolding two children. Una followed, staring all around her. Characters from other Districts seemed to do their shopping in Fairy Village, for she saw more than just fantasy folk. She saw a couple who looked like pioneers, and a man in a long black coat with a frilly shirt and tight trousers. She caught up with Peter over by a merchant with baskets of fruits and vegetables for sale. He filled a canvas sack with squashes and then scooped up a small pouch of interesting-smelling spices.

"Just need to get the bulbs for the garden now," Peter said. He turned down a crooked alley that opened up in front of a little greenhouse tucked away. The side of the greenhouse was covered with autumn flowers— mums and marigolds, red and orange roses, and trailing purple clematis. Una pushed open the glass door and led the way inside. The air was instantly humid. Peter set off to find the section with the autumn bulbs, but Una poked through an ivy archway to a tiny room. A murmur of trilling voices mixed in with the sound of tinkling water.

Una looked around, but there was no one else in sight. The room was full of plants of all kinds, the greenery broken only by a small wooden door at the opposite end of the room. She saw movement out of the corner of her eye, and she peered closer. The flowers were nodding and chattering to one another. Every so often a small pixie interrupted, bossing the flowers and shushing them. She leaned in to study a beautiful glass waterfall surrounded by little stones. A tiny woman perched on one of these, singing in a whispery voice. Great teardrops were falling from her eyes.

"Are you all right?" Una whispered.

The pixie fluttered up and disappeared behind a pile of gardening gloves on the next shelf over.

"Don't mind her," a soft woman's voice called from

behind her. "Can I help you find something?" Una turned and found the dryad Griselda.

Una forced a smile on her face. *Remember, she doesn't know you saw her last night. You're just a customer in her shop. Nothing more.* "Why is she crying?"

"She's lost her bulbs, that one, and the sooner she realizes that," Griselda said pointedly to the gardening gloves, "the better off she'll be." The dryad explained that she had planted the pixie's tulips just that morning. "She attached herself too young, if you ask me. Best for the pixies to wait until they're grown to choose a flower."

Una glanced back at the shelf, but the pixie was nowhere in sight.

"It's nice to see you again," the woman whispered.

So much for just being a customer. "Did you ever find your tree?" Una asked.

"No." The woman's mossy eyes filled with tears as she shook her head sadly. "This is where it came as a seed, you know. And where did you grow up, little girl?"

Una inspected the nearest plant and dodged the question. "Oh, my name is Una. I go to Perrault Academy. Just doing a little shopping."

All of a sudden Peter appeared at Una's elbow.

"There you are." His voice was strained.

"Why, Peter! I've just been talking to the shop owner," Una said. "I met—" She caught herself just in time. "I'm sorry, I don't think I know your name."

"Griselda." She held out a bony hand for Peter to take. "I'm a dryad. But not really if I don't have a tree."

"Nice to meet you," said Peter. "Do you have any daffodil bulbs?"

"Right this way," Griselda said. "We keep them separate because they're so noisy. They don't like the long winter sleep," she explained. "Come spring, won't they be pleased with their new home?"

"I'll wait here, I think," Una said. "I'd like to catch another peek at that pixie."

As soon as Peter and Griselda were out of sight, Una hurried to the little door she had seen earlier. Griselda had come from behind there. She pushed it open and found herself in a tiny cubbyhole that looked like Griselda's office. A ledger lay open on a low desk, which was crammed full of papers and parchments. A thick shelf ran over the length of the desk with dark-looking ivy trailing down over it.

Una sifted through the stacks of papers. Who exactly was this Griselda? And did she know anything else about the Muses? Most of the papers seemed to be receipts, cataloging the sales of everything from herbal remedies to potted plants. Una didn't know how much time she had left. Hopefully the dryad was going on about her tree to Peter.

Una had almost given up when her fingers caught something. It felt like a lever. She pulled, and a catch gave way with a click. A small drawer she hadn't seen popped open. Holding her breath, Una gingerly reached into the drawer and pulled out a little black folder. Inside were several pages covered with a spidery hand. Una let out her breath in a sigh. Each line held the title of a book. She skimmed the pages: *The Tale of Marina Goodwife*; *The Tale of Thomas Fielding*; *The Tale of Ebenezer Lionheart*; *The Tale of Sarah Witting*. They were all the same. Just like the book that had brought her to this world.

Una sat down on the rickety chair that perched in front of the desk. *What could this mean?* Was this a list of everyone who had been Written In like her? That didn't make much sense, since next to each title was a notation of who had told Griselda the Tale and when. As best Una could tell, this was a list of the characters Griselda had talked to about the old Tales.

Una flipped through each page until she got to the very last. It was crumpled, as though someone had read it over and over again. The ink had been blotted, leaving smudges over the angled script. Una smoothed the page. At the top of the paper, someone had neatly lettered, "Muse books." There was a little star by three of the names. Una read through them all: *Sophia, Alethia, Clementia, Spero, Fidelus, Virtus, Charis.* So these were the names of the infamous Muses. Next to each name were cryptic notations. "Talked to Sullivan in Hollow District about Virtus." Or "Felicity remembers her mother visiting Clementia. Characters in Enchanted Swamp think Archimago was a fraud." The final line made her heart speed up. It was a footnote for the little stars. "Muse books found after the Unbinding." Una couldn't know for sure, but it seemed that Griselda had been collecting information about the Muses for a long time. And if her notes were accurate, the Talekeepers *had* lied. Three Muses, or at least three Muse books, were still around.

There was a nearly illegible marking at the bottom of the page. Una drew near to the doorway to catch the greenhouse light in an effort to make it out. She rubbed a hand over the ink, which sketched the shape of a flowering tree. Underneath that someone had written in the same careful lettering: *Servants of the King*.

Una read the names thrice over. She flipped back to the first page to look for more clues, and it was then that she heard Peter's voice. He was speaking loudly, but if Una hadn't been by the door she wouldn't have heard him in time.

She shoved the folder back into its hiding place, pushed the drawer shut with a click, and gave the little room one last look. She didn't believe the desk was in any particular order to begin with. Hopefully Griselda would think all was as it had been. She dashed through the door and was out by the pixie's plant before Peter ducked his head in.

"Ready, Una?" he asked. In one fist he clutched a canvas bag that was moving with fits and jolts.

"Those are feisty daffodils." Griselda's face appeared behind him. "Plant them soon, and they'll calm down."

"I'll make sure he does," Una said, following Peter out to the front door. From across the shop, they heard the sound of breaking glass and an anguished shriek. "That'll be the orchids," Griselda said. "Snobbish, if you ask me. If you don't come right away, they show their tempers. Excuse me, please. So nice to see you again, Una. You will let me know if you find my tree?" She hurried off to the far end of the greenhouse.

Peter turned to face her as soon as they were out of sight of the shop. "What did you find out?" he said. "I can tell. Your face is all flushed, and you looked guilty when we found you."

"Do you think Griselda noticed?" Una asked as Peter wrangled the daffodil bag into some semblance of order. Finally, he tucked it inside the parcel with the squashes, which seemed to stifle the fussing.

"I don't think she notices much unless it looks like a tree," Peter said. "She wouldn't stop talking about the one she lost."

"That's how she was when I met her, too," Una said. "But never mind all that. I found her office." She pulled him into a deserted alley. "It's bad news, Peter."

"What do you mean?"

She told him about the list of the Muses. And Griselda's notes at the bottom. "If she's right—and I'm not sure why she'd lie about it on her own list—the Muses weren't destroyed after all."

Peter's face had gone white. "Are you sure?"

"As sure as I can be," Una said. "There's one more thing. Have you ever heard of the Servants of the King?"

Peter raised an eyebrow. "The King? I told you before: there's never been a King in Story."

Una grabbed his elbow and propelled him back out into the market square. "Well, maybe you're wrong. What about the Tale your mom told your brothers? There was a King in that one."

Peter protested. "But that's just made up for little kids, to teach them manners and stuff, like Bastian said. It's not Backstory or anything."

Una bumped past a weathered fisherman in a yellow slicker. "Made up or not, for some reason Griselda wrote *Servants of the King* on her list of Muses. Maybe there are children's stories about a King because once upon a time there really was one."

Peter snorted. "That's crazy. It's like saying . . . Well, what are some bedtime stories in your world?"

"Snow White. Cinderella. Little Red Riding Hood. You know, the kind of stories that have turned out to have actually happened here in this world." She crossed her arms. "Didn't the scroll say something about the Muses and the King? That they were waiting for the King to return?"

"Yeah, in between the part where the Muses killed everyone and ruined Story."

"You don't have to be so touchy," Una said. "I'm just trying to help us find some answers."

"I'm sorry," Peter said in a softer voice. "I'm just worried what you've found out is true. What will happen to Story if the Muses come back? Archimago's gone, and do you think Elton could save us from them? It's hard to care about a King nobody's ever heard of when something horrible might be about to happen."

"I get it," she said. "I don't know what to think either."

Peter kicked at a stone on the path. "But was there anything in there about how Griselda knows my parents?"

Una shook her head. "The only connection I could find is that she's been talking to people who might remember the old Tales. I suppose the Talekeepers can lock up books in their Vault, but they can't do much about characters' memories."

"The Vault again," Peter said as they approached a trolley stop. "Well, let's get on with it. One more stop and we can find out what books they've managed to hide in there." They waited until a pair of startlingly white horses pulled up, and Peter helped her into the carriage.

"Heart's Place," Peter called to the driver.

★ ★ ★

Una must have slept, because when the carriage jolted to a halt, she came to with a start. Rubbing bleary eyes, she followed Peter down the carriage steps into a noisy street. She rubbed her eyes again. The colors were still there, red and pink of every shade glaring out at her. The air smelled of a fruity perfume that overpowered Una. She could feel a headache coming on.

"I hate shopping for fabrics," Peter said.

Heart's Place also seemed to be a market town, and all the shop fronts here were filled with fashionable displays. Sheer fabrics draped the doorways and blew in the crisp air. Una followed Peter under a sparkling gold banner with giant pastel polka dots.

Despite its exterior, the shop wasn't so bad inside. Tables were stacked with rolls of beautifully woven fabrics. Brightly colored fleeces were piled against the wall. Next to that, reams of calico tottered up against glistening silks. Peter disappeared to place his mother's order, and Una made her way around the tables, holding up first one print, then another. She was trying to decide between a nice blue-and-white check and a more daring floral print, when she bumped into someone. She mumbled an apology, but the person didn't move.

Una glanced up and almost dropped the fabric. Snow stood in front of her, surrounded by girls, all of them dressed in smart blue dresses and hooded capes. Snow held a beautifully made gown in her fingers and eyed the fabric in Una's hand scornfully. She twisted her too-red lips into a smile.

"What have we here, girls?" Snow asked, looking Una up and down. "Dreaming about a new dress, Una? Tired of the same old ugly things?" The girls around her giggled. "I thought I wouldn't have to see you for a whole weekend, but I guess life is full of disappointments."

Una sighed. If Snow wanted a fight, she could have it. "Oh, hi, Snow. Have you missed our roommate chats? I haven't."

"Oooh," said Snow. "The little kitten has her claws out. Me-ow." She clawed the air and laughed over her shoulder at the other girls.

Perhaps it was the cloying atmosphere of Heart's Place. Or maybe it was that Snow had made fun of her one too many times. Whatever the reason, Una was through with playing nice. "You know, I was wondering," Una said as she put one index finger up to her mouth. "What's your mother doing for the weekend? I heard there was a coven gathering over in Horror Hollow. Maybe she went?" Una knew that this was Snow's soft spot. She didn't know what the deal was, but anyone who called her mother "Professor" had some issues. "Not going to join her, Snow? Why *is* that, anyway? Doesn't your own mother even like you?"

The girls weren't laughing anymore. A few of them trickled off to the other side of the store. Snow's white face went red. She notched her voice up. "I heard you're staying with the Merriweathers. That won't last long," she said. "They'll take in anything out of pity! Everyone knows that. What do they pity you for?" she asked. "No money for clothes?" she laughed.

"Just drop it, Snow," Una said, trying to keep her voice even.

"Or no family?" Snow pounced on that. "You really shouldn't judge my mother, when your parents haven't so much as sent you a letter. Oooh, look, girls! She's blushing!" But the girls were gone.

"Don't. Talk. About. My. Parents." Una would have slapped her, but the shiny look in Snow's eyes stayed her hand. Instead they stood glaring at each other with much more than a table of discounted fabrics between them.

Peter found them like that. "Una! There you are," he said. "Oh. Hey, Snow. We don't have time to stop and chat." He grabbed Una by the arm.

Snow tossed out a halfhearted, "See you, roomie."

Una spun on one heel and followed after Peter. Had Snow been about to cry? And why? Because of what Una had said about her mother? Una felt a pang of guilt, remembering all the times she had been teased about her own parents. *I shouldn't have said that about her mom.* Finding the chink in Snow's armor might mean the end of the dress jokes, but Una still wished her words unsaid.

Peter held up an ugly polka-dot paper bag. "I've already got the silk, so buy your stuff and we can get out of this place."

When they left the store, there were even more people crowded in the street than before. Peter grimaced as they pushed through a cluster of women covered in frilly lace and bypassed a flock of swans being driven through the center of the street. Finally they arrived at the trolley stop. This time, a red heart-shaped carriage with coal-black horses pulled up. They climbed in and shut the small door behind them. Inside, there were cushions of all shapes and sizes, so many that Una had to perch on the edge of her seat, clutching the carriage walls as they bumped and jostled along the road. She looked at the two tidily wrapped parcels bouncing around next to her. Those dresses had better be worth it.

Snow peered out from the shop window and watched Peter and Una's carriage drive away. She shouldn't have introduced Una to her mother like that in class. Una had noticed something. And now Una knew that Snow cared what people thought about her mother. Snow had tried not to mind, to brush it off as easily as she ignored Aunt Becky's diatribes. But, no matter what she did, no matter how often she blew off their weekly teas or glared at her mother during class, she actually wanted other people to like her mother. Maybe if everyone else could accept her mother's reasons for leaving her days-old daughter on someone else's doorstep, Snow would be able to, too.

Well, what did Una care anyway? It's not like Una's family was something special. No one had come to settle her in at Perrault. And whenever Snow asked her about her family, Una just changed the subject. Maybe Elton was on to something. Maybe Una *did* have something worth hiding.

At least now she could tell Elton she had tried to

talk to Una. Snow had decided to follow Aunt Becky's demands to the letter. She would report to Elton if that was what it took to show her *gratitude* to the Wottons. But she would camp out under the stars before she actually gave him any useful information.

What could she say? She guessed she could tell him that Ms. Fairchild seemed to be on the lookout for a new costume. That ought to keep Elton busy for a while.

A salesgirl appeared next to her. "Do you like the gown, miss?"

Snow set down the fine dress she had been admiring. "It's cheaply made," she said. Snow would never admit that she couldn't afford such a dress. Perhaps she would wait until it went on sale. The giant cuckoo clock in the square chirped the hour. She frowned up at it. Why the Wottons chose to live in Heart's Place was beyond her. The saleslady had moved on to the crowd of tittering girls, who now were ogling two boys dressed as gentlemen. Snow breezed out of the store. She wouldn't have said good-bye even if she'd had the time.

She painstakingly made her way down the crowded main street and, glancing over her shoulder, took a hard right. What Una had implied stung, because it was true. Not because her mother was part of a coven, which, come to think of it, was likely. No, it was the ever-present mystery of who exactly Professor Adelaide Thornhill was. Where had she been for the past thirteen years?

Her aunt and uncle knew nothing. Horace had been nearly a year old when they opened the door one winter morning to find a baby girl inside a basket and a note from Becky's sister that read, "I've named her Snow, for my heart has turned to ice."

Snow passed between tall buildings with clotheslines strung between them. Neighbors shouted noisily out the windows to each other, and Snow could hear the sound of a baby wailing. But the farther she went, the quieter it got. There were only closed doors, and even these got fewer and farther between as she walked. The cobbled route zigzagged through forlorn little squares, and Snow chose turning after turning without hesitation.

A heart of ice. There was the ugly truth. Her own mother's heart was cold toward her. And whatever she said, however much she claimed to want to make amends, all Snow could ever see in her mother's sad face was a woman who had abandoned her daughter.

Around one more bend, under a weathered stone archway, and she was there. Only the residents who had lived in Heart's Place longest knew about the subway that went directly to the City Hub. And she had arrived just in time, too. She studied the little group around the station. A few scattered passengers, a group of children flocking around a tall redheaded girl with a snub nose, and the cloaked figure she knew was her mother.

Every weekend she could, Snow followed her. So far, all her mother ever did was take the same train to the same street in the City Hub. But tailing her for the past term had given Snow more than just an activity to help her endure her horrible weekends at the Wottons'. It had given her questions. And Snow wanted answers. When her mother boarded the train, she pulled up her blue hood and got on behind her.

Chapter 15

The carriage dropped them off in a plastic booth that Una thought looked exactly like a city bus stop. Cars and taxis whizzed by on the street outside. Tall buildings stretched up on either side, blotting out the sunlight. Peter kept fidgeting, crinkling the paper of his polka-dot bag and looking around like an excited tourist.

"How do we get into the Vault?" Una asked.

"Well, there's this thing called a safe-deposit box," he said importantly. "My father has one key." He held up the old-fashioned-looking key he had stolen from his father's study that morning. "And we go to the Vault, and they have another key. That way only the person who owns the box can open it, see?" He said this in little more than a whisper, as if it were some great secret. "You can put whatever you want to keep safe in it. Important papers. Money. Or, in my father's case, books."

"A bank transaction?" Una said. "You mean the Vault is just a boring old bank in the middle of a city?"

Peter didn't bat an eye. "Let's hope it *is* boring. If the Talekeepers catch us with the old Tales, we'll be in trouble. Even worse, if my father finds out." He checked the small paper in his pocket again. "Forty-second and Fifth. Come on, then."

Una had to walk fast to keep up. At last she would get her hands on some books. She was itching to read something, anything. They passed a cat and dog chatting amiably over a milk shake in the shop on the corner. Peter stopped to ask a samurai carrying a briefcase for directions. The man pointed off to the left, and soon Una and Peter were there.

The skyscraper looked like a giant slab of black marble and took up the entire city block. Dark glass covered the steep sides that, from Una's spot on the sidewalk, seemed to lean into the overcast sky. She followed Peter through the revolving doors into a pale foyer. In the center of the room was a giant circle etched into the white tile.

"Peter, look!" she said, and pointed with her toe. In the center of the circle was an image of a sword piercing a stack of books, just like she had seen at the statue of Archimago.

"So?" He went back to scanning the directory posted on the far wall. "There it is. The fifteenth floor."

"Don't you think it means something?" Una asked as they waited for the elevator. Outside each elevator stood a guard clad in a dark suit and matching sunglasses.

"Of course it does," Peter said as the elevator doors opened. When they had closed again, leaving them alone, he continued. "Archimago built the Vault after the Unbinding. That's his symbol."

Once they were on the fifteenth floor, he took off around the corner. They went up to the front desk, and Peter presented the Merriweather key. The bank manager took the key and disappeared. A moment later he returned with a stern-faced woman. She consulted a clipboard and pinched her lips together before addressing Peter and Una.

"The Merriweather box?" She raised one very thin eyebrow and looked at Peter, who held his ground. "Very well." She ticked something off on a chart and led them down a hallway with floor-to-ceiling white tiles, her heels breaking the cavernous silence with their staccato clicks. Una tried to peek at the chart, but the woman whisked it out of view.

She finally stopped at a giant metal portal sandwiched between two more guards. The door had a huge padlock on it, which was apparently just for show. Instead of producing an equally giant key to unlock the door, the woman placed her palm on a shiny panel to the right of the door. The door's seal hissed open. "Wait here," she ordered, and disappeared inside.

Soon she returned, wheeling a cart with a large metal box on top. Tiny white letters marked the box MERRIWEATHER. The cart had one squeaky wheel, which stuttered as the woman led the way down another immaculate hallway. Spaced at regular intervals were bright red curtains. She stopped at the third one of these and pushed it aside to reveal a wood table. She frowned at Peter and Una. "Do your parents know you're here?"

Peter gave her a winning smile. "We have the key, don't we?"

The woman didn't look happy. "I suppose that's true," she said as she heaved the box onto the center of the table. "You have ten minutes." She inserted her master key, twisted it once, and left Peter and Una alone in the small compartment.

Click, click, went her heels as she walked away. With shaky fingers, Peter put his own key into the lock, turned it, and nearly jumped at the loud hiss as the box opened.

Four large books were fitted snugly into the box, their bindings so weathered with age that they looked brown.

"You do it," Peter said. He looked as though he thought the books might bite him.

Una had to use both hands to pick one up, and she laid it flat on the table. Ever so carefully, she pulled back the crumbling cover. The title page was blank. She slid a finger under the next page. Blank. And another, blank. Abandoning care, she picked up the volume and paged through to the end. There was no writing, not a single speck.

"Are you kidding me?" Una asked. The rest of the books were blank as well. She tried flipping one upside down.

"I don't know what to think," Peter said, who had grown bolder. He ran his fingers all around the binding of another. "I mean, what's the point of forbidding us to read books if there aren't any Tales written in them?"

"Well, if these were some of the ones Archimago

and his Talekeeper friends were supposed to keep safe, they didn't do such a great job." Una held one of the books up to the fluorescent ceiling bulb. All the pages stayed stubbornly bare. She sneezed, and tiny particles of dust floated down onto her forehead.

Peter whispered every concealment charm he could remember from Beginner's Enchanting, but nothing happened. He tried tapping one of the books with his finger and even hopped up and down on it.

"What help is that going to be?" Una asked after he had tried unsuccessfully to tear a page out of one of the books.

"I don't know. Maybe there's a special trick to getting it to reveal its secrets," Peter said, tugging hard on the cover.

Una heard the clicking of the bank manager's stilettos. They stopped outside the cubicle. Una tried to grab three books at once and ended up dropping them all. They landed on the white tiles with a thud.

"Do you need any assistance, young man?" the woman's voice drifted in.

"Nope," Peter managed, glaring at Una. "Everything's fine."

"Sorry," Una mouthed, and waited for the clicking

shoes to walk away. They didn't. The bank manager wasn't going to leave.

"It sounds like you're having trouble," she said. Peter silently motioned for Una to come closer. He crammed one book into the polka-dot bag.

"We might as well put the others back," Peter whispered. "They're no good to us blank anyway."

Una looked longingly at the three other worn volumes as she arranged them back in the drawer. Peter was right, of course. The books were heavy and big. They would have trouble hiding just the one.

"Are you finished?" The woman's strident tones interrupted the moment. "I'm coming in."

Peter slammed the lid shut and twisted his key just in time. The bank manager frowned down at them as she clicked the lock into place. They followed the squeaky cart back to the Vault. *Click, click*, went the woman's heels. *Squeak*, went the cart. With every sound, Una's nerves tightened. What would happen if they got caught taking a book with them? She hoped Peter had a plan.

One of the security guards and a wizened old woman got onto the elevator with them. The old lady had a brightly printed scarf wrapped around her head, and her shoulders bent under a thick woolen shawl. "First floor, please," she said in a reedy voice.

They rode in silence for a while. Peter stared fixedly at the lit numbers on the elevator panel. Una could feel the old woman's eyes on her. She cleared her throat and pretended to study a wad of chewing gum mashed into the elevator floor.

"If you are too fond of books," the old woman whispered in Una's ear, and the words sounded like they would catch in her throat.

Una felt her face flush. "Excuse me?" How could the woman tell she liked books? Did she know they had a book with them?

The old woman's face was hidden by the shadows of her scarf. Her throaty chuckle took Una off guard. She reached out a wrinkled hand and patted Una's shoulder gently.

"Never mind, dearie. Just humor an old woman." The elevator dinged open on the sixth floor, and the security guard got out. Once the doors closed, the woman turned to Peter. Her gnarled fingers patted the square shape in the polka-dot bag. "I knew you were fond of books," she said with a sly grin.

"I don't know what you're talking about," Peter said.

This didn't seem to bother the old lady at all. "That's for sure. Young people of today don't know anything about the old days."

"Oh, but we want to!" Una said. "Do you remember anything about the Muses?" She peered closer at the woman's wrinkled face.

"Yeah, do you remember what it was like when they killed everyone?" Peter scowled. "And it's not our fault we don't know anything about the old days," he said to the lady. "No one will tell us."

"Aye," the woman said. "I remember. And I remember the day my parents disappeared, too. They were asking too many questions about the new Tale Master." She rubbed her hands together briskly. "The days of the Muses were dark days, to be sure. But trading one form of tyranny for another isn't freedom."

Peter's mouth dropped open. "What do you mean?"

The old woman smiled at him. "You're the Merriweather boy, aren't you? You have the look of your father." She pulled a weathered piece of parchment out from under her shawl and handed it to him. "Tell him that Story would do better with a King. You must remember that the roots of the tree are buried deep in Story's soil," she said, and leaned in so close that Una could see her toothless smile. "Schoolchildren should always learn their Backstory." The elevator doors opened. "Have a nice day," she said, and disappeared into the lobby.

Una peered over Peter's shoulder while he unfolded the paper. She gasped and snatched it out of his hands. In the middle of the page was the same tree she had seen on the bottom of Griselda's paper. "Hurry up, Peter. We have to catch her."

But the old lady was nowhere to be found.

"She knows something about the King, I'm sure of it," Una said as they made their way outside. "You can't pretend you didn't hear her, or that it's just a coincidence about the trees."

"Right, Una. An old crone knows all the secrets of Story." Peter rolled his eyes. "I wonder how she knows my father. Too bad I can't ask without him knowing I was at the Vault."

They reached the end of the block, and Peter heaved a great sigh of relief. "No one's following us. We made it."

Una tucked the paper back into her pocket and tried a different approach. "Have you ever talked to any other characters who were alive back then?"

"Not really," he said. "Most retired characters live in the country. Trix is probably the oldest person I know, but even she was just a baby back then."

"Well, if you don't know any old people, where else could we learn the Backstory?" Una prodded.

"I've told you before. The Museum is our best bet."

Peter pointed to a sandwich shop. "I'm starving. Let's get something to eat."

Una followed him in. "Maybe the Museum will have something about the King." It was in that instant, when Una realized that she didn't want to admit her theory to Peter, that she knew she truly believed it. She had gone from speculating to knowing, the kind of knowing that pricked her thumbs, that the King was real—and that he had something to do with what was happening in Story.

They ate most of their meal in silence. Peter had told her before they sat down that anyone could report them for what they had done, and it seemed to Una that everyone was watching them. The man with his daughter. The woman in the green uniform. The cashier who rang them up. She tried to concentrate on her food.

Peter popped another french fry into his mouth and washed it down with some orange soda. "I can't believe we just broke the law!" he whispered. He sounded halfway horrified and halfway delighted. "No one in my family has ever committed a crime. All of them—and the Merriweathers go way back, further than anyone can remember—have been law-abiding, upstanding citizens. The model of character lineage."

He tilted back his cup to get at the ice.

"So far as you know," Una said. "Maybe they haven't always been the Heroes you think they were. Just look at your parents." She took a bite of her fish sandwich and stared out of the shop's window. That was when she saw Snow. She would recognize her saunter anywhere. And that bright blue cape.

"Look who else is visiting the City," she said to Peter. The saunter slowed as the blue cloak came to the end of the block, and Snow ducked under an awning, scanning the crowd. When the cluster of people crossed at the crosswalk, Snow hurried on.

"She's tailing someone!" Peter peered out the window.

"Well, come on," Una said as she made for the door. "Don't you want to know why?"

For five blocks they followed Snow, who kept straining to see past the cluster of people the next block up. Then, right in front of an outdoor café, Snow came to a dead halt and stared ahead of her. A tall woman clad all in gray was crossing to the opposite side of the street.

"She's following her own mother?" Una asked. For it was Professor Thornhill who ducked down a crooked little alleyway that snaked off to the left.

"Let's go," Peter said as Snow's blue form disappeared behind Thornhill.

Professor Thornhill glanced over her shoulder twice as she made her way down the almost deserted alley. This was doubly tricky for Una and Peter. First Snow would stop and press against the brick wall. Then, they had to do the same. Once, Una was almost certain Thornhill saw them before they jumped behind a nearby trash can. But Thornhill only looked back for a fraction of a second and kept on moving. Snow never turned around at all. The trash can smelled like fruit gone bad, and the five seconds they waited felt like forever. After Snow had gone a ways ahead, they popped out to follow her.

Soon the alley emptied into a busy pedestrian street. This one was packed with people, and it looked like most of them were tourists. Small vendors had set up booths and were selling wooden knickknacks and charms.

"Care for a blessed necklace?" an old woman asked, and shoved a hideous beaded thing in front of Una's face. "It'll keep evil at bay."

"No thanks," she said before plowing on after Peter. A tiny icon, two more gaudy necklaces, and a gargoyle pendant later, they had lost sight of Snow. They were in the heart of the market now, but most of the tourists weren't buying. Instead, a steady stream of people walked two by two toward a Gothic stone building.

Una got a glimpse of Snow's hooded cape. "There!" she yelled to Peter above the noise. They pushed their way forward. Soon they were only a few paces behind Snow, who was pretending to look at some miniatures of the cathedral. Her mother had stopped on the stairs to talk to someone. Una craned her neck, but she could only see the person's back.

Thornhill's companion wore richly colored robes that draped gracefully over his form. Thornhill bent in close to whisper something in his ear, and he escorted her up the steps and into the cathedral.

So intent was Una on watching Thornhill, she didn't notice that Snow had turned until Peter's elbow jabbed into her ribs. Snow was headed right toward them.

Una grabbed Peter by the arm and plunged into the interior of the nearest stall. "How much for this?" she asked, and grabbed up the first talisman she could find.

"A bronze mark," the toothless man said.

"Okay," Una said, and dug the coin out of her change purse.

By this time Snow had passed them. "Do you think she saw us?" Una asked Peter.

Peter shook his head. He wasn't looking at Snow. He was staring at the thing in Una's hand. "You paid a bronze mark for *that*?" Una looked down. Nestled in her palm, cast out of some sort of cheap metal, was an exact replica of the flowering tree.

Chapter 16

Una didn't mention the City Hub to Snow when she returned to Grimm Dorm later that night. Or what had happened at Heart's Place. Snow was already back when Una arrived, and she gave Una the barest of nods. Their room felt like a tomb. Una wasn't sure whether she liked silent, stoic Snow or pouty, mocking Snow better. Neither one was the Snow she had glimpsed earlier that day in the fabric shop. The real Snow. Una couldn't bring herself to apologize, and Snow didn't seem interested in conversation anyway, so when Snow settled in to study, Una headed for the Woodland Room.

While Una didn't exactly enjoy the forced silence of her dorm, she wished a little of it would rub off on Peter. He couldn't stop talking about the City Hub. She and Peter were sitting with Sam in a corner booth. Una flipped through the sheaf of papers titled *How to Win Your Hero* that Peter had given her to memorize before Heroics class. The only reason she actually read the thing was to mock it. The assignment was addressed to Village Girls. "Ready yourself. Make sure you look refreshed before you wait on the Hero. Take a few moments to freshen up. Smooth your hair. Tighten your corset. Remember, you may be the nicest thing he's seen all day."

She tossed the papers aside and pulled out the one book that had consumed her attention all day.

Peter's eyes widened, and he darted a panicky glance round the room. "Una! Put that away!"

She shifted it closer. "No one's around. I checked." She ran her hands over the now familiar cover. They had taken turns trying to decipher the book. She had examined the cover for something, anything, that would help them read it. Peter had looked for hidden clues on the creamy pages, and Sam had smelled the bindings for suspect ingredients. All to no avail. The blank book was just that. A blank book. Nothing spectacular. Nothing about the Muses or the King or, well, anything.

Sam stretched and batted at the book's cover. "Feels old," he said, and licked his paw. "And tastes bad."

Peter grabbed the book from Una. "It doesn't matter, anyway. There's nothing in it." His mouth twisted into a bitter smile. "Maybe I should just give it back to my father. He's the one who thinks it's important enough to save." He shoved the book into his satchel. "Besides, if we get caught with it, then what will we do?"

Una didn't answer. She let her thoughts wander as she watched a cluster of pigs the next booth over laugh and slap a large wolf on the back. *What would we find if we could read the book? A Tale? Heroes? Villains?* Sam curled up next to Una and started a reassuring purr. Soon he was asleep.

Peter went back to memorizing his outline for Heroics. Una reached across Sam and picked up a discarded magazine from the floor. *Today's Faerie* was emblazoned across the front in flowing letters. A pixie face looked up mischievously from the cover, and Una scanned the articles. "Tinkerbelle: How Short Is Too Short? Why Fashion Matters in Today's Tales"; "Take Our New Quiz—Which Flower Is Right for You?" Una flipped through the pages and settled on an interview with a fairy named Lenora who recently had been given the title "Queen of the Newest Fairy Tale."

Peter set his slate aside and grabbed the magazine from her. "Most of this is nonsense, you know."

"I really wish you'd stop taking what I'm reading." Una snatched it back. "What I don't understand is whether she was actually a character in a Tale or not. I mean, has anyone read this"—she glanced down at the page—"this 'Lenora in Neverland'?"

Peter shook his head. "It's not like that. *We* don't read the stories. Oh, we know about the famous characters and all," he said, and pointed to Lenora. "But it's people out there, in the land of the Readers, who read our Tales."

Una looked at the pixie's smiling face. *The land of the Readers.* Like the one where Una had come from. *Like home.* "So when someone reads 'Lenora in Neverland,' Lenora is acting it out here?"

Peter was staring back at the kitchens. "Right. Although it's not acting so much as living out a Tale. You want some pie?" he asked, already halfway out of his seat.

While he was gone, Una studied the pictures of

Lenora's buttercup home. It wasn't that the idea of living out a Tale was weird. It just mattered what kind of Tale you had to live out.

"If you're characters in stories, or characters in training or whatever, don't you need to know what happens in books to live out a good Tale?" she demanded when Peter returned with half a pumpkin pie, still in its pan, and two forks.

"Not really," Peter said around a mouthful of pie. "Any character worth anything has it all stored up here." He tapped his head. "Besides, I don't think characters have ever been big readers. Too busy doing." He scraped his fork around the side of the pan to get at the crust. "Professor Allister went on and on about it in Character Formation last term."

"And?" Una prodded.

"And what?" He stopped shoveling in pie. "I didn't do so well in Character Formation."

Una rolled her eyes, and Peter set his fork down. "It's not all bad. Our studies have to be really practical, to help us learn how to be our type, you know? The Talekeepers say that reading too many other Tales might muddle our motivation."

"And you believe the Talekeepers?" Una exclaimed.

"We already know they've lied about the Muses. And what about the King?"

"Sh!" Peter warned as the Truepenny boy walked by.

Una lowered her voice to a whisper. "I just mean that the Talekeepers seem more and more untrustworthy. If they've lied about the really important stuff, who's to say they aren't lying to you about other things as well? If the people of Story can't read things for themselves, how will they know the truth? Seems fishy to me."

"Well, when you put it like that," Peter said.

Sam stretched and yawned. "Did someone say 'fish'?" He eyed Una's piece of pie.

"It's pumpkin," Una said as Sam sniffed at what was left of the crust. "You can have the rest, Sam." She repositioned herself in the booth and looked out the diamond-paned window next to her.

"I'm not saying I think it's the way things should be," Peter said as he stood to go refill their mugs with cider. "I'm just saying it's the way things are."

It had been storming all evening, and the rumbling thunder shook the windows. Una watched the lightning from her perch near the window and listened to the patter of raindrops.

After an especially bright flash, the Truepenny boy appeared in front of her. She hadn't seen him since she'd spied on him at the Merriweathers', and she had never seen him up close. He seemed older than the other students. Tall and thin, he towered over Una's chair. His skin was very brown, and his dark hair fell over one eye as he looked down at her.

Una felt her face grow hot. Her mind went blank. *Say something. Anything.* But she couldn't help but stare at his eyes. In the dim room they looked dark purple. And when the firelight hit them—

Sam belched, and the moment was gone.

"Um," said Una. "Hi."

"I thought I heard you talking about books."

Before Una could answer, Peter appeared. "Can I help you with something?" Peter asked, looking from Una's face to the other boy's.

"Never mind," Truepenny said. And he left.

Una watched the mysterious boy walk away. "He was so . . ." She trailed off as the boy left the room.

Peter cleared his throat, and Una was sure a lecture about being careful was forthcoming. She spoke first. "Look, he's probably not that bad if he's meeting up with your parents' secret group, right?"

"Maybe." Peter sounded doubtful. "But his father's a Talekeeper. What if he is spying on you for Elton?"

Una chewed her lip. She *had* seen him watching her an awful lot.

"Well, there's only one way to find out what he's up to," Sam said, and gave a tremendous yawn. "Let's follow him and see where he goes."

Chapter 17

By the time they left the Woodland Room, the Truepenny boy was already disappearing into the gardens. Sam, being the best at sneaking, scampered ahead, while Una and Peter drew the hoods of their cloaks up and followed behind. The rain had let up, but everything was still wet and soggy. As they left the lights of Birchwood Hall behind, it got harder and harder to see which way Truepenny had gone. Not many students were out this late, and the few who were hurried by without saying anything. Birchwood Forest grew thick around them, and all Una could hear was the soft squish of their footfalls in the mud.

Suddenly Sam appeared in front of them. "He's gone into the Talekeeper Club," he said, his eyes wild with the hunt.

Una exchanged glances with Peter. As they hurried down the path, her heart sank. She wasn't sure what the Truepenny kid was up to, but she had secretly hoped that he wasn't one of the bad guys.

They arrived at an imposing brick building with no windows. A sloping ramp curved up to the front door, and the three friends stood in the shadows staring at it.

"There's got to be another way in." Una crept over to the side of the building and peered down a dark alley. "Sam? Are you up for a little reconnaissance?"

Sam disappeared into the blackness, and Peter and Una leaned up against the cold bricks. "What do the Talekeepers do at the club?" she asked.

Peter stuck his hands into his pockets. "Make up the latest lies to tell? Play games? Figure out ways to torture WIs?" He shrugged. "Your guess is as good as mine. It's a private club. Invitation only."

Una rubbed her hands together. She was chilled through before Sam appeared.

"There's a kitchen entrance," he said. "Back by the garbage."

They followed him around the building to an even smaller alleyway. A rickety staircase led up to a door. Judging from the awful smell, the garbage hadn't been taken away in some time. Holding her breath, Una followed Peter up the stairs. As they reached the top, the scent of sautéing onions and garlic blended in with the rotting trash.

"There's no way they'll overlook a cat in the kitchens." Sam paused at the top landing. "I'll wait out front. See if our prey comes out and hunt him from there."

Una and Peter slipped in and found themselves in the coatroom of a steamy kitchen. A mustached man in a chef's hat was shouting orders to the workers, who wore starched white uniforms. Peter shoved one into her hand. "Put it on," he said as he pulled another off the hooks behind them. He took Una's cloak, wadded it up with his, and stuck them both outside on the landing. "We'll get them later."

The jacket was too big for Una, but, paired with the long apron, it didn't look too bad. When she was finished, Peter leaned in close. "I've been watching them carry the food out. The dining room must be through those doors. Let's go." He sidled over to a counter and grabbed a tray of desserts.

Una was about to follow him, when the mustached man saw her. "You, there!" he shouted. "Carry this to table forty-two." The man shoved a tray into her hands, pointed her toward the doors, and pushed her through. The sound of quiet conversation and tinkling glasses met her. Dark-brown fabric was draped in artful folds around secluded tables, giving the illusion of privacy for the diners. Servers dressed in white moved silently between the alcoves, and Una was relieved to see that they largely went unnoticed.

She caught the eye of a girl hurrying back to the kitchen. "Table forty-two?" she asked.

The girl gave her a sympathetic glance and pointed toward a particularly well-hidden table. She nearly dropped her tray. The curtains in front of it were parted, and even though he was hidden in shadows, Una could still make out Elton's face. She watched him sip at a goblet of wine, then set the cup down and begin tugging on his pinky ring. Una followed his gaze and saw that he was staring across the dining room at Professor Thornhill, who was bent over a sheet of parchment, a cup of coffee forgotten at her elbow. *Interesting.* How had the Villainy teacher managed to get an invitation to dine at the Talekeeper Club?

Elton leaned forward and began speaking to whoever was sitting across the table from him. Una raised her eyebrows. *So he's not alone.* Maybe the Truepenny boy was with him. Taking a deep breath, she made her way over to table forty-two. Keeping her gaze cast down, and hoping the white hat helped her blend in with the army of other servers, she set the platter of roast duck down. She sneaked a peek, but the fabric blocked his companion from view.

She swiveled on one heel, when Elton's voice called out. "Miss?"

Una painstakingly turned back around and bobbed a curtsy.

"The curtain." Una began to pull the fabric shut with trembling fingers. Elton raised his voice. "And see that the other tables remain empty." He pointed to the booths on either side, and, with a flick of his finger, she was dismissed.

Una breathed a sigh of relief as she ducked behind the curtains around the neighboring table. She arranged their folds to hide her presence and hoped that it would be good enough. It took a moment for her ears to adjust, but if she pressed backward, she could catch the conversation from Elton's table.

"Only two left," someone said. "We've nearly broken one, and the other is the last."

Una took off the ridiculous white hat and eased herself onto her knees. Slowly and carefully, she peered over the half wall dividing the two tables. Una's heart thumped in her chest. Elton wasn't eating dinner with Endeavor Truepenny. Someone dressed all in red sat against the wall, her hood pulled up to hide her face. Elton sat opposite, gnawing away at a bone from the roasted duck.

"With each one, I sense his power growing stronger."

Elton held the bone in midair. "You've seen him?"

"No, you fool. But I do not need to see him to feel his presence. Such is our union." The woman clasped her hands together. "Now you must do your part. Find Alethia."

Una held her breath. Alethia was a name from Griselda's list of Muses.

Elton's words sounded thick in his mouth. "But how would I—"

"We know her book is somewhere at Perrault."

Una swallowed, and it sounded noisy to her ears. But the pair on the other side of the curtains didn't seem to notice.

"Where?" Elton's voice was a low whisper.

The woman slapped her hand flat on the table. "If I

knew that, I wouldn't have called you here, would I?"

"But it's taken years to find the others." Elton sounded frightened. "How am I supposed to—"

"Remember your vows. You must find the book."

A commotion at the dining room entrance caught Una's eye, and she slid back away from the divider. One of the servers had dropped a tray. Una's heart beat wildly. He was dressed in a white uniform, but Una knew him at once. It was the Truepenny boy. He bent down to scrape up the spilled dishes, and Una resituated herself as close to the half wall as possible.

"You fool," the woman was saying. "You waste your time with these pitiful characters."

Elton's voice was icy. "You forget, milady. I have other responsibilities. The Talekeepers were in an uproar once they found out a book had been erased."

"And they needed *you* to calm them?" His companion snorted. "Do you think anything you do will make them *respect* you?" She spat the word at him. "That because you bear the title of Tale Master, it makes you someone important? Don't forget. I know what you once were."

Without a sound, the red-cloaked figure emerged from the alcove. One pale hand grasped her hood down over her face. A red-stoned ring nestled on the last finger of the stranger's hand. Una's heart beat faster, and her mouth went dry. *It has to be Red.*

Una was so busy watching Red leave the restaurant that she nearly cried out when someone plopped down beside her. She gasped, and Peter shushed her.

"Quiet!" He laid a hand on her shoulder. "I've only just now made it out of the kitchen. Did you see that Truepenny works here?"

Una pointed a thumb behind her. "Elton," she whispered. "And Red was with him." A rustling sound from that direction ended their hushed conversation. Elton soon eased himself out from behind the table, brushing the crumbs off his front as he stood. He dabbed his mouth one final time with his napkin, tossed it onto the ground behind him, and left. Another server appeared and began clearing the table.

"We better wait until he's finished," Peter whispered.

The server turned and called after Elton. "Sir!" He held out a wad of paper. "You dropped this!"

But Elton was already at the front doors. Una jumped up. "I'll take it," she said, and snatched the packet from his hands. "I'll take it to him."

She heard a squeal from behind her and spun around

to find the mustached man pulling Peter by the ear. "No time for chatting!" The man dragged Peter back to the kitchen. "The supper rush is upon us."

Una shoved Elton's papers into her skirt pocket. There was no way she was going back into that kitchen. When the time was right, she edged her way around the dining room and out the front door.

Chapter 18

Peter was late for Heroics class. Chef Gaston had kept him until past midnight at the Talekeeper Club. Splitting tips with the other waiters didn't make up for his sore feet and aching head. He had overslept, and now he had to sprint across the campus just to make it to class. He raced up the broad sandstone steps into the white clapboard building. The warning bell had already rung by the time he pushed his way through the crush of students and into the indoor amphitheater.

Peter scanned the dozens of chairs that circled a low platform and finally spotted Una sitting by a leprechaun. He raced down the stairs and slid into a folding seat right before the class bell rang.

Just in time. He handed Una the cloak she had left at the club.

Professor Roderick turned from the blackboard. Today he was dressed like a lumberjack. He wore a green flannel shirt tucked into thick woolen pants that were held up by yellow suspenders. His cherry-red cheeks stood out below his black, shiny eyes as he beamed up at the class. "WELL, WELL, WELL!" he shouted. "ANOTHER DAY OF LEARNING. ANOTHER DAY OF FUN."

Peter scrunched down in his chair. Why had Una decided to sit so close? The pounding in his skull intensified. The only benefit was that Professor Roderick always looked at the upper rows of students. That, coupled with his robust volume, meant that Heroics was the best class in which to hold a private conversation.

"Well?" Una whispered while Professor Roderick went on about how well everyone had done on the latest pop quiz. "What happened?"

"I'll be happy if I never have to see another roast duck." Peter rubbed his temples. "I have new respect for Trix now. Cooking food and waiting tables is hard work."

"Probably good for you," Una said unsympathetically. She eyed the teacher and tossed a packet onto Peter's lap. "The papers Elton dropped. You've *got* to read them."

"I ALWAYS SAY," Professor Roderick was saying, "THE HERO WINS THE DAY. ARE YOU READY TO WIN TODAY?"

Peter slouched down in his seat and untied the ribbon on the little bundle. A childish scrawl covered the kind of lined paper that little Oliver used to practice his letters. Peter bent close to read the smudged ink on the first page.

> *Dear Mother,*
>
> *What an adventure I've had! Walter told me to write it all down so that I can show you these letters when I see you. Walter is the man who helped me on the pirate ship. It was like this, Mother. I found an old book in Grandpapa's library and, because it was raining outside and because Morris was being so mean, I decided to read it.*
>
> *It was a pirate story and, do you know, Mother, halfway through I was there on the boat! It was stormy and there was a great battle and everyone got all wet.*
>
> *Walter was there and his wife. I don't remember her name. They had been reading a book on the bench*

in the park together when they found themselves on the ship, so they were just as surprised as me. His wife kept crying. And then we found an old man who kept talking about going crazy. Walter helped us all hide under an old rowboat that was upside down on the deck.

It was a bully spot for watching the fighting, Mother. I'm going to draw it all out at the end of the letter. The sailors fought the pirates until the pirates went back to their own ship and sailed away. And then our captain gave a very fine speech about being brave and said we were going back to the land. But before we arrived, it all disappeared and we were in a cave.

The captain said he would take care of us and take us to meet some special people. He said there would be a big party and a feast and presents. I held Walter's hand like he asked, I promise I did, Mother, but then I got lost again. There were so many people. I looked everywhere, but I couldn't find the captain again. Or Walter. Or the old man.

But a nice lady found me and took me to her house in the woods and fed me soup. I told her all about our adventure and she said, "That's nice, dear." And I asked her about the presents, but she said that was all a mistake. There wasn't to be a feast. I didn't like that,

Mother, so I started to cry. But then the lady said,
"Hush, dear. Tomorrow, we'll find your mother."
And I guess we will.

I'll see you tomorrow, dearest Mother, and oh what
fun we'll have!

Your Son

"LISTEN UP!" Professor Roderick yelled.
"TODAY WE ARE GOING TO TALK ABOUT
THE IMPORTANCE OF . . ." He paused dramatically
and whispered, "LEADERSHIP." Even his whisper
was louder than an ordinary speaking voice.

Peter glanced around and leaned in closer to Una.
"Who was this kid?"

Professor Roderick boomed, "A HERO LEADS.
WHO CAN GIVE ME AN EXAMPLE OF A
GREAT LEADER?"

Una's violet eyes were suspiciously shiny. "Keep
reading."

He picked up the second letter. This one was even
harder to read, the lines of writing slanting crookedly
across the ruled paper. But Peter could still make out
the words.

Dear Mother,

I put another mark on the wall by my bed tonight. I've been here twenty-two days already. Are you coming for me, Mother? Wherever you are, whatever you are doing right now, I'm thinking of you. Have you gotten my letters? I didn't mean what I said before, Mother. I want to come home.

The people are taking good care of me. They give me tasty food and let me sleep in my very own room. But I wish there were windows. Or that I could go out in the daytime. Sometimes I go out at night, and the moon seems very bright after all the candles.

Today, my tutor brought me a book. It's very old, and it smells bad. He wanted me to try and read it out loud, but now all the words are made up of strange letters that make no sense. He says it's very important that I pronounce them just so. If I read them right, I'll get to see you and Father. I'm trying my hardest, dear Mother, I really am.

Sometimes my tutor asks me a lot of questions about how I came to be here. If I tell it right, he brings me ice cream. I get a bigger scoop when I tell the bits about the others who came in with me. What their names are and where they went after we got here.

Maybe I'll get to see them again someday too. I hope so.

My candle is running low, dearest Mother, or I would write more.

Your Son

Peter set the letter aside as Professor Roderick shouted, "PRINCE CHARMING, FOR EXAMPLE"—he wrote the name on the chalkboard—"IS THE IDEAL LEADER. HE KNOWS WHAT HE IS SUPPOSED TO DO. HE GETS IT DONE. HE WINS THE GIRL. HE LIVES HAPPILY EVER AFTER. A HERO."

Peter looked around. Not too many of the students appeared to be listening. "One more," he said, and swallowed. "Please tell me this has a happy ending."

Una didn't meet his eyes, and Peter willed himself to pick up the last sheet. It was rumpled like it had gotten rained on. A few of the words ran together in places, but when he smoothed the paper, Peter could make them out.

Dear Mother,
I've made twenty-nine little marks by my bed,

Mother. My tutor saw them today and told me to stop. I told him I had to keep track so I would know when it was my birthday. He said he would tell me when. You know, Mother, I don't believe him.

But I do like it when he laughs at my stories. Today he wanted to know about you and Father and what it was like to live at my house. I told him everything I knew, but he must have forgotten about the ice cream, because I didn't get any after my dinner.

Sometimes a cat comes down to my room. It's a nice cat with big gold eyes and a loud purr. I don't tell my tutor about the cat. I don't want him to disappear too.

I read the book out loud today, Mother, and I thought I had done it all wrong. When I got to the end of the first page, there was a loud noise like a cannon. I covered my ears, but then I had to cover my eyes, because the light that came into the room was so bright. When I could see again, I saw that the book was gone and there was a huge shimmering mirror in its place. It looked like it was going to catch fire. I wanted to cry then, Mother, because I knew my tutor would be angry.

But he wasn't angry at all, Mother. He cried. But

he said it was because he was so happy. I said that Father was always upset if I lost his books, but that only made my tutor laugh all the more. I asked him if I could see you since I read the book right, and he said I could. So I guess this is my last letter to you, dear Mother, for soon I will be able to give you a great big hug.

Your Son

Peter sat and stared at the paper for what felt like a long time. But when he looked up, Professor Roderick was still rapping his chalk against the chalkboard.

"WHAT ELSE ABOUT THE HANDSOME PRINCE? WHO CAN TELL US WHAT MAKES HIM A GOOD HERO?"

Peter felt sick to his stomach. "Do you think that kid got to see his mother?" he asked Una.

Her mouth said, "Sure, he did," but her eyes spoke differently. Peter didn't think the kind of people who would lock up a little boy and only let him out at night were the kind of people who would make sure he made it safely home.

"That's horrible," Peter said. "Why did you even show me these? It's not like we can help him."

Una tucked the letters back into her satchel. "Peter, don't you realize? That little boy, whoever he was, was Written In."

Sam joined them for lunch at their usual table in the Woodland Room. Una kept folding and unfolding the letters.

"Another WI. I wish we knew exactly when he was here," Peter said, and took a bite of roast beef sandwich.

"These letters are pretty old." Una spread out the last letter again. "So he must be all grown-up now, right? He was just a little boy when he wrote them."

"Why do you think Elton had the letters?" Peter set his sandwich aside and sipped at his root beer.

"Why else?" Una tied the letters up with an old hair ribbon she had swiped from Snow's bureau. "Because he's a Tale Master and it's his job to take away any shred of information having to do with the Muses or the WIs they wrote in."

"Or maybe it wasn't him who had the letters," Peter said. "Maybe it was Red who dropped them at the club. Maybe she has the rest."

"What if there are no other letters?" Sam asked, looking up from his second tuna fish sandwich. When

Peter gave him a pointed look, he said, "Well, it doesn't sound as though he was in the best place, does it? 'They don't let me out during the day. They make me read the book.'" Sam spread out his claws to nibble at a little piece of tuna he had overlooked.

"Sam!" Peter said sharply.

"You don't have to try and protect me, Peter," Una said. "I already know the other WIs were killed. But this is the first real clue we've found that might tell us why someone Wrote them here in the first place." She tried not to think about the little boy from the letters. She hoped he had really given his mother that hug. "I wonder who his tutor was."

"No one I'd like to meet." Peter took a big bite of sandwich and kept talking around it. "Whoever he was, he forced the boy to read the book. Sounds like some kind of enchantment or something."

"More questions! Can't we get any answers around here?" Una propped her head up in her hands. "Well, whatever it was, that's what made the mirror appear. I think it was something only a WI could do." She shivered at that. Despite how normal it felt to be in Story, she'd never gotten used to the idea that someone had brought her here for some specific reason.

"Maybe we'll find something in the Museum,"

Peter said. They had decided to visit the Museum the next day during their morning free period. Peter said that students went there for field trips, so it would be easy to blend in with the other visitors.

"Maybe," Una said, but she felt doubtful. Besides getting their questions answered, she and Peter wanted to find proof that the Talekeepers had lied about everything. Then maybe the characters would rally and throw the Tale Master out of office before he and Red did whatever they were planning to do with the Muse books. She chewed her lip. They were pinning too much hope on the Museum. She hardly thought they'd find information about the Muses and the WIs and the King all in one place.

She reached over and scratched the top of Sam's head. Sam flattened his ears, but then gave himself over to the scratching.

"A little to the left," Sam said. "This makes me hungry. Cow, please." Sam pointed a paw at the burger line.

Una grimaced. "How can you eat other animals, Sam?"

"Like cows?" Sam glinted one green eye toward her. "Why, those aren't the talking kind, of course." He licked his chops. "I mean, eating talking animals would be . . . well, it would be cannibalism."

Una didn't feel that this really explained anything and picked at her macaroni and cheese. "Eating an animal really doesn't bother you?" she asked Peter when he returned with two giant hamburgers.

"It's like Sam said." Peter slid a burger across to Sam. "We'd never eat a talking animal."

Una looked around the dining hall. She had gotten so used to seeing animals in her classes that it seemed totally normal for that wily-looking fox at the next table to be chatting with a dog. Maybe it was because nearly all of her classes were full of students from the Fantasy District. Peter had told her that most talking animals appeared in fantasy stories, so, unless they were horses or cows or other barnyard animals, which stayed out on the Ranch, they lived in Birchwood Forest.

The dog winked at her, and she realized that she had been staring. She supposed that going to school with animals was no worse than having a talking cat for one of your best friends. She smiled at Sam, who was listening to Peter describe his experience at the Talekeeper Club. Peter punctuated each description with a big bite of hamburger. Una listened for a while, and then lost the rest of her appetite as Peter licked his greasy fingers.

She laid her head down on the table and muttered words which, in her old life, she never would have imagined saying: "Wake me up for Villainy."

Chapter 19

Snow was on her way to grab a quick lunch before class when her mother caught up with her in the middle of the quad.

"Professor," Snow said, and nodded at her. Her mother had never sought her out during the week before.

"I've been looking for you, Snow." Professor Thornhill's usually smooth face was creased with worry. "I don't think it can wait." She touched Snow's shoulder lightly and steered her toward an iron bench.

"I don't have long," Snow said. What was she supposed to do, drop everything just because her mother had come to find her? Over the weekend her mother had met the strange man at the cathedral again. But this morning when Snow asked if she had a nice break, her mother claimed to have spent the whole time on campus. Snow pursed her lips and sat stiffly on the edge of the bench.

Professor Thornhill folded her hands in her lap. "I'll get straight to the point. Why is Mr. Elton interested in you?"

Snow stared down at her hands. "I don't know what you mean." She fidgeted with her satchel. Why should she feel guilty for agreeing to help Elton? Her mother was the one who was sneaking around and lying about it. *I'm not doing anything wrong.* She stuck out her chin and stared defiantly into her mother's eyes. Eyes that always looked sad.

"Snow, he is an evil man," she said.

Snow laughed at this. "He's a stupid old fool, but he's not evil."

Her mother didn't argue. Instead she said, "Whatever he's asked you to do, please don't do it."

Snow stared hard at her mother. "Are you two having some sort of . . . fight?" she asked slowly.

Her mother brushed at her skirt and shook her head. "Snow, that's really none of your business. The point is: he's evil. And he must be stopped. Please. Don't do whatever it is he wants you to do."

Snow stiffened. "I hardly think his requests are evil."

"So he *has* asked you to do something."

Snow looked into her mother's sad eyes and said, "That's really none of your business."

Her mother flinched.

Snow stood. "I have to go."

When she glanced back at the bench, she saw her mother folded over, her head in her hands. Well, let her be upset! Why was she trying to interfere with Snow's life anyway? What did she expect? A cozy little chat? *Why sure, Professor, we can talk about dresses and boys and, oh yeah, where you've been for the past thirteen years.*

She walked briskly across the quad. It wasn't like she was telling Elton anything important. Besides, as much as she hated Elton, she could understand what it was like to have someone not like you back. Didn't she feel like slapping Una's smug little face whenever she saw her laughing with Peter? And Elton had it worse than she did. He must have really fallen hard for her mother. His suits hung a little looser these days, and his face looked gray and old. Maybe she would toss him a bone. It would probably make his day if she told him her mother had asked after him. Was her mother still sitting on the bench? Snow resisted the urge to look

over her shoulder. Instead, she held her head up high
and didn't turn back.

Una stifled a groan when Snow popped through the
Villainy classroom door and slid into the seat next to
her. Neither said anything, and Una felt lucky that
their mutual silence was holding outside of their dorm
room. A tiny woman dressed in a black jumpsuit swept
in next, a line of students emptying into their seats
behind her with a minimum of fuss. Somewhere, a
class bell rang.

The woman had a veil over her face that bobbed as she
clapped her hands. "Good afternoon, class. I am Mrs.
Underwood, and I will be substituting for Professor
Thornhill, who was called away unexpectedly. I hope
you have come prepared for a practical lesson today."
It was an ordinary enough sentence, but Una drew in
her breath when she heard it. Something about Mrs.
Underwood's voice compelled Una to listen and want
to do what she said.

"The power of the human voice to enchant its
hearer is one essential to Villain and Hero alike," Mrs.
Underwood said.

Una didn't know whether it was an enchantment

or a magic trick, but she craned her head with the rest
of the students. Mrs. Underwood settled herself in the
front corner of the room. Where was Thornhill? And
what had she been doing last night at the Talekeeper
Club?

"Today, we will have a Battle of Words," Mrs.
Underwood announced, her rich voice at once
beckoning and commanding. An excited whisper ran
around the room.

Mrs. Underwood instructed the students to line
up facing each other. Once everyone had situated
themselves to her satisfaction, she raised both hands.
The two girls at the front of the line curtsied formally
to each other.

Mrs. Underwood called out, "Mystery."

"Secret," the girl on the left said.

"Riddle," the other answered.

Mrs. Underwood held up her right hand, and the
first girl smiled. She moved to the back of the line. The
other girl went to the side of the classroom. *Thornhill
is one big mystery.* If Una hadn't seen them both at the
Club, she might have guessed that Thornhill and Red
were one and the same. *What is Thornhill's secret?*

Una hadn't participated in this sort of challenge
before, but it looked easy enough. She just had to say

a word similar to the one Mrs. Underwood called out. And remember to curtsy. No matter how often she practiced, her curtsies usually came out all wobbly.

"Silence," came the voice from the front of the room. Una shuffled forward in line as the other students replied.

"Quiet."

"Solitude."

And on and on it went. When Una stepped up to meet her opponent, it was none other than Endeavor Truepenny. She felt the heat rise to her face as she dropped into a low curtsy. It worked well enough until the last minute, when she had to slide her foot out to catch her balance. The boy smiled at her. He had a nice smile.

"Stranger," Mrs. Underwood's voice called out.

"Villain," Truepenny said as though it was a question.

Una looked him directly in the eye. "Misfit," she said. She didn't know why the boy was involved with the Merriweathers' group or what he was doing at the Talekeeper Club the night before. But he had to know she was not a Villain.

His smile this time was lopsided, and Una followed his gaze to Mrs. Underwood's raised hand. She had won. She gave him another curtsy and slowly turned around to walk back to the end of the line. She almost felt bad for beating him.

While she was waiting for her next turn, she wondered at Mrs. Underwood's choice of word. Did she suspect that Una was a stranger? Peter would say it was a coincidence, but she wasn't so sure. *And where is Peter anyway?* He had disappeared after lunch, but he should be here by now. The Battle of Words continued, getting harder as students were eliminated. "Sincerity." "Phenomenal." "Execution." "Lascivious." "Foppish." She swiveled around as a carroty-haired boy in front of her lost his match. She was next, and standing opposite her was Horace Wotton.

Una gave him a scathing look as she curtsied. Horace smirked back and didn't even bother to bow.

"Victory," Mrs. Underwood called out. The challenge word echoed off the walls.

Horace lifted his head back and laughed. Then, he looked right into Una's eyes and shot his word at her. "Superiority," he said, and didn't even watch for Mrs. Underwood's raised hand before sauntering off.

Una stared at his spiky hair. That jerk thought he had already won. She clenched and unclenched her fists. "Mastery," she said in a clear voice that sliced the air.

Everyone watched Mrs. Underwood's hands. They wavered for a moment, but then the hand on Una's side went up. Most everyone cheered, and Una tipped her head toward Horace as she went to the end of the line. Horace scowled and slumped down next to the other students who were out of the game.

The class was dismissed soon after, and Una floated out of the room, buoyed up by her victory over Horace and the fact that she had won every round she played. Maybe she was starting to fit into this world after all.

Sam caught up with her as she was crossing the quad.

"Have you seen Peter?" she asked.

"Cutting class," Sam said, unconcerned. "The Museum."

"Without us?" Una demanded. "We're supposed to go tomorrow!" He was probably trying to protect her. *He'll need protecting when I get my hands on him.* What if he found something interesting without her? *He won't even be looking for clues about the King!*

"He said he'd fill us in during Outdoor Experiential Questing," Sam said as he loped along. "I guess we'll find out soon enough."

*C*hapter 20

*P*eter crossed his arms and scowled down at the floor. His plan wasn't working at all. Losing Una on the way to Villainy wasn't the hard part. Nor was skipping class. Neither was getting into the free tour of the Museum. The problem was that he couldn't break away from the group.

The tour guide watched everyone like a hawk, his turquoise umbrella held aloft as he said in a crisp voice, "This way, please. Follow me. Keep up, please." His stories were interesting, but how he could go on and on about dates and facts and minute details *and* notice every person in the tour group and where they were headed was a mystery to Peter.

Twice he had deliberately tried to linger in corridors, feigning interest in plaques of celebrated Talekeepers shaking hands. Immediately, the tour guide popped up next to him, crossing from the front of the group to the back in seconds. "We're leaving this area now. Please keep up with the rest of the group." Each time Peter fell back in line with the others.

The Museum itself was beautiful. Peter's last visit had been the year before on a school field trip, and he had only cared about getting to the gift shop at the end. Now he kept a sharp eye out for anything remotely connected to Muses, books, or being Written In—but so far, no luck.

The building sprawled like a palace, corridors sprouting off in every direction. Long ballrooms with painted frescoes connected to immense bedchambers, the king-size beds tiny compared to the vast rooms and high ceilings. And desks were everywhere. Ornate wooden pieces took up entire walls, their massive doors hiding who-knew-what. One room was filled with polished wood desks that reflected the chandeliers above. Another had only glass-topped tables with quills and ink set at jaunty angles.

The guide went on and on about which Talekeeper had stayed in which room, but what he never said was whether anyone's Tales had been written here. The closest he had gotten to anything remotely interesting was when he said there used to be rooms dedicated to each of the Muses. But then the whole group had gone all quiet, and it wasn't like Peter could ask a follow-up question about the Muses. The tour guide hadn't said another interesting word since.

Peter squared his shoulders and pretended to be captivated by someone's question about an ancient-looking printing press. If he could just find one of those Muse rooms. Peter felt a chill and shrugged it off. He kept reminding himself that the Muses weren't hiding in the Museum. But it didn't make him feel any braver.

The tour guide paused his lecture and stooped to tie his shoe. Now was Peter's chance. He ducked out of the group, slipped under a maroon rope with a Restricted sign hanging from it, and hurried down a narrow corridor. With any luck, the guide wouldn't notice he had left.

Peter had only gone a little way when he heard approaching voices. His heart sank. If he was caught now, he would certainly be kicked out and, no doubt, reported to his parents. He glanced quickly about and slid into a small room off to the left. It was barely furnished: a few chairs, low tables, and a marble-topped desk that took up most of one corner. Opposite it, a curving iron staircase twisted up to another floor. The voices were getting louder.

"Books are disappearing from the Vault," a man said. "One has even been erased. It's time for us to read them. And why shouldn't we? We're Talekeepers, after all."

They were right outside the door. Peter ran over to the massive desk and flung himself beneath it, pulling the desk chair in front of his body. Anyone who looked closely would spot him, but it was the best he could do. A moment later, three figures entered the room, deep in conversation.

"You're Talekeepers and you've never read any of the Tales?" one of them said. The voice was familiar, but Peter couldn't quite place it. He peeked out from under the desk, but he could only see one of their faces.

"No." The Talekeeper scratched at his beard and scuffed his foot on the floor. "I actually believed that Story was better off without them. Until now."

"And you? You've swallowed everything you've been told as well?"

Peter strained his ears. Where did he know that voice from?

The other Talekeeper shrugged apologetically. Peter thought he looked too young to be a Talekeeper. "But we want to read them now."

"Which is why you've called me here."

"Of course. We've heard that you were the best. That you knew the most about"—the bearded man's voice dropped—"the old ways."

They moved toward the staircase, and their voices faded. Peter leaned forward, straining his ears. The floor beneath him creaked, sounding exceptionally loud in the little room. The three paused at the bottom of the stairs.

"Did you hear that?" One of them turned to peer back at the doorway. Peter stifled a gasp. He should have known! The familiar voice belonged to Professor Thornhill! He had listened to her often enough in Villainy. The seconds dragged on. Peter held his breath.

After a long pause, Professor Thornhill leaned back against a low table. "And what do Talekeepers hope to find in the old Tales? I thought it was your policy to lock up anything the Muses had written. Don't you people set the enchantments yourself so that no one can read them? Why, Mr. Elton himself just—"

"The Tale Master doesn't know." The young

Talekeeper clasped his hands together as though he were praying. "And he is the one who sets the enchantment. Look. Some of us just want to read the Tales."

"Elton doesn't know." Thornhill raised her eyebrows. "Now, that's interesting. But I need more. Tell me what you hope to learn, and I'll decide if it's worth the risk."

The young Talekeeper seemed to come to some sort of internal decision, for his nervousness disappeared as he answered. "We want to know about the Muses. What made them go bad? And what kind of Tales did they write?"

Thornhill's face was unreadable. "And how am I to know you won't turn me in for practicing the old ways?"

The bearded Talekeeper dug in his pocket and opened his palm to Thornhill. "We want to find the Muses."

Peter's mouth dropped open. Thornhill didn't question his statement or scoff at the idea that the Muses weren't really gone from Story, like Peter's father had done. She studied the Talekeeper's palm. "And what makes you think the Muses want to be found by you?"

The Talekeeper had no answer, but he stubbornly

held his hand out. Whatever was in it, it apparently satisfied Professor Thornhill. "Very well," she said decisively. "The old saying goes, 'Books that you carry to the fire and hold readily to hand are the most useful of all.' Take me somewhere private and I will show you."

The trio disappeared up the stairs, and Peter didn't waste any time after they had gone. Things were worse than he had thought. He crept up the narrow staircase and followed the sound of muffled voices. They were moving farther away. He paused at the first landing and tried the door. It clicked open, and Peter peered into a dark room. Everything was quiet now. *So all the books in the Vault are blank.* It sounded like something the Tale Master would do: enchant them blank just in case a character actually got ahold of one. He tried not to think about the other thing, the part about looking for the Muses. He moved quickly through the room to the door opposite.

The voices moved farther from the door, and however much he strained his ears, after a while Peter heard only silence. He tried the door handle, but it didn't budge. He slumped down against it. So much for learning more about the books.

The shaft of light from the stairway entrance bathed everything in shadows. As his eyes adjusted, he saw that the room was full of oddly shaped furniture. The thing closest to him was covered with an old sheet. He reached up, pulled it off, and a cloud of dust sent him coughing. Underneath, he found a solid-looking round wooden table. He moved past it and uncovered an imposing thronelike chair, a set of wooden benches, and an old jousting lance. He turned around and nearly bumped into someone. Choking back a scream, Peter was halfway to the door before he realized it wasn't a real person. He crept closer and tugged off the figure's sheet to uncover a set of rusted knight's armor. His heart sped up. This stuff was old. He made his way around the room, sorting through the jumble of odds and ends: old tent frames leaned up next to some ancient-looking swords, and a few splintered spears were mixed in with cartographer's instruments and old saddles. This room wasn't like the rest of the Museum, full of desks or disproportionate beds. This was a forgotten armory.

In the farthest corner, he found a pedestal that looked just like the ones in the Tale station. But where the exam packet would have gone, there was a layer of dirt. Peter leaned in close and rubbed the grime off with his sleeve. It looked like there was some sort of symbol carved into the stone. And the letters above it were much clearer. A few more scrubs, and he could make them out: VIRTUS. Peter stared at the letters. *Virtus. The Muse.* His skin felt all crawly. He bent closer and studied the pedestal. Characters must have entered the Muse books from these rooms at the Museum. Now that he thought of it, it was obvious. It wasn't like they'd have had a Museum about the Muses back in the days of the Muses. This building must have been something else at one time. A place especially for the Muses.

A sound from the next room startled him. Thornhill and the Talekeepers were coming back. He moved swiftly toward the open doorway and stumbled out into the light.

Chapter 21

Una's fingers were stained red from berry juice. The afternoon's Outdoor Experiential Questing class was about camping essentials, and Professor Edenberry thought they were advanced enough to identify poison berries in the row of bushes planted in a clearing. It sounded straightforward enough, but Peter and Sam wouldn't stop grumbling.

"What a pointless assignment," Sam growled. "Everyone knows you don't eat poison berries in the woods." He seemed to have no trouble sorting out the shiny red berries.

"I can't tell them apart," Peter said. "What the heck kind of project is this? They're *all* shiny and red."

Una took small comfort in his difficulty. He didn't seem regretful at all that he'd sneaked off to the

Museum without her.

"And if you'd gotten caught?" he had said in a perfectly calm voice. "What then? Me, they'd just expel."

Una couldn't argue with that except to say, "I wouldn't have gotten caught."

Professor Edenberry picked his way behind her as he went from student to student. Una had a hard time thinking of him as anything but a nice old man who lived a secret double life. Along with the Merriweathers. And Elton. And Endeavor Truepenny. Was there no person in Story who was actually as they appeared to be?

Una heedlessly tossed berries into her tray. Who cared about learning to avoid poisonous berries when the Muses were still in Story? She moved a bit closer to the bush Peter was eyeing as though it was a dragon needing slaying. "Tell me about Virtus's room again," she whispered. "And the pedestal."

Peter plucked a black berry, scrutinized it, and tossed it aside. "Stop torturing yourself, Una. That pedestal hadn't been used in ages."

Una choked back a nasty comment. Peter hadn't sounded so sure of himself when he first got back from the Museum. Whatever he said now, he had been creeped out.

"Right," said Sam as he popped a dangerous-looking white berry into his mouth with no adverse effect. "You'd need a Muse book to work it anyway."

"And the symbol on the pedestal?" she asked. "You said it might have been a tree. Did it look anything like this?" She pulled a crumpled paper out of her pocket and shoved it at Peter. It was the drawing of the tree the old lady at the Vault had given them. "And you didn't see anything about the King? If *I* had been there, I *know* I could have found out something."

"Una . . ." Red berries thumped forcefully into Peter's tray. "Forget about the King. We need to focus on the Muses." He reached for another berry, and his tray hit a branch. Berries spilled everywhere.

Una pretended not to hear Peter swear. "But the King's important," she said under her breath. "What do you think, Sam?" she asked to distract herself.

"Actually"—Sam sat back on his haunches—"I tend to agree with Una. According to Animal Lore, there was in fact a Good King, a great friend to cats and other furry beasts. Of course, our ancients say the King had some feline aid when he ruled long ago, but who's to say? We have quite heated discussions about it in the Quorum."

Una and Peter both stared at Sam. Una had never heard him say so many words all at once.

"The Quorum?" Peter asked.

"Animal Lore?" Una said. "You mean you know something about the King?"

Sam inelegantly raised his hind leg over his head and began to lick. "In general, the affairs of humans are of little interest to us. No offense, Una."

"Sam! Why haven't you said anything before?" Peter demanded.

"You never asked," Sam said as he squinted at them.

Just then Horace, who was two bushes over, began to choke and gag. Professor Edenberry approached with a resigned look on his face. "Remember. Do not eat any of the berries until I check your work," he said in a loud voice, and looked at Horace's eyes. "Off to the Healer with you, son."

Una picked berries in silence until Edenberry moved out of the clearing. "What else do you know, Sam? Anything about WIs?"

Sam yawned. "We care little for such disturbances. Yes, there have been cats who claimed to have once been in another world. But a patch of sunlight here or there, what's the difference?" He blinked his eyes like some ancient philosopher dispensing wisdom.

"You can't be serious," Peter said.

Sam widened his eyes at Peter, and then they became slits. "If you're not interested, I won't bore you with the secrets of the Feline Quorum," he said, and curled his tail neatly around his forepaws.

"Of course we're interested!" Una exclaimed, but despite all her well-aimed compliments and the scratching of Sam's favorite spots, he remained silent.

"Way to go, Peter," Una said after class. "Maybe he knows other stuff! I can't believe I never asked him what he thought." She looked over at Sam, who was now talking to a pretty calico.

"Animal Lore's all right for stories around the campfire, Una, but you can't go believing everything you hear. They'd just as soon tell you the King was a giant tiger as tell you the truth about anything. Most of their Tales are full of poems called 'Lines on a Rat in the Sun' and stuff like that."

Sam was heading their way. She elbowed Peter in the ribs. If he would just shut up, she might be able to find out something else.

"Can you tell us anything about the Muses? What do you think, Sam? Do any of the felines know why they Wrote characters In?" she asked courteously.

"Who are we going to ask next, Una?" Peter asked, rubbing his ribs. "Squirrels? The ponies down at the farm? That's crazy!"

"I *said*, 'What do you think, *Sam*?'" Una turned her back on Peter. *Like I haven't heard Peter's opinion a hundred times already.*

Sam didn't deign to reply to Peter. Instead he brushed by Una. "You people are just distracted by the nonessentials." They crossed a little footbridge, and he hopped up onto the railing.

Peter crossed his arms. "Which are?"

"Which of you is right, who should have gone to the Museum, blah, blah, blah." Sam leaped down from the railing, landing softly in the fallen leaves. "What you need to do is work with what you have. Have you figured out a way to break the enchantment on the book from the Vault?"

"He has a point," Una said, giving Sam a quick scratch.

Peter was looking at Sam with something akin to respect. "You're absolutely right, Sam. I've been so caught up with what I found in Virtus's room, I almost forgot about the book." He reached for Sam, who easily moved out of his grasp.

"I think, Peter," he said archly, "you are confusing me with a dog." And, with a polite nod to Una, Sam walked off into the woods, his tail arched in a perfect question mark.

Una laughed out loud. "I think you have offended an esteemed member of the Feline Quorum," she said.

Peter didn't smile. He was looking back toward Birchwood Hall. "'Books that you carry to the fire and hold readily to hand are the most useful after all.' That's what Thornhill said. What do you think it means?"

"There's only one way to find out." Una led the way back to Birchwood Hall, but she said little. Sam was right. Reading the book was important. If what she thought was correct, finding answers wasn't just about discovering why she had been Written In. It was solving a mystery that stretched back to before the Muses. And somehow the missing pieces—the books, who it was that Wrote her In, what had happened with the Muses—they all fit together to form a picture of the King.

Chapter 22

Peter and Una met at the entrance to the gardens later that night. "Are you sure no one will find us here?" Una asked.

"I'm not *sure*, but it's the best place I can think of," Peter said, leading the way down the twisty garden path. "Besides, most of the students are in bed, and it's too cold for doing much outside anyway."

Una followed silently after him. Her breath made little puffs in the frosty air. Above her, wooden bridges connected the upper levels of Birchwood Hall. She hoped nobody was looking down at them.

The path led them under arbors and through hedges. Little offshoots trailed into the surrounding forest, but Peter didn't take one of these. Deeper and deeper into the gardens they went, until Peter finally ducked around the back of a little shed and set his lantern on the ground.

Una drew her cloak snug about her and tucked her hands inside. She watched as Peter gathered a tiny pile of kindling and lit it with the flame from his lantern. The small fire took the chill off the air. "Well?" she said. "Don't tell me you forgot to bring it."

"I brought it, all right," Peter said and pulled out the book they had taken from the Vault.

Una took it from him and ran her fingers along the weathered cover. "'Books that you carry to the fire and hold readily to hand are the most useful after all.' Well, here goes nothing," she said, and moved close to the fire.

The book didn't change. Maybe it had to do with the "readily to hand" part. She tried switching the book from hand to hand. They tossed the book back and forth over the fire. She and Peter even danced around the fire, just in case there was a special way you had to bring the book to the fire, but its pages stubbornly remained blank.

Peter stared into the dying flames and then gently took the book from Una's hands. He approached the fire, one slow step after another, holding the book overhead.

"Peter, no," Una whispered. Was this how the book

from the potting shed had become a little pile of ash? She put her hands up to shield her eyes, but in the last second she felt compelled to watch. With one quick movement Peter threw the book into the flames. There was a little spout of sparks and then, nothing. The book didn't catch fire. Which was, in Una's opinion, a good thing. The tiny sparks glowed for a moment and then died. The fire slowly burned down next to nothing, and the book sat untouched in the ashes.

Peter squatted down. "Maybe Thornhill didn't know how to break the enchantment after all."

Una patted his shoulder. "We did the best we could." Her mouth twisted in disappointment. She had been so sure that once she could read the books the Talekeepers worked so hard to keep hidden, she'd find out some answers. She sat back on her heels and then gasped. Something was happening to the book. The dull brown changed, warming into a rich chocolate. Gold flecks sparkled and made the whole thing look like it was shimmering. Embossed letters trailed across the front. *The Tale of Jedediah Lionheart*, it read. Underneath, faintly first, and then with clarity, more words appeared: *A long life, well lived.*

Peter gingerly pulled the book from the fire and opened its cover. The first page was blossoming into print. In the center of the page, flowery script grew and twisted, the ink somersaulting and climbing until the entire creamy page was beautifully illuminated. An etching of a silver tree stretched over the center of the page. From its roots flowed a stream of water, cascading down to the bottom of the page. Underneath the image stood finely wrought letters that read, *Ex Libris*. And underneath that: *Rex*.

"The tree!" Una reached out a finger to touch the scripted page. It was warm. "It feels . . . alive," she said.

At first, they huddled together and pored over the book by the lantern's flickering light. It told a Tale about a character named Jedediah Lionheart. After a while, they gave that up and took turns reading the Tale out loud. With every passing page, Una's heart sank. Why would the Tale Master bother to censor these books? Jedediah's Tale wasn't even remotely interesting. Jedediah lived out in the country. He cared for his estate and grounds. He gave his wife nice presents. He played with his children. He helped the peasants on his lands who were hungry. Boring old everyday stuff. The most exciting thing that happened was when his son, Royal, got in trouble for fighting with some other kids.

Una yawned and began to skim yet another chapter

where Jedediah went for his morning walk before having breakfast.

Peter stood and rekindled the fire's remains. "Might as well be warm," he mumbled.

Una was about to call it a night, when something caught her eye. "Peter, look at this." There was an entire chapter in which Jedediah traveled to funerals for each of his three brothers. After a period of mourning, he set out to find the Muses who had killed them. He journeyed throughout Story, and the descriptions of what he saw around the time of the Unbinding made Una's stomach turn. Orphaned children. Families who fled their towns only to freeze, homeless and starving, in the mountains. Characters who disappeared and the loved ones who were constantly searching for them. And the many, many who were dead. No village in Story was left untouched. The characters who weren't too terrified to leave home were furious, angry that their rulers had betrayed them, a fact made worse by their inability to confront the Muses. By the end of his Tale, Jedediah, hardened and embittered by the Muses' silence, had nearly given up hope. No matter where Jedediah went, no one could find a Muse book.

Una stopped reading. "I can see why the Talekeepers

locked these books up," she said. "I can't believe all this stuff really happened to people."

Peter had a sickly expression on his face. He didn't say anything.

Una forced herself back to the book, and there, near the end, was where she saw it. Jedediah came across an old stone cairn, and the place had the feel of Muse magic. Una skimmed ahead and gasped. "He found a Muse, Peter! This is what we were looking for! Listen!" She yanked Peter down next to her and read: "'Jedediah moved the stones to reveal a small book, covered with black leather, with a marking on the binding. A black dragon in flight was surrounded by a border of royal blue. He raised the book above his head with a triumphant cry.

"'Jedediah checked to make sure his sword was strapped securely to his back, hid two more daggers in his boots, and turned his attention back to the Muse book. His tall form bent low over the cover, and, after tracing the dragon markings according to the pattern, he entered the book. It took him straight to Sophia's house.'"

Peter tugged the book closer.

"Hey," Una exclaimed.

"It *took* him to Sophia?" He read the words for himself and whistled. "Sounds like he finally found one of the Muses."

"That's what I said." Una shivered. Her arms were breaking out in goose bumps. "Let's keep reading."

Jedediah arrived on a deserted beach. He climbed the coastal path and strode up to a weathered cottage. When the door opened, Sophia stood there, and her dark beauty matched the storming ocean. Jedediah silently followed her in and seated himself at her table.

"What is the one thing you seek, Jedediah Lionheart?" Sophia asked.

"It's my son, Royal," Jedediah said. "Whatever I do seems wrong, and I fear he will become a weak-willed man."

"Really?" Una said out loud. "He's sitting down with one of the Muses, the ones he's been hunting forever, and he asks her about his nincompoop son? What was he thinking!"

Peter snorted. "Obviously he wasn't."

They turned back to the book, and Una groaned.

Sophia was giving Jedediah some parenting advice over tea. Una skipped ahead:

> *"Tell me how the characters fare," Sophia said then. "For it seems many ages since I have had a visitor."*
>
> *Jedediah shook his head vigorously, and stood so quickly that the chair behind him toppled from the table. In a flash, his sword was out and pointed toward Sophia.*
>
> *"Murderess," he hissed. "I almost fell for your enchantments. Are you blinding me with your feigned hospitality before you kill me like you did my kin?"*
>
> *"Peace," Sophia said. She stood and, with a fingertip, directed the blade down to the floor. "Why are you troubled?"*
>
> *"Three deaths at least I lay at your feet." His voice cracked. "My brothers."*

Una and Peter had seen Jedediah do a lot of things through all his travels. But they had never seen him weep, and Una found her own eyes watering at the account of his grief. She wiped them with her sleeve and went back to the Tale.

When Jedediah's grief was spent, he told her of all the suffering he had witnessed in Story.

"This is a grave thing," Sophia said. "Your brothers died before their time. This is not the Tale we purposed for them. Nor did we write these many sorrows for the people of Story." Sophia bowed her head. "We swore to never harm the characters of Story. We obey the King's orders and have only ever framed the Tales. To ink death would be wrong."

"So you admit it then," Jeremiah spat. "You confess your oath breaking."

"Broken my oaths?" Sophia's smooth face wrinkled in concern. "But this is an untruth."

After that the house began to shake violently. The window cracked and shattered into pieces. Chairs toppled, books fell off the shelves, and dishes clattered to the floor. Lady Sophia was thrown onto the edge of her desk. A tremendous peal of thunder reverberated through the sky. Then, all was silent.

In a matter of moments, her house was destroyed. The sea air blew the smell of salt in through the broken window. And something else. Something that smelled like decay. A seagull lay silent in the shards of glass. Dead.

Lady Sophia cried out in dismay, but it wasn't about the bird. She ran to a little trunk under her window and flipped the lid open. From its depths, she pulled out a packet. It looked like she had torn a chapter out of a book, and she crushed these papers to her chest.

"His bonds are weakening. You must warn Alethia," she whispered to Jedediah. She cupped his head in her hands and spoke fiercely. "You must find her and warn her."

"Alethia!" Una cried. "That's the Muse whose book Red was telling Elton to find. The one that is somewhere at Perrault!"

"Maybe Jedediah talked to her as well," Peter said. "Keep reading."

Sophia swept Jedediah out of the house and down to a tiny rowboat that lay hidden in the cove.

"Someone will be coming now. I will not see you again, friend Jedediah." The sky grew dark, and a cold sleet began to fall. Lady Sophia's fingers worked the air, weaving a charm. When the glowing strands had sunk into Jedediah's skin, she sighed. "Your Tale will be bound," she said, "though it be my last." The air

began to shimmer, and Jedediah looked around sleepily.

From farther down the beach, horses were galloping toward them. "We do not have much time," Sophia said. "They are coming."

And then Jedediah's eyes closed, the scene around him fading into mist. When he woke, he was back in the forest by the cairn. Except the stones were all smashed, as though someone had come through and destroyed them. Beneath the biggest fragment of all, Sophia's book was splayed, a blot of ink pooling under it. The symbol on its spine was bent at an odd angle, the dragon's head severed from its body. In a few moments, the book's cover had turned to ashes.

"Just like the one Wilfred brought to my parents," Peter breathed. "Do you think that's why Elton wants to find Alethia's book? So he can crumble it to ash or whatever?"

Una shook her head. "I don't know." She gripped the cover of the book tight. "But I do know one thing for sure. Griselda was right. The Talekeepers have been lying all along. The Muses aren't gone. They never were. And now Elton's looking for them. I don't think he intends to try and destroy them. I think he means to bring the Muses back to Story."

Peter shivered. "Let's see if Jedediah ever found Alethia later on." But there wasn't much left to Jedediah's Tale. The next day as he traveled home through the forest, he was caught by rogues and killed.

Chapter 23

Una accepted the mug of tea Professor Thornhill held out to her. She sat in the stuffed plaid armchair and wished that she was somewhere else. Though she and Peter stayed up very late the night before, they had learned nothing new from Jedediah's Tale. Una had tossed and turned in her bed, running the Muses and the Talekeepers through her mind in circles to no avail. She needed more information about the Muses and the old ways. And there was only one person she could think of who might have it. Setting up a fake advising meeting with Professor Thornhill had seemed like a good idea back in her dorm room. She had thought keeping her meeting a secret was payback for Peter sneaking off to the Museum without her, but now spying on Thornhill seemed like a very bad idea. As did meeting Thornhill alone in her apartment above the Villainy classroom.

Una wrapped her hands around the mug and scanned the room. Every corner was crammed with squatty-looking furniture and soft lamps that gave the space a sleepy air. Tapestries spanned the cracking stone walls, and rugs in warm reds and golds covered the floor. She was sure that Thornhill was hiding something. And her instincts said it had something to do with the old Tales. After all, Thornhill had known how to break Elton's enchantment on the books from the vault.

Three purring and meowing cats paced the floor between Una and the professor. "Hello there," Una greeted the cats, glad to find she wouldn't be alone with Professor Thornhill after all. "What are your names?"

The cats meowed in response.

Professor Thornhill said quietly, "They're not the talking kind."

The striped tabby jumped up and settled on one side of the professor's couch, and a soft calico curled up in Una's lap. Una focused very intently on her tea. How was she supposed to tell talking animals and regular animals apart anyway?

She could feel Professor Thornhill watching her, her

own tea left untouched on the side table.

"Well," Una finally broke the silence, "about tomorrow's exam . . ."

"Yes," Professor Thornhill said. "We'll talk about that in a minute. I always like to see how my students are getting on at this point in the semester." Her pale hands reached for her mug of tea, and Una couldn't help but stare at the long, spidery fingers. "You are a transfer student," Professor Thornhill was saying, "from D'Aulnoy's, isn't it?"

Una nodded, but stopped midnod when Professor Thornhill added, "I studied there as a girl, you know."

Una's mouth went dry. Peter had said D'Aulnoy's was an all-girls school somewhere up in the mountains, but that was all she knew of it—certainly not enough to pass Thornhill's scrutiny.

"Do you have more sugar?" Una managed. She waved at Thornhill. "Oh, don't bother. I'll get it." She hopped up, spilling the calico from her lap, and headed for the side table and the little sugar jar. She almost made it. In one fluid movement, she stumbled over the edge of a rug, tripped over a chair leg, and somehow ended up in a heap on the floor. In that moment, everything changed. She was only on the floor a few seconds, but that was all it took for Una to see behind one of the tapestries. She couldn't be sure how many were there, but she had no doubt that she had seen some books hidden behind the beautiful fabric.

Professor Thornhill jumped to her aid in a very motherly fashion and helped Una to her feet. Una stammered a flustered thank-you.

It was some time before Una was settled again with a fresh cup of tea. Her mind was whirring. Did Professor Thornhill know what Una had seen? Could any of them be Muse books? Stirring her tea with a tiny spoon, Una said in her most businesslike way, "This will be my second practical examination."

"So I've heard," Thornhill said dryly.

Una hurried on. "What exactly should I expect?"

"Well, you'll need to get there early tomorrow morning so you can meet your traveling companions. The exam will last two days, so make sure to pack camping gear."

A bell rang in the distance. Thornhill left the room, telling Una that she wouldn't be long.

"Take your time," Una said. *Enough time for me to figure out what to do.* She didn't trust Thornhill, but she couldn't shake a nagging impulse to tell her the truth. If the Talekeepers themselves went to the Villainy teacher as the expert on the old ways, surely she knew something about the Muses. Una wondered what Thornhill would make of Jedediah's Tale. Besides all that, Una had the feeling that Thornhill wanted something from her. Information? Confirmation of her suspicions that Una was lying about something? A chat with her daughter's roommate? She looked at the small framed picture on the table next to her. It was Snow and Professor Thornhill. Both stood stiffly, an awkward space between them. Their arms were linked, but neither was smiling. Two sets of clear, striking eyes gazed into the camera, one pair ice-blue and angry, the other a bewitching green and very sad.

Just then, Thornhill rushed into the room, grabbed a small handbag, and raced back out. "I must go," she called over her shoulder. "You'll do fine in the exam. Lock up when you leave." And then she was gone.

Una waited until Thornhill's footsteps faded. *Finally! My luck pays off.* She hurried over to the tapestry and ran her fingers along the intricate scrollwork around the frayed edges. The calico joined her and started frantically tugging on the loose threads that dangled to the floor. "Oh, I know something's there, little kitty,"

Una said, nudging the cat away. "I already know."

Una pushed the heavy fabric aside, sending tiny particles of dust flying. Spitting and hissing, the frightened calico scampered off. Una paused in the doorway, waiting for her eyes to adjust to the dimness.

And then she waited for her eyes to adjust to the shock. The hidden space seemed to run the whole length of Thornhill's apartment. It didn't have all the odds and ends that were crammed into the other rooms. There were no colorful fabrics draped here. And it didn't have just the few books she had seen after her fall. Except for a small walkway, the compartment was *filled* with books, piles and piles of books of all shapes and sizes. Some were propped up against each other. Others sat in tottering stacks that looked near collapse.

Una found a candle on a small shelf just inside and lit it. Letting the tapestry fall behind her, she sat down on the floor and greedily grabbed for the nearest stack of books. She flipped open the cover of the first, expecting to see blank pages, but was momentarily surprised to see the now familiar tree. The same one that was on Jedediah's Tale and Griselda's notebook. She picked up another book. More words. Of course Thornhill would have used the fire trick to make the books reveal their secrets! She sorted through the nearest pile. Surely some of these books had to have clues about the Muses. Una's heart sped up. Or maybe even the King. She gave a great sigh of contentment. Then Una did something she'd missed doing since she first arrived in Story. She began to read.

Snow was tidying up the dorm room when the pounding started. She hurried to answer the door. Her mother stood there, breathless, her face filled with panic. She grabbed Snow in her arms and stood, gently swaying back and forth, muttering, "You're all right. You're all right."

Snow stiffened against her mother's embrace. They had never hugged before; they barely even touched.

Her mother stood back and ran her hand over Snow's hair. Her eyes shone with tears. "I was so worried."

Snow stepped back and looked away. *My mother? Crying?* "I'm fine," she said. "What's going on?"

Professor Thornhill sat down on Una's bed and looked hard at Snow. "Are you sure?"

"Of course I'm sure. Why are you so worried?"

Her mother pulled a crumpled piece of paper from her pocket and handed it to Snow. Snow sat down next to her and read, "'Come immediately. Snow gravely injured.'"

She turned it over, but there was no writing on the other side. "That's all? What does it mean?"

"I don't know." Her mother frowned down at the paper. "Especially since you're all right." She crumpled up the paper in her fist. "Why would—?" She froze, the paper forgotten in her hand. "Una. I was meeting with Una."

Una sat with one of Thornhill's books open in her lap. It was about a girl named Gretel Butterworth, and it didn't take long for Una to guess that it told the Tale of Hansel and Gretel. It was a story Una had never had much patience with. Why had the children been so greedy? Couldn't they have just paid better attention in the forest? But this version began earlier, when Hansel and Gretel were very small children, and Una had curiously read through their short history until she got to the chapter where they entered the forest. Sure enough, they came upon a candy-covered house, and the description of the marvelous treats made Una more sympathetic to the children's lack of self-control than she ever had been before. But that was where the similarities ended. Una read through the whole segment several times, *but nothing else happened.* There was no witch. There was no kidnapping. No vengeful oven scene. They just ate all the candy, and then they went home.

Una wondered if they went back later, but the next chapters quickly moved through Gretel's girlhood and on to her life as a baker and young woman. Gretel was just about to receive her first proposal of marriage when Una heard footfalls in the room outside. She froze and held her breath. *Is Thornhill back?* What would she do if she found Una in her secret room? The footsteps grew fainter. Una painstakingly got to her feet, crept to the tapestry door, and peered through the crack at the edge of the heavy fabric.

On the far side of the room Mr. Elton was opening drawers, pawing through their contents, and shutting them. When he finished with the sideboard, he felt the couch cushions. *He's looking for Alethia's book.* She stepped back from the tapestry. And Una thought she knew where it must be. Somewhere in Professor Thornhill's secret book room.

Maybe Elton would just keep looking in the furniture. At that moment, the little calico darted into view. It went back to playing with the string. Una glared at it. It tumbled over onto its back and tossed the string up in its four paws. The tapestry jiggled. She fruitlessly shooed the air, as though the cat could see her through the thick fabric. Elton was looking at the stuffed armchair now. Beads of sweat shone on his forehead. He punched at the seat cushion. The cat froze at the movement and then bolted. The tapestry flapped open wider. Elton looked up. Had he seen? He peered closer. He was coming over. Una pressed back against a mound of books. Her shoulder knocked the top volume off. She twisted and caught it expertly, gripping it tightly in her shaking fingers. The tapestry began to move.

From somewhere in the direction of the kitchen, a voice shouted, "Someone's coming."

She heard Elton curse, and the tapestry flapped back into place.

It only took a moment for Una to decide what to do. She looked out into the apartment. *Empty.* She started pawing through the mounds of books. It didn't matter if Thornhill realized someone had been digging through them. This might be her only chance to find the Muse book before Elton did. She worked her way through another stack. How could she tell which one might be Alethia's book? She grabbed her satchel and began shoving books into it. She had to take as many as she could. The one Elton was looking for might be in there. Besides, any of the others might hold more clues. Thornhill was probably planning to burn them, or explode them, or whatever it was she did to them.

Her fingers hurt as she crammed more books into the corners of her bag. She didn't have much time. She tipped over a low pile, and then she saw it. The faintest hint of blue. She climbed over the fallen books and snatched it off its little ledge. A dragon rimmed in blue. *Alethia's book.* That was when she heard the footsteps on the stairs. She'd never make it. Una wedged Alethia's book into her cloak pocket. Then she pulled the tapestry closed with shaking fingers and held it taut. It would have to do.

"Una?" Snow said. "Why were you meeting with her?"

Her mother put a hand up to her mouth. "Of course. How could I have been so blind? He's after Una."

Snow had never seen her mother so animated. "Why is everyone so interested in her, anyway?" Snow asked.

"First Mr. Elton. And now you."

Her mother gasped. She grabbed Snow by the shoulders. "*Una* is why Mr. Elton came to you? He wanted information about Una?"

Snow shrugged her mother's hands off. She didn't like how horrified her mother looked. "It's not like I told him anything. Just stuff anyone would have known. He wanted to know about you, too, you know."

Her mother let out a little choked cry. "We've got to get to her first. Come on, Snow!" Her mother whirled around and sped out of the dorm.

Snow grabbed her cloak and followed her mother. Students milled about, returning from their final class of the day. They stopped to gawk as their Villainy teacher tore through the quad. Snow glimpsed staring faces and open mouths as she sped by. They ran on, through the forest and down the path. She felt on the edge of a great discovery. Was her mother finally about to tell her something important? But why did she need Una? And what was Una doing in her mother's flat, anyway?

They hurried over the little bridge. They were nearly there. Into the dark and musty Villainy classroom. Up the rickety stairs. The door to the flat was ajar.

Her mother quietly pushed it open. "Hello?" she called. "Una?"

There was no answer. Gingerly, Snow followed her mother into the flat. A tabby cat bounded around the corner, and Snow gasped, her heart pounding. Everything was quiet.

Snow followed the cat into the main sitting room and down the hallway. She didn't see any sign of Una.

Her mother met her in the living room. "There's only one place left to look," she said. She walked over to the wall and pulled hard on a tapestry. It came up easily and there, in a hidden space in the wall, was Una Fairchild.

Chapter 24

Una saw Snow first. She was standing behind her mother, blue eyes filled with disbelief. "Una!" she exclaimed.

Professor Thornhill reached out a hand. "Come out of there, child."

Una stepped backward. What could she say? *Oh, hi, Professor. I'm just hanging out in your secret illegal book room. Don't mind me. Oh, and by the way, what are you doing with all of these? Smuggling them? Hunting for Alethia's book? Getting ready to bring one of the Muses back?* None of those was a good option.

Professor Thornhill was looking at her with wide eyes. She didn't seem angry, just determined somehow.

Snow moved forward a step. She reached out to touch Thornhill's cloak but stopped just shy of it.

"Professor?" she asked.

Professor Thornhill didn't answer her. Instead, she grabbed Una's hand and pulled her out. She looked Una up and down, studying her fingers, her face, her feet.

Why was Thornhill looking at her like that? She tugged her hand back.

"I know," Thornhill said. "I know what you are."

Una's stomach leaped up into her throat. *She knows.* Her heart pounded. She backed up a step, and the side of the armchair pressed into her.

Thornhill moved toward her. Her face looked hungry, and she reached out her hand again. On the third finger of her left hand was a ring, a black pearl that looked like liquid smoke.

Una stared at the ring and sank over the arm into the chair sideways. She felt like a turtle scrambling about on its back. She flipped around and got to her feet. Now the chair was between her and Thornhill. She eyed the distance between the chair and the door. *Not enough to make a run for it.*

Snow stood looking back and forth between the two. "Can someone please tell me what's going on?"

"Una can," Thornhill said. "But I'm not sure she will."

Thoughts of the Muses returning and the Tale Master's lies swirled around in Una's head. All that she had learned made her mind cloudy. She had to get somewhere where she could sit and think. Could she trust Thornhill or not? "I need to know about the books," Una said. "What are you going to do with the books?" It all came down to the books. Was Thornhill hiding the books or destroying them? Was Thornhill part of the Merriweathers' secret rebellion or something more sinister? Was she a Hero or a Villain? The air pressed close, and Una's chest constricted. Her breathing was shallow, and she felt light-headed. She reached out a hand to steady herself, but it was too late. The room started to spin, and everything went black.

Snow held one of Una's arms and legs as she and her mother shifted her up onto the bed in the spare room. Una moaned but didn't wake.

Snow's mother reached out and wiped a wet cloth over Una's forehead. "Tea, perhaps, Snow, and something sweet."

Snow went wordlessly to the kitchen and put the kettle on. Her mother hadn't answered any of her questions. About Una. About the books. About the strange man in the cathedral. She tossed a tin of cookies onto the tray and clattered the teacup down next to it. *More secrets.* She poured out a stream of hot water, and the soothing scent of peppermint wafted up.

There was no way to make that woman talk. Her mother would purse her lips and gently shake her head to each question. "I can't answer that, Snow," she would say in a patronizing tone. Snow banged the kettle back onto the stove.

Her mother appeared in the kitchen doorway. "She should be stirring by now." She handed Snow the damp cloth. "I'm sending a pigeon for the Healer. Keep her face cool, and give her the tea when she wakes."

Snow schooled her face to passivity. "Whatever you say, Professor." It didn't matter. Her mother was already gone.

Una's eyes were still shut when Snow returned. Snow set the tray gently down on the nightstand. Una looked small and frail as she lay stretched out on the bed. Vulnerable. Snow hated her mother in that moment. Wasn't it enough that she had ruined Snow's life? Did she have to terrorize some other girl as well? She sat down carefully and pressed the cloth to Una's face. "Una," she whispered as she dabbed. "Don't worry. It'll be okay."

Una's eyes popped open. She reached up and grabbed Snow's wrist. "Is she gone?" Her voice was a jagged whisper. "Snow," she pleaded. "I've got to get out of here. Please. Help me."

There was none of the old challenge in Una's eyes. None of the mocking superiority. There was just fear. And tears.

Snow didn't even have to think about it. "Do you think you can walk?" she asked.

Una nodded and swung her legs over the edge of the bed.

"Here," Snow said as she shoved the tin of cookies into her hand. "Eat one of these." Her mother kept the pigeons out on the back balcony. With any luck, they had a few more minutes. Snow peered out into the hall. No sign of her. She led Una back through the apartment. Just as they reached the front door, Una grabbed her arm. She held up one hand, but before Snow could stop her, she had disappeared back into the apartment. A moment later she returned with her bulging satchel.

Snow led her down the rickety stairs and across the classroom. Everything looked spookier at night, and Snow kept stopping to look over her shoulder. Was her mother following them?

It wasn't until they had reached the windswept plain around the tower that Una spoke. "Thank you, Snow." She pulled the hood up on her cloak and started running toward the path.

"Tell me what's going on," Snow demanded.

"There's no time," Una called over her shoulder. "I've got to get to Peter." She took off at a dead sprint.

Snow didn't wait to follow her. She wanted answers. And Una had them.

Snow had to run hard to catch up. Una was much faster than she expected, especially considering she'd just woken from a faint. Snow saw her small form a little ways up the path, the bulging bag thumping against her back. She was close now. Una started across the bridge with Snow right behind her.

In front of her a shadowy form darted out and reached for Una. The next moment, someone pummeled into Snow and knocked her to the ground. She heard Una's scream, then a man's groan.

"She's getting away," he yelled.

Snow didn't even have the breath to scream. The cold started at the bottom of her spine and crept up and out to her fingertips. A hand grabbed her hair and jerked her head back. A masked face peered into hers.

"It's Thornhill's brat," he rasped, and yanked her to her feet. He twisted her arms around behind her, and Snow cried out in pain.

Just then, her mother's voice carried across the still air. "Leave her alone," she said. It was commanding, as though every creature in the woods was compelled to obey her.

But the masked man just laughed. It sounded like metal dragged over stone. He twisted harder on Snow's wrists, and she gasped.

Her mother lifted a pale hand, and a web of light shot out, blinding Snow. There was another flash of light, a brilliant collision that burned Snow's eyes. She couldn't see anything.

She heard a thump. A moan. And then: "Bring her," said the man with the rasping voice.

Chapter 25

Una tore through the underbrush. The satchel of books bumped against her side as she ran. Her heart was galloping in her chest. Every muscle in her body felt tense and alive. She sprinted in what she thought was the direction of Birchwood Hall. She had to get to Peter.

Was it Thornhill who had grabbed her? Elton? Red? The cold air was sharp in her lungs. She tried to control her breathing, tried to listen for sounds of pursuit. But all she could hear was the crashing of her own feet as she sped through the leaves.

She could see the glimmer of Birchwood's lights up ahead. The Hall burst into sight, and she slowed to a walk, bending at her waist to catch her breath. A few students were out, but no one looked twice at her. Everyone was too busy cramming for tomorrow's examination to notice one girl running through the woods.

She found Peter in the Woodland Room. He was sitting in a leather chair by the fire, his boots propped up on a coffee table. She walked straight up to him.

"Una." He set his feet down and sat up. "You look like a mess."

"Peter! You've got to come with me."

"But the exam. I was just reviewing the unit on Showing versus Telling. I could really use a—"

"We can't wait any longer." She plopped her bag down on the table with a thud. "We're breaking into Elton's study. We need answers about the Muses. Tonight."

The rocking of the wagon woke her. Snow opened her eyes. Then the pain hit. Her head throbbed, and with every jostle and bump she thought it might split open. She reached up to rub it, but her hands were firmly bound behind her. That was when she started to panic. Her ankles were also tied together. She threw her body backward, pulling hard against her bonds. The knots were strong, and she flopped about, bruising already sore muscles even more. Once her energy was spent, the pain in her head returned, heightened by the new, deeper paths the ropes were making in her flesh. She screwed her eyes shut, counted slowly to three, and opened them again.

She was in a covered wagon, the hard slats of one side pressing into her back. Boxes of all sizes were strapped securely to the side opposite her, and a pile of old rags sat jumbled up against the driver's seat. The rags twitched. Snow squinted her eyes in the dimness. More movement, and then Snow spotted the hair.

"Mother!" she gasped, and her own voice sounded foreign and raw. What was her mother doing here? Then she remembered. The sprint through the darkened forest. The blinding flash of light. The rasping voice.

The wagon was slowing down. Then it stopped.

Peter glanced over his shoulder. The door to the Tale Master's study flickered in the light of Peter's travel lantern. Una was slumped in the outer-office desk chair, her head nodding as she dozed. At first, it had been hard to find a window in the building that would do. Some were too high up, and others were too small to squeeze through. Then Una had seen it. The tiniest crack. A wooden peg holding a basement pane open. After that, it had been easy to sneak through the deserted corridors and into Elton's quarters.

But that was hours ago. The satchel of books perched on the desk in front of her, its contents spread across the surface. *All those books.* "The Tales are wrong," Una had said when she first started reading through them. "I know these stories. I've read them before—back in my old world—and these are different. Missing characters. Boring endings. Something isn't right."

But Peter hadn't had a good chance to look at them. He had been too busy with the door. Now Una's head bobbed over the one book she clutched in her hands. That book had a dragon binding. Peter felt chills every time he touched it. What would happen if they opened it? After all this time, would the book even work? And what would they find if they arrived at Alethia's house?

The problem was that the book was locked. It wasn't a matter of using the fire trick like they had on Jedediah's Tale. This book wouldn't even open. The dragon's tail snaked around the side and clasped the pages securely shut. He and Una had argued about it, but neither could remember exactly how Jedediah had opened Sophia's book.

But that wasn't their only problem. Peter had searched the entire outer office for a key but found nothing. The Tale Master's study was shut fast against them. Peter studied the door's surface. Above the old-fashioned-looking keyhole, an ornate metal-worked seal was fastened to the center of the thick wood planks. Peter lightly traced the intricate pattern. Black vines twisted around pieces of armor. Shields and helmets were tangled up with swords and spears. The strange weaponry formed a thick border around a collection of little iron books. He guessed it was supposed to represent how the Tale Master protected the old Tales.

Peter leaned his forearms against the sharp surface of the seal and hung his head down between them with a sigh. *We might as well go back to Birchwood before someone catches us.* He pushed back to wake Una and tell her the bad news. That was when he heard the click. He jerked his head back and stared. A tiny helmet had moved a fraction of an inch toward the books.

"Of course!" he shouted. "The seal *is* the lock!"

Una woke with a groan. "What is it? What's happened?"

"I've almost got it open!" Peter pushed hard against one of the vines, and it slid aside. "Una, what do you

know about Elton? What kind of lock would he set?"
His fingers worked faster now, shifting the moving
parts across the seal. "Let's see. He grew up in the
Hollow. He's in love with Professor Thornhill. What
else?"

Una came up behind him, rubbing her eyes. "Um.
He's the Tale Master," she said in a sleepy voice.

"Thanks, Una," Peter said. "Really helpful. What—"
He pushed away from the wall. "*That's it!* This was
someone else's office long before it was Elton's. The
first Tale Master of Story, Archimago Mores."

He scanned the metal pieces until he found the
sword he had seen earlier. He slowly maneuvered each
of the pieces out of the way, until the sword was right
over the pile of books.

Una sounded wide awake now. "Go on, Peter," she
said over his shoulder.

Peter's heart thumped hard in his chest. He shifted
the sword down, and it sank into place on top of
the stack of books. There was a loud click this time.
"Gotcha," he said, as he picked up the little lantern.

"Very clever." Una pushed the heavy door back.
"Nice job, Peter."

Elton's study looked bare and severe. Someone had

been in recently to tidy up. Peter lifted his arm, but the little pool of light only illuminated a small circle in the midst of the dark room. Filing cabinets lined one wall. Opposite them was a cupboard, its doors hanging open and slightly askew. Next to that was a broken glass-fronted bookcase, but there was one thing they all had in common. Everything was empty.

"Oh no!" Una cried. "We waited too long!" She clutched the dragon book to her chest. "Elton has cleared everything away! Now how will we learn why he's bringing the Muses back? Or anything about the King?"

Peter cleared his throat, but Una spun to face him.

"Don't bother to argue, Peter," she said. "Every book in Thornhill's room had that tree on it. I know—Peter, I *know*—this all has something to do with the King."

Peter swallowed. He wasn't about to admit that he didn't know what to believe anymore. Instead he said, "We only have one lantern." He lifted it higher. "Come on. Maybe there's some stuff left in his desk."

The Tale Master's desk was also nearly empty, except that a few forgotten scraps of paper lay in the bottom drawer. Una snatched them up eagerly, but they were blank. Peter and Una carefully worked their way around the rest of Elton's study. The room was quiet except for the sound of their soft footfalls on the old wood floor. They scanned everything for a single clue, but it didn't matter. There was nothing.

Peter sat down hard on a nearby chair. They had finally gotten into the Tale Master's study. *But we're too late.*

"We can't give up now," Una said, taking the lantern from him and peering into the open cupboard, which was honeycombed with slots for scrolls. "Maybe he overlooked something."

They decided it must have been Elton himself who cleared the place out. Maybe he was worried that the people of Story might find out about the Muses. Or maybe he was afraid Talekeepers curious enough to try and break his enchantments might come nosing around other places as well. Whatever the reason, Peter was ready to go home.

He thought he heard something and stopped to listen. All was silent. He put his head in his hands. This was pointless. They could search all night and still not find anything. This was as worthless as his trip to the Museum. He studied the pattern on the floorboards. He doubted that the Tale Masters—either Archimago or

Elton—would have kept anything that told what really happened in the time before the Unbinding, anyway.

If they wanted to open Alethia's book, they were going to have to take the risk and ask for Professor Thornhill's help. He was about to tell Una so when he noticed it. In the dim light of the lantern, he saw that the pattern on the wood floor wasn't just any pattern. It seemed remarkably familiar. The space around him looked like the top of a flowering tree. Peter got down on his hands and knees. His brothers hid stuff under the floorboards of their old house. Maybe someone else had done the same. Someone who wanted to keep something hidden. He began wiggling the nearest boards.

He was nearing the roots of the tree now, and the floorboard beneath his hand was a little loose. He grabbed an old fountain pen from the top of Elton's desk and wedged it under splintering wood.

"Bring the lantern over, Una," he said with a grunt, as the panel came up.

Una joined him, and the light illuminated a hidden rectangular compartment.

"Under the Tale Master's nose," Peter said, and pulled out a slim scroll. It didn't look like it had ever been opened. The center of it was tied with a cord and sealed with wax. In the middle of the wax was the tree.

The hair on the back of his neck stood up. He pulled out his pocketknife and began to ease it under the wax seal. Una hovered nearby, one hand holding the lantern aloft and the other clutching the dragon book. Would the scroll help them open it?

Peter's knife sliced through the last of the wax, and he gingerly spread the scroll out on the floor.

The Last Confession of Archimago Mores was written in a spidery script across the top.

"Archimago!" Una gasped.

"He must have hidden it here," Peter said and drew the lantern near. "I wonder why." They knelt down, shoulder to shoulder. The first paragraph told about the reliable character of said Archimago Mores. Peter rolled his eyes. Why would Archimago hide a description of how wonderful he was?

When he heard the noise this time, Peter was sure of it. Someone was walking around in the Talekeepers' headquarters. He pulled out his pocket watch.

"Una," he said, yanking her to her feet. "It's half past five in the morning! We've got to go."

Peter let the scroll roll up and slid it into his pocket.

He shoved the floorboard back in place and followed after Una.

"Elton will *know* someone's been here for sure," Una said as they hurried back through the Tale Master's study and into the outer office. She was right. They had messed it up in their search for the combination, and there was no way they could put it back in order.

"But he won't know it was us," Peter said as he helped Una cram Thornhill's books back into her satchel. "And if we hurry, we'll be in our practical before he even comes to work."

Chapter 26

$\mathcal{U}$na was sharing a desk with Peter while they waited for all of their classmates to arrive. They had made it through the Talekeepers' headquarters without any trouble, and now they had a few minutes before their practical examination. The classroom entrance to the Tale station loomed behind Professor Edenberry's withered frame.

"Professor Thornhill has been unavoidably detained," he said in a serious voice. "I will administer your practical today." A low murmur went around the room, but Edenberry had nothing else to say about Thornhill's absence. Una wondered if Thornhill knew she had taken Alethia's book yet. If she suspected, surely the Villainy teacher would be here now to confront Una about it. She patted her satchel reassuringly. Nothing would make her give up that book.

"Move closer," Una whispered. Soon Professor Edenberry would start grouping students together and sending them into the exam. She and Peter spread *The Last Confession of Archimago Mores* out on their laps and tried to look inconspicuous. She skimmed the first paragraph and found the spot where Archimago's testimony began.

> *Of those who know what happened, three have lied, seven are bound, and the others are dead. I am one who lied. And, before they come for me, I record here for all time the way I've served the Enemy of Story. Fidelus was the Muse who Wrote me here.*

Una pointed at the line. "Archimago was a WI! Peter, what do you know about Fidelus? Or this Enemy?"

"Nothing," Peter said. "I've never heard of the Enemy before. Keep reading."

> *Fidelus trained me and taught me all he knew of Story. He told me he purposed me to lead the characters into a new era. And I believed him. But that was before he became the Enemy.*
>
> *Who was I to question him? His words seemed*

good to me, and I had no reason to doubt him. Fidelus
taught me to fight. He wrote me adventures. And I
became a Hero. Because of Fidelus, I became famous.
Because of him, I won Story's trust. Soon, I was the
Hero the others came to with their troubles. When
Fidelus told me the King would only enslave us when
he returned, I believed him.

"The King!" Una whispered. "I knew he was real!
Why do you think he left Story?"

"How should I know?" Peter sounded irritated.
"Let's just keep reading, okay?"

I didn't know then that he was a great deceiver.
I became his servant, spewing his lies to all of
Story. Fidelus started wars across Story, and I blamed
the Muses. He brought famine and suffering, and I laid
it at their feet. Fidelus broke every oath he had taken,
and I said it was all of them together. I said that the
fault of everything that happened in those dark days
belonged to the Muses, that their oath breaking led to
the loss of so many character lives, when all the while
every other Muse was fighting against Fidelus's evil. I
turned the characters of Story against the other Muses,
the only ones who could save them.

Una's scalp prickled. Archimago's testimony was no fairy tale with some happily-ever-after ending. And Peter had been right to be afraid of at least one of the Muses. No wonder Archimago called Fidelus the Enemy of Story.

> *I will not write of Fidelus's great betrayal. What happened there is to me as a dream, but one thing I can never forget. That night I saw what it was to anger a Muse. And I saw Fidelus for what he was. His face twisted ugly as he spewed his hate. How could I have suspected such a heroic frame to hide such a villainous heart? He boasted of his great evil. Of those he had killed. Of the others he had imprisoned. Of his lies.*

Students were filing into the classroom now. She hunched lower over the paper and continued reading.

> *And his lies were his undoing. His oath bound him as surely as he himself was locked in a prison of his own making. Fidelus was lost to Story, and I thought his evil had come to an end. Though Story's Enemy was bound, the terror and confusion he had wrought lived on. The Muses had disappeared, and no one mourned their absence. I had done my job well, for all of Story hated the Muses.*

My readers must know that I meant only good for Story. The land was in chaos. It needed a Hero. And who was better positioned to lead than I? The Red Enchantress came to me then. She claimed to want to rebuild Story, to undo the lies and evil we had done as the Enemy's servants. Fool that I am! I should have known that she was an evil Enchantress. That her voice could fell the strongest warrior.

First, she told me to gather all the old Tales. What good would it do for Story to know the truth of the Muses? She said that Story needed a fresh beginning, one unencumbered by the past. Her words seemed to me wisdom, and I did not know that her heart was filled with the Enemy's lies. Together, we locked up the old Tales. I swear to you, I didn't think it possible that she still worked the Enemy's will.

Next, she told me to find the Muse books. We both knew that the Enemy had scattered them far and wide throughout Story. Hadn't I built one of the stone cairns myself? "To give the Muses peace," Fidelus had said then. "To make sure meddlesome characters bother them no more." The other Muses didn't know Fidelus had hidden their books. Alethia. Charis. Spero. Clementia. Sophia. Virtus. They couldn't guess that this was why no characters visited them anymore. I *found Virtus's first, for that was the cairn I had built. The Red Enchantress came with me, and had I known then what I know now, I swear to you I wouldn't have done it. Virtus was surprised to see us, eager for news of Story, lonely and a prisoner of his own house. I knew why no one visited him, for I had hidden his own book myself, but I do not know why he couldn't leave.*

The Red Enchantress took him then. She fought him, and the magic of the Enchantress overpowered the Muse. Never have I seen the like in Story. After that I knew the Red Enchantress for what she was. She never intended to help the land of Story. Always, she was seeking her lost Fidelus. She told me the truth after that. She said there was a way to free Fidelus. If she could but find all the other Muses, the spell imprisoning him would be broken and she could bring Fidelus back to rule Story. And that is what she seeks to do.

The characters of Story already hated the Muses, thanks to Fidelus. It was a small thing for the Red Enchantress to grow their fear, to hide any trace of the Muses' goodness, and to make sure her Tale Master was in control. And, one by one, she hunts the Muses. Not because they are Oathbreakers, but because they are Story's protectors.

Perhaps I should have done things differently.

Perhaps I could have told Story the truth. Perhaps we could have overpowered the magic that felled the Muses. Perhaps the Red Enchantress would have let me live. Perhaps death would have been better than this lifetime of lies. I don't know.

But I am done with that now. My death draws near, and the burden of my life weighs me down. And here is my confession: We have wronged the Muses. All our hatred and bitterness falls on those who swore to protect us. And, one by one, our protectors vanish. Soon, they will be gone, and Story will be laid bare to the will of a very great and terrible Enemy.

I am finished. I know she is coming for me. Perhaps I could have done more once upon a time. But this is what I am doing now and for those who come ever after. May they be braver than me. I write this, dear people of Story, because I am ashamed of what I have done. I am not the Hero you thought. I never was.

I was there when he rebelled. I was there when he was bound. I will not be there when he returns. Here ends my confession.

Una stared at the paper. While she had been reading, Professor Edenberry had been busy grouping students for the examination.

"Peter." She couldn't make her mouth form the words. She licked her lips and tried again. "Peter. I think we know why Red wants the Muse books."

Peter froze in the middle of rolling up the scroll. "You think Red is . . ."

"I do," Una whispered fiercely. "If she's the Red Enchantress from Archimago's confession, it all fits. The way everyone hates the Muses. Why the Talekeepers have censored all the books so no one can read what the Muses were really like. Peter"—she swallowed hard—"I don't know whether Story has a King or not. But it sure does have an Enemy."

". . . and Una Fairchild. That will make three." Edenberry's voice broke off any further conversation.

Una stood on shaky legs. "Come on, Peter. Let's go."

Peter didn't move. "I'm not in your group." He set the scroll down on his lap. "I'm not in your group," he said again, as though this was a completely unforeseen turn of events.

"Una Fairchild?" Professor Edenberry called, louder this time, and looked up from his clipboard.

Peter nudged her. "Go on," he whispered. "You'll do just fine. I know you will."

Perhaps it was the leftover effects from her encounter with Thornhill. Or the discovery that nearly everything Story thought about the Muses was a lie. Maybe it was just the result of going on only an hour of sleep. Or the paralyzing knowledge that there was an Enemy out there somewhere. Whatever the reason, Una thought she might dissolve into tears on the spot.

Peter gave her another little shove, and she propelled herself up to the front. There, standing next to Professor Edenberry with a pleased sneer on his greasy face, was Horace Wotton. She blinked hard. Horace mustn't see her cry. Then, it got worse. Their third and final group member came up behind Horace. And it was none other than Endeavor Truepenny.

Professor Edenberry handed them a packet of papers and pointed at the far door. His white puff of hair bobbed up and down as Una's group headed over. He patted her gently on the shoulder. "Good luck, Una." Una wasn't sure, because she was almost out the door, but she could have sworn he added under his breath, "You'll need it."

With a crash, the back of the wagon bounced down. Canvas fabric closed tight over Snow's head, and rough hands dragged her body out into the cold. The air felt wet, like it might start to rain at any moment. Snow gagged. Something smelled like milk left out too long in the sun. Whoever was carrying her tossed her up over a shoulder and set off at a steady pace.

"Get the other one." Muffled thumps followed this command. Snow wondered if her mother was awake. She strained her ears, hoping that they would at least be taken to the same place, but all she could hear was the panting breath of her captor. She thought of Perrault. Had they been missed yet? *Will anyone care if I don't show up for the practical?* Thump, thump went her aching head against the sharp shoulder of the person carrying her. With every thump, the pounding in her skull got worse. *Did Una escape? Is she all right?*

Snow thought she heard something. She tried to listen closely. It was hard to focus with the throbbing in her temple. "I have taken . . . ," someone was saying. His voice sounded familiar.

Just then, Snow's captor deposited her in a crumpled heap on the wet earth. A hand ripped off the canvas sack, and cold, damp air flooded in. The morning sky was cloudy, but after the dark wagon ride, Snow squinted in the gray dawn.

"I have taken the woman, Milady Duessa."

Snow snapped her head up and saw Elton's stout form bowed low before a red-cloaked figure.

"And the girl?" Duessa's voice sounded like steam when water is thrown on a fire.

Elton bobbed his head up and down. "Her daughter. She was with her. I could not leave her free." Then there was silence.

"Very well," Duessa said, drawing the hood of her cloak farther over her face with one hand. Snow caught a glimpse of a huge red ring on one of her pale fingers. The Lady continued talking. "We are very close now. You may go. Stand ready for my command."

Although she wasn't sure why, Snow hoped Mr. Elton would stay. It was clear he had betrayed her and her mother, but maybe some tiny part of him would pity them. With every passing moment, the knot in her stomach was growing bigger. She struggled against her bonds, and a booted foot knocked her to the ground.

"Better to stay still," Elton's voice ordered, "Ms. Wotton." The pressure of his foot lifted, but Snow kept her face pressed into the wet earth. She wished she knew some horrible curses. The sounds of Elton's departure were soon overcome by heavy footfalls, which grew louder as they approached Snow. When they stopped, her mother's form crumpled to the ground. She, too, had the canvas sack over her head pulled off, but her head hung at an awkward angle, and her eyes were closed.

"Wake her," Duessa said, and someone poured a flaskful of water over Snow's mother. With a sputtering gasp, she opened her eyes. Snow expected to see the usual calm indifference in her mother's green eyes. Instead she saw fear.

"Where is Alethia's book?"

A hand pulled Snow's mother to her knees.

"Answer the Lady," a voice from behind commanded. Snow watched her mother draw herself up, squaring her shoulders and leveling out her chin. She looked queenly, somehow, even with her bound wrists and twisted cloak.

"I cannot say," she said in a clear, even voice. At this, Duessa really did hiss, her breath coming out in a rush.

"I do not have time for games," she said. She tipped a finger at the figure behind her mother. "Make her talk. Bring them to me when you finish." Her cloaked form disappeared into the growing light. Snow didn't see what happened next, since the bag was roughly pushed back over her head, and she was lifted once more onto someone's back.

"All right," her captor said over his shoulder. "Have your fun. But keep her alive."

Snow heard a low, coarse chuckle in response. Then her mother began to scream.

Chapter 27

The Exam Room was much as Una remembered. The space glowed with the same faint light, and the stone circular dais took up most of the room. She stood between Horace and Endeavor in front of a tiny pedestal. That first meeting with Peter seemed a lifetime ago. *If only Peter were here now.* A small pamphlet, stapled together carelessly, sat on the pedestal. "Exam A" was written in large block letters on the cover. Underneath that, a much-smudged list read:

Endeavor Truepenny: Villain
Una Fairchild: Lady
Horace Wotton: Sidekick

"Oh, that's rich," Horace said to Endeavor. "*You're* the Villain?"

Below the smudges, a small note instructed, "Enter when ready."

Endeavor looked at the others. "Well? Maybe we should talk about strategy. What did you guys bring?" He upended a standard-issue knapsack on the floor, and Una bent down to see the pile of items: a piece of flint, a small pot for cooking, a change of clothes, a leather pouch, a travel lantern, and a compass. He also had a long sword strapped to his back.

Una shifted her satchel from one shoulder to the other. She hadn't planned on being in Elton's office all night. What did she have in her bag—besides the books? She knew her dagger was in there. She thought her flint might be somewhere in the bottom, along with her slate. *Not helpful.* Endeavor was looking at her expectantly.

"Um," she said. She didn't think they would be pleased to see a satchel full of books. Not the least because they were perfectly useless for the practical. "I'd rather not. If you don't mind, Endeavor. Personal reasons."

Endeavor grimaced. "Call me Indy," he said.

Horace crossed his arms over his chest. "If she's not showing hers, I'm not showing mine." He gave Una a dirty look.

This was going to be a long two days.

"Fine then," Indy said, and tucked his goods back into his bag. "Looks like we're off to an excellent start." His tone was thick with sarcasm. He took the pamphlet from the pedestal and led the way back to the stone dais. "Sidekick Horace. Lady Una," he called. "Come along now."

She turned to go, but Horace pushed in front of her. "Ladies last," he said.

She took the toe of her boot and knocked the outside of his left foot in toward the right. It was just enough to throw him off balance, and he stumbled to the side. "But then, I'm not much of a Lady," she said as she pushed ahead of him.

Chapter 28

Peter thought his name would never be called. One by one his classmates had been grouped together and disappeared into the Tale station. Now only a handful of students were left, and even Professor Edenberry looked bored with the process.

A trio was arguing in the front about whether they should bring an extra lantern or not, which left two other students with Peter. He guessed they must be his group. He was just going to introduce himself when the classroom door burst open, and Mr. Elton nearly fell in. He was soaked in sweat and breathless with the exertion. His greasy hair hung in disarray around his mud-streaked face. He leaned against the doorframe. "Una Fairchild," he gasped. "Where is she?"

Edenberry's gaze darted to Peter and then back to

Elton. It was so quick Peter thought he might have imagined it.

"Run along," Edenberry said to the group of arguing students and practically pushed them out the opposite door.

"Una!" Elton wheezed. "It's an emergency! We have to find her!"

Professor Edenberry's face tightened in alarm. He went over to the desk and looked carefully at an open ledger before consulting his watch.

"I'm very sorry to say, Mr. Elton," he said, "that Una Fairchild, Horace Wotton, and Endeavor Truepenny have already left for their exam, and I cannot let you detain them."

Una didn't know what to expect from a Villainy practical. Thornhill had said that the goal of this practical was to try and understand the mind of a Villain, not to try and act villainous. Una wasn't sure she understood the difference and halfheartedly wished she could have actually finished her advising meeting with Thornhill the day before.

The stone dais had taken them to a woodland clearing, and Indy found their instructions posted on a tree. Their assignment was to journey to the Caverns of Tears. Once there, they were to set up camp and look for an enchanted ax. They would have to unlock the enchantments of the ax by dusk of the following day. It sounded simple enough, but, as Indy reminded them, these things were never that straightforward. Inevitably there would be challenges along the way.

"What kind of challenges?" Una asked.

"Yeah, tell her," Horace said. "She failed her other practical."

Una ignored him and followed Indy, who set off through the trees.

"Delays," Indy said. "Weather or trouble crossing a stream. Villainy exams usually have a lot of logic problems. That sort of thing."

"What happens if you don't make it back in time?"

"When we finish the quest—when we unlock the ax—we'll all just be back in the Tale station. If the exam ends before we finish the assignment, we'll go back just the same. There's no extra time. No exceptions."

Delays she could handle. Weather couldn't be that bad. But could other things happen in the exam? Bad things? Ever since fighting the dragons, Una had wondered what would have happened if Peter hadn't saved her just in time. She voiced her fears. "What if something, say, attacks us? I mean, can bad things really happen here?"

"Nothing permanent," Indy reassured her. They had come upon an open field with tall grasses. He unsheathed his sword and cut a path forward. "Whatever happens during an exam isn't lasting in the real world." He swiped the other direction. "On my first practical, I lost an arm—it hurt like crazy, but as soon as my mates and I came out of the exam, we all were just the same as when we went in."

"Has anyone ever . . . well, died?" Una asked.

He was cutting faster now, the rhythm of the sword matching his steps forward. "Of course. Lots of people 'die,' if you want to call it that. If your character dies, though, you immediately exit the exam, and it's an automatic F. You have to be pretty dense to fail a beginner's practical, though."

"If you know so much, why are you in the first level of Villainy anyway?" Una asked.

Indy adjusted his grip on the sword. "I was held back—missed too many classes last term," he said.

Of course, the class where they had learned how to unlock basic enchantments was one from before she arrived at Perrault. By the time they had reached the other side of the field, Indy had filled her in on the proper procedure. But his instructions were hard to follow. Something about looking for inconsistencies and manipulating them with the tools at hand. He said that enchantments were just little deceptions, a twisting of the way things actually were. Horace didn't say anything but stomped through the newly cut path behind her.

But passing the exam was the least of her worries. *What about the Red Enchantress?* She couldn't have found all the Muses yet, since Una still had Alethia's book. She thought about the conversation she had overheard at the Talekeeper Club. Red had said there were only "two left." If Una's theory was correct, the Red Enchantress was very close to freeing the Enemy. Perhaps Alethia's book alone now stood in the way.

The three didn't speak much more for most of the day. They plodded along the narrow trail, heading toward a large cliff with dark openings that appeared to be the Caverns of Tears. It was an uneventful trek, with not even a rain shower to slow their progress. But when they arrived at their destination, Una understood a little more what Indy had meant about deception. What had appeared to be openings were actually shadows on the rock. And no matter what they tried, they couldn't find a way inside. The day was fading fast, and, after a short discussion, they decided to build their camp near the cliff, so they could rise early in the hope of seeing the stone in the morning light. Indy seemed to think that the dawn would bring out the impurities.

After they had picked a spot, Indy left to find something to eat before darkness fell. Una gathered sticks and twigs for a fire while Horace went to fetch water from a creek they had crossed earlier. She was right. Her flint was at the bottom of her satchel. In no time at all, she had the fire crackling and plopped down by it to await the boys' return.

Indy came into the clearing first, toting a small rabbit over one shoulder and a cloth full of berries in the other hand. "Roasted rabbit," he said.

Una wrinkled up her nose, but she knew that a meal full of berries wouldn't be enough after skipping breakfast that morning. She watched Indy skin the rabbit. His deft hands worked quickly, the shiny muscle of the rabbit's flesh emerging under the swift strokes of his knife.

This was the first time Una had ever been alone with him. And for once she knew what to say. "Why do you always watch me?"

The methodical scraping stopped. Indy stared hard at her. "What do you mean, fair lady?"

Una clamped her mouth shut. She had already forgotten that this was an exam. Though Peter had told her the examiners couldn't know her thoughts, they were reading everything she and the boys said and did.

"Never mind," she mumbled, and added a "kind sir." She stood. What would a Lady do to help set up camp? *Might as well try for an A.*

She swept the leaves off to the edge of the clearing. Tidying up seemed ladylike. Once the rabbit was roasting over the fire, Indy left to get the water himself, since Horace had returned only to sit under a tree where he appeared to be sleeping.

Every so often, he would open his eyes long enough to say something rude like, "When's dinner, woman?" Or, "Where'd our Villain go? I need to kick him in the side."

Una was never gladder to see anyone than when Indy returned. It had gotten cold once the sun disappeared, and the three of them gathered around the little fire to share their meal. The berries disappeared too quickly, and Una forced the rabbit down, because she was so hungry.

They all sat in silence together for a long while. Soon the quiet was broken with the sounds of the night animals. The stars overhead looked like little cut holes in black velvet. The fire popped and crackled, tiny bursts of heat blending with the cold air.

After a while, Indy stood. "I'll take first watch," he said. "You two get some sleep."

Una didn't have to be told twice. Not sleeping the night before coupled with the day's hike made it nearly impossible for her to keep her eyes open. She found a relatively flat spot on one side of the fire and set her satchel down for a pillow. It didn't matter that she only had her cloak between her and the hard ground. It didn't matter that Horace's snores were nearly as loud as Professor Roderick's voice. Almost as soon as Una shut her eyes, she was out.

When Indy woke her several hours later, her body was still heavy with slumber. Everything tingled. "I'm up. I'm up," she said to Indy, who, once he saw that she was sitting, went over to the other side of the fire. Soon, she could hear the sound of his regular breathing.

Despite the chill of the night air and the newness of her surroundings, Una had a hard time staying awake. She rubbed her eyes and tried to clear her mind, but her thoughts were jumbled and foggy with sleep. That was when she remembered what was in her satchel.

Wide awake now, Una waited until she was sure that Indy was fast asleep. She pulled out a few other books first, but then her fingers found the dragon book. She glanced over at Indy, and then at Horace. *So far, so good.* The book felt like it belonged in her hands, a solid weight, and she ran her fingers lightly over the black dragon that snaked up the spine. She had to figure out how to open it. In the firelight it was hard to see the blue border. Una felt along the edges. If she did open it, would it take her to Alethia's house, just like the one that had taken Jedediah to Sophia's cottage? And if it did, what would she find there?

Even though the heat from the fire was warm, she shivered. She examined the binding. It looked sound. The cover was a soft brown leather with a dulled pattern set into the front. No matter what she did, no matter how she turned it or thumped it or pulled on the edges, it remained shut fast. For a long time she traced the dragon on the spine. She sighed. After all this, and she didn't know how to open the book. Maybe there was a way to ask Professor Thornhill about Muse books without making her suspicious. *Fat chance.* Or was there another teacher they could ask? Una remembered Peter saying that his Backstory professor had been fired for talking about the Muses. Maybe he knew something about their books. That seemed like her best shot. As soon as the practical was over, she and Peter would find him. Una's eyes grew heavy, and it wasn't long before she nodded off again, the book clasped tightly against her chest.

Chapter 29

Elton hadn't stayed in the classroom after Edenberry told him Una wasn't there, and Peter waited until Edenberry's back was turned before he slipped out the classroom door. This would probably mean another failed practical, but Peter didn't care. He rushed down the hall and outside.

Elton must know that Una had the book. What else would have him in such a panic? Where would Elton go next? Peter watched groups of happy students who had no exams today and were relaxing on the quad. That was it! The Tale station. Elton might follow Una there.

Peter couldn't go back to the classroom since Edenberry would be there, waiting to send him into his own exam. He was halfway to the Tale station's main entrance when Sam found him.

"I'm going to ace it, Peter," he said with a self-satisfied smile. "Eating practicals are a piece of cake. Literally. I just have to find the room and—"

Peter interrupted him. "Una's in trouble." He explained about Elton.

"Forget Eating!" Sam's eyes grew wide. "Lead the way."

It didn't take them long to find the right examination wing, empty now that all the students were in the exams. The hallway was well marked, and they soon found the correct door. Sam pawed Peter's leg. "Wait. I smell something, Peter." He opened his mouth to take in more of the scent. "There are beasts here." His back was arched, his fur puffed out, and his eyes round.

"Beasts?" Peter swallowed. "Really?"

Sam's nostrils flared. "And not the talking kind."

Peter shivered. Talking animals were one thing. Wild ones were another. *And wild beasts!* He pulled his sword from its sheath.

Sam slinked forward. They could hear the snarls before they were halfway down the hall. The air smelled of wet fur, and the growls and snaps up ahead set Peter on edge. He crept along the passageway. How many were there? Three, maybe four?

The noises grew louder, and soon Peter could see around the corner. It was worse than he thought. There were five of them. And they were the wolf kind. Each was packed into a wooden crate, but, instead of taming them, their captivity whipped them into a fury. Their powerful muscles flexed under matted fur as they threw their bodies at the crate walls, rocking them from side to side. Frenzied howls filled the air, and they snarled at each other through the slats. Peter caught glimpses of gleaming yellow eyes and sharp fangs glistening with saliva as the beasts tried to snap through the crates. The howling escalated. They knew Peter and Sam were there.

Elton stood next to them, mumbling something incoherent as he squinted at a tiny book. Every so often, he dabbed his sweaty forehead with a handkerchief. "Shut up!" he screamed at the beasts. "Just shut up!" He looked over, and Peter didn't duck quickly enough. Elton had seen him. "So that's it, my delicious creatures," Elton said. "We have a visitor."

Peter ran out to the middle of the room. Sam galloped close behind. "We know what you're doing, Elton," Peter said. "We've come to stop you."

Elton looked at Peter's brandished sword and laughed. "Oh really? The little Hero has come to save the day?" He shook his head. "I don't think so. You're too late." The air behind him was shimmering into an oval. With a flick of his wrist, Elton dropped the doors of the crates, and the snarling beasts crashed out.

"Gog! Magog!" he commanded, and two of the beasts looked at him. "The boy and the cat are yours." The beasts paced warily, eyeing their prey. "Farewell, Peter Merriweather," Elton said with a sneer. "I can't say that I'll miss you." The strange oval behind him now looked like a smooth mirror. Elton stepped backward into it and disappeared. As soon as he was gone, the beasts attacked. Peter moved to the right, and Sam went left, his fur standing all on end and making him look twice his normal size. Peter gripped his sword tighter, hoping that all his Weaponry practice would pay off. He felt the adrenaline pulse through his veins.

The larger of the two, Magog, sprang at Peter. Peter rolled instinctively, and the beast hit the wall directly behind him. Growling, Magog turned and paced the length of the room, her yellow eyes fixed on Peter.

He braced himself. Perhaps if he was quick, he could stab the beast as it attacked. Before Magog leaped, however, a furry, spitting ball flung itself onto the beast. "Sam!" Peter yelled. "No!" Peter took two steps forward, then a crushing mass slammed into his left side, and his sword clattered down out of reach. Gog had found him. On the floor now, Peter fought blindly, pummeling the beast's foul flesh with his fists. He felt Gog's hold loosen. He stretched down for the dagger in his boot. He stabbed the beast with it, sinking the blade deep into its body, and the creature shuddered and collapsed onto Peter. He heaved the creature off his face, but his torso was still pinned. The rank smell of the beast filled his nostrils, and Peter shook his head to clear it. And then he saw Sam.

Sam clawed and bit like a wild thing, and Magog yelped in fury and pain. Sam bit hard on the beast's neck and began working his hind legs, digging deep into Magog's chest. Peter gathered his strength once more and wrenched Gog's dead body a little farther to one side. One leg was free.

Magog flailed her great head from side to side, hitting Sam against the stone wall with each blow. Peter could hardly watch. He pulled frantically at his pinned leg. He had to help Sam. With one final shove, he freed himself from the huge carcass and crawled to his feet. Sam's grip had grown weaker, and as Peter raced across the dais, Magog violently flung the little form across the room, where it lay still.

"No!" Peter yelled, and threw himself at the beast. He grabbed his discarded sword, and struck out. The blade hit soft flesh, but Magog was strong. Her jaws snapped at Peter unfailingly, and as he tried to dart away, she sank her teeth into his shoulder.

Peter yelled in pain as she bit down, clawing at his back with her forepaws. He flipped his sword in one smooth movement and stabbed blindly behind him. Magog's teeth loosened. But Peter was on his knees. Black spots were in front of his eyes. The walls were turning a strange color, and then an incredible weight toppled onto his back, and everything went black.

It was still dark when Una awoke. Indy's boot was nudging into her side, and she sat up groggily. Her neck was stiff from slumping back against the tree. The fire had nearly gone out, and her fingers felt numb with cold. She had slept through her watch and, it looked like, Horace's as well. *That should make Horace happy.*

"Horace is gone," Indy said in a monotone.

Una looked across the campsite. The ground where Horace had slept was flat and empty. "Maybe he went for firewood?" she said.

Indy kicked at a pile of dirt. "The little coward's deserted. And, wouldn't you know it, he took his supplies with him. I bet he's off to find the enchanted ax on his own. Just like a Villain."

She stretched to work the knots out of her back. Then she remembered. *Alethia's book!* She felt around on the ground frantically and, finding no success, hopped up to shake out her skirts.

"Looking for this?" Indy said. The book sat in his hand. In the dying firelight it looked like any other book. Except for the dragon snaking up the side. "Where did you get it?"

"Give it back." Una grabbed for the book, but he held it up out of her reach. "Indy"—she stood up on her tiptoes, but he easily moved away—"you don't understand. You've got to give it to me. It's important."

"I know," he said as he tucked the book into his cloak pocket. "Which is why you shouldn't have brought it into a practical examination."

Chapter 30

Peter felt like he was racing down a tunnel, faster and faster toward the light at the end. When he got there, he opened his eyes slowly, and pain washed over him as consciousness returned. His shoulder throbbed. He could smell blood, the metallic scent of it thick in his nostrils. Slowly, things came into focus. The stone ceiling arched above him.

Peter wriggled out from under the beast's carcass and sat up. Magog's dead body sprawled next to him. The memory of the fight came crashing in. "Sam?" he whispered.

There was no answer.

Peter saw the little body, lying in a crumpled heap on the other side of Magog. He limped over and fell to his knees beside him. Sam's eyes were glazed over, his mouth bared in a fighting snarl. "Oh, Sam," he said, the tears falling now. "You fought well, my friend."

When his tears were spent, he bent forward. *Elton will pay for this.* He scooped Sam's body up with both hands. That was when he saw the flick of a whisker. Peter leaned in close. He felt a puff of air. He looked at Sam's chest—was it moving?

Another puff. A tiny movement. Sam was alive.

Una kicked dirt over the remains of the fire. With each vigorous kick she chided herself. It had been stupid to look at the book in the exam. Now, at the very least, the examiners would know she had a book. And if Elton was reading, he would recognize the description and know it was Alethia's book. He'd probably be waiting for her the moment she stepped out into the Tale station.

The spot where the fire had been was now buried in dirt, and the only light now came from Indy's travel lantern.

"Very thorough, milady," Indy said as he finished packing up his things.

Una stopped kicking. Maybe she could hide the book somewhere in the exam. Or disguise it somehow. She had to get it back.

Indy strapped his sword into its scabbard. He was adjusting it over his shoulder when Una came up behind him. "Let me help you, milord."

Indy's hands stopped. "Um, that's really not necessary. Milady."

"I insist." Una grabbed the leather strap and wiggled it a bit so it was more in the center of his back. *Now, which pocket did he put it in?*

"Forget it. Milady." Indy's voice sounded flat. He turned around. "I'm keeping it."

Una clasped her hands together in front of her. "You don't get it. If they find that bo—" She caught herself. She had to make him understand without revealing too much to the examiners. She ran over and grabbed a stick from the edge of the woods. In crooked letters she wrote *destroy* in the soil next to the lantern. "Like what happened at the potting shed."

Indy looked down at her. "How did you know—?"

"It's not important," Una said. She underlined the word *destroy*. "But we've got to do something."

Indy crouched down and traced the letters in the dirt.

This wasn't helping. Maybe if she could get Indy to take the book out, she could steal it back. Una volunteered, "I never figured out how to open it."

Indy stood and readjusted his pack. "What do you mean?"

Una tried to phrase things so that the examiners wouldn't understand what she was talking about. "It's locked. Didn't you recognize the dragon?"

Indy looked puzzled. "I saw it. So?"

Una didn't know how to tell him. She scratched *Muse* in the dirt with her finger.

Indy stood up slowly. "You brought one into the *exam*? You idiot!" He began muttering under his breath in another language. He sounded mad.

"Indy," Una began.

"Unbelievable! We have been seeking them for years. Risking life and limb to beg one of them to return. And some little girl"—Una huffed at this—"brings one of their books into the Talekeepers' exam. We have got to get it out of here." He started walking.

"Wait. You want them to come back?" Una asked, struggling to keep up. "You don't think they're all dead?"

Indy snorted. "Immortals don't die."

Immortals! Una stopped short and blinked at Indy. He was halfway across the clearing before she found her voice. "Have you found any?"

Indy didn't look at her. "We haven't."

"We?" She doubled her stride to catch up.

He gave her a curt nod.

Una wanted to shake the answers out of him. What else did he know? "What will you do with it now? We can't open it, remember?"

"*You* can't open it. I can. My family has passed on the tradition for generations." Indy scowled back at her. He wasn't even out of breath. "But there's no way I'm going to do it in some stupid Talekeeper exam."

"Show me," Una demanded. "Open it now."

"Now? Are you crazy?" Indy asked, but it wasn't Una's voice that answered him.

"I think that would be very unwise," Elton said as he moved into the lantern's little circle of light. Una spun around to face him, and Indy stepped forward so that he and Una were standing shoulder to shoulder.

Elton's face was streaked with lines of dirt. He was snugly buttoned into an old-fashioned tweed suit, but the shirt had come untucked and all the fabric was rumpled. Behind him stood three horrible creatures. Their bodies were hidden in the shadows, but they began to growl as they skirted the clearing. Una reached out for Indy's hand, and he grasped hers firmly.

"Is something wrong with the examination?" Indy asked in a strained voice.

"Something is wrong, yes," Elton responded, turning to Una. Una squeezed Indy's hand.

"The book, child. Give it to me," Elton said.

The creatures behind him were shaking now, scenting the air hungrily. Una didn't doubt that they were carnivorous. Her tongue was stuck to the roof of her mouth.

"Give it to me!" Elton screamed, and the beasts went into a howling frenzy. They circled around one more time. The moment seemed to stretch on forever. Then everything happened in a flash. Indy threw something flaming at Elton, which exploded in the air right in front of him.

"Run!" he yelled, whirling Una back around and out of the clearing.

"Elton is working for the Red Enchantress," she said as they blindly sped up the path. "They've been hunting for Alethia's book." What did it matter now if the examiners knew what they were talking about? She tried to match Indy's long strides. "And I think they mean to destroy it."

"We've got to get back to the Tale station," Indy

said, with an even voice that had no strain of the run in it. "The Talekeepers may try to make us hand over the book there, but at least they won't destroy it. The professors won't allow it. Edenberry will help us."

They could hear the sound of pursuit in the forest behind them. Una sprinted on. It was nearly impossible to see anything beyond the ground right in front of her. How much farther did they have to go? They weren't even close to the exam entrance, and Una was having a hard time breathing. There was no way she could run the entire way. Even Indy was showing signs of tiring.

"Need to . . . rest . . . soon," she managed, and had to double her pace to make up for the distance lost while she talked. As they sped through yet another clearing, they heard a crashing off to their immediate left, and an animal burst into the path in front them. The unicorn was a hugely majestic creature, and its fur shone with silver light. Una and Indy stopped instinctively and stared in wonder.

"What do you seek?" the unicorn asked, his voice deep and resonant. He was looking straight at Una, as though Indy wasn't even there.

Una didn't hesitate. "We are being followed," she whispered. "By evil creatures. We seek your aid."

The unicorn looked at her for a moment. "An unusual request," he said. "What will you exchange for my aid?"

Una's heart felt like it was going to explode out of her chest. She could hear the beasts' howls coming from somewhere behind them. They didn't have time for her to figure out how to manipulate the reality of the exam. Besides, she didn't know the first thing about unicorns or what they liked. She thought hard. *What could a unicorn want?* But even if she knew, it wouldn't have mattered.

"I don't have anything to exchange," she said simply. Una locked eyes with the unicorn for a moment. She could see green flecks in the golden depths. "If I did, I swear I would give it." She could hear Indy's intake of breath next to her, but she ignored it. "Please," she whispered. "We're desperate."

After a long moment the unicorn spoke. "Agreed. We will delay those who follow you."

The next moment the unicorn bayed, his call one long melancholy note that filled the forest. Even though Una couldn't understand the cry, she felt it deep in her spirit. The leaves around them shook with the sound. Soon, small noises carried across the air. The forest was stirring. In a very short time, she and Indy were alone in an almost silent clearing.

She could feel him staring at her. "Do you have any idea what you've done?"

Una couldn't tell if he was angry or not. "We needed time. I bought us time. We've got to keep going, though. Who knows how long they can hold Elton back?" They set off at a slow jog, to pace themselves for the journey ahead. "What *were* those things?" Una finally asked.

Indy's faced tightened as he answered. "Beasts. Trained fighters. Believe me, you don't want to mess with them." He touched a hand to his sword. "Why does Elton want Alethia's book so bad?"

"I'm just guessing," she panted. "He's been helping the Enchantress destroy the Muse books. I read about what happened to Sophia. The Enchantress came for her. And Sophia's book got destroyed." It was getting harder to talk. "It's a long story. But if they capture all the Muses and destroy all their books, they will bring back the Enemy."

"What Enemy?" Indy demanded.

Una licked her lips. With every breath her mouth was getting dryer. "Fidelus. He broke his oaths. It's all lies. Everything the Talekeepers have said about the

Muses has been a lie."

Indy snorted. "We've always known they were liars. But no one else believed us."

"But your dad's a Talekeeper!" It came out like an accusation. "I saw you at the Merriweathers' house," she explained.

"The Merriweathers head up the Resistance." Indy shrugged. "My dad's part of it. Staying a Talekeeper is a good way to find books and other stuff."

"Other stuff?" Una managed.

Indy sounded embarrassed. "Stuff about the King."

Una stopped running.

"I know, I know," Indy said as he slowed and turned around. "You think he's not real."

"No! I believe in the King," she laughed. "I just don't know anything about him."

Indy grinned. "My family says that once upon a time, the Muses were watching for his return. Since the Muses disappeared, we have taken up their watch. Though he left long ago, we serve the King of Story."

The Servants of the King! Una knew what she and Indy had to do. And, if they were lucky, it would help them escape Elton as well. "Then open the book, and let's go find one of the Muses."

He wiped a hand over his mouth. "What if the

book's just blank inside? Like all the ones in the Vault?"

"Don't worry about that." If he would just open it, Una knew it would work. "They'll take it anyway when we get back, and if Elton gets it first, he'll destroy it. Do you really know how to do it or not? We don't have much time."

In the pause that followed, the silence of the forest was broken by the sounds of a struggle. Una thought she could hear the deep tones of the unicorn. Could that be Elton's high-pitched laugh? "Something's happening," she said.

Indy peered back the way they came as if he could see what was going on. "All right," was all he said, and he pulled the small book out of his cloak.

In the blackness of the forest, Una couldn't see the book's binding, but the blue around the dragon sparkled like some strange jewel. She wanted to touch it. "How do you . . . ?" she began.

Indy shushed her and carefully began running his fingers over the cover. Una's anxiety returned, and she felt a panicky feeling around her heart. The sounds of the struggle behind them were growing louder. She hadn't heard the unicorn's call for a long time now. That couldn't be a good sign. *Hurry*, she thought madly. *Hurry. Hurry. Hurry.*

Indy seemed in no rush. His hands moved smoothly and rhythmically across the book's binding. Back and forth, around to the other side, his long fingers crept carefully, his face furrowed with concentration. Una couldn't restrain herself any longer. "Come on!" she whispered fiercely.

"Shut up!" Indy said without looking up. "I've got to focus."

Una could hear Elton directing his creatures. What had happened to the unicorn? Her heart jumped as the sound of trampled branches and Elton's awful voice drew nearer. Una moved closer to Indy and could barely stop herself from reaching out to grab his hand.

"Almost done," he muttered, pausing to wipe the sweat out of his eyes.

With a shout of triumph, Elton crashed into the side of the clearing, followed by one of the ugly beasts. "Gotcha!" he cried.

Una gasped and grabbed Indy's hand.

Indy tensed and muttered something under his breath.

There was a loud clash like a thunderclap, and the air flashed with a blinding light. Una and Indy fell to their knees and covered their eyes. She heard Elton cry out. For a moment, everything was chaos. The noise was horrific, filling everything and paralyzing Una. She held tightly to Indy's hand and screwed her eyes shut. She could see the light burning into her eyelids. Inside her head everything was bathed in a red glow. Then the world began to spin.

Chapter 31

After the noise died down, all was silent. The air was warm and fragrant, and Una felt strangely at peace. She was lying on her back and could feel Indy's hand clasped in her own. It seemed that the events in the clearing were playing through her mind in slow motion. *Is that really me, crouching in the clearing, clinging to Indy's hand? Was I really frightened by that grasping Mr. Elton?* The playback in her head was replaced by the soothing quiet around her. Joy bubbled up from somewhere deep inside, and curiosity soon followed. It seemed imperative that Una know where she was, as though it was the most important thing in the world. And whatever else she was feeling, Una wasn't afraid. She sat up, opened her eyes, and stared about her.

It was no longer the middle of the night, but Una didn't find this peculiar. She was more interested in the world of Alethia's book. She was sitting on a soft mound of the greenest grass she had ever seen. Indy lay next to her, his eyes still shut and his hand folded in hers. The grassy hill gently sloped down to the edge of a forest clothed in brilliant colors. Bluebells nodded to one another, while above them purple wisteria trailed on branches of slim trees. Crimson peonies mingled with white daisies, their heads bobbing in the perfumed air. It was quiet, and Una could hear the sound of grasses and leaves blowing in the softest breeze she could have imagined. She didn't know how long she sat there, soaking up the deep silence, letting the ocean of color and scent wash over her senses. All too soon, Indy stirred.

Una gently released his hand.

He sat up, rubbing his head. "Where are we? I remember opening the book, and then . . ."

"And then this," Una finished for him. "We actually made it through the Muse book. Isn't it wonderful?" The compelling curiosity was rising up in her again. They got to their feet and wandered about. Everywhere she looked, brilliant colors soothed Una's soul. The contrasts were breathtakingly beautiful—the brightest purple violets set against crimson geraniums. Lavender clematis next to the yellowest sunflowers Una had ever seen. She couldn't help but smile.

Indy was smiling too, and it softened his whole face. *Was he always this courageous and kindhearted? How did I never see it before?*

"What a brave, true, noble little soul you have, Una," Indy said, and looked at her with admiration.

This didn't embarrass Una. It seemed right that in the beauty of the garden they would only think the best of each other. "When you talk like that, so peacefully, it makes your whole face look stronger," she told him. She knew it was true as she said it. And the good things in him made her want to be better, stronger, braver, and truer.

Una could have wandered around the little wilderness of color forever, were it not for the fact that she heard the sound of tinkling chimes behind her. Together, she and Indy turned to follow their call. They discovered a charming wooded path at one end of the grassy slope and started off. The path was just wide enough for two to walk side by side, and they strolled into the friendly woods. Under the dappled shade of the trees, they could hear the sound of small woodland animals, birds calling cheerfully to one another and squirrels flying from tree to tree.

Soon the twisty little path crossed a small creek, and they lingered on the footbridge for a while, looking out over the busy waters. The creek curved out of sight, but right before the bridge it hopped down layers of stones.

Indy ducked below and then emerged from under the bridge with a small piece of willow bark that he had cleverly fashioned into a cup. It was full of crystal-clear water. "Have a drink?" He offered it to Una. No water ever tasted so sweet, and Una drained the cup, wiping her mouth with her sleeve. She tucked the little cup into her bag, and they continued on.

Before long, the path opened up, and they found themselves in a valley rimmed by hilly forest. In front of them lay the coziest cottage Una had ever seen. It was cobbled together with bits of stone and brick. A small front garden overflowed with more of the brilliantly colored flowers, and a crooked path tripped up to the round front door. Smoke trailed out of the chimney, and Una could hear the tinkle of the chimes they had been seeking. They made their way up the path and found themselves before a bright-green door with a Cheshire cat knocker on it. Una grasped it firmly in her hand and rapped three times.

In no time at all, the door was opened by a tall boy wearing a brown cloak. He looked familiar, but Una couldn't quite place him. He bowed low and held the door open.

"Come in," he said, and Una was enchanted by his rich, smooth voice. He introduced himself as the servant and bid them sit in two squashy armchairs placed at angles before the cheery fire.

They were in a cozy room, pillowed and cushioned with deep reds and browns. Una felt as though they had left the spring of the forest outside and were now ensconced in the beauty of autumn. The servant left them, and Indy and Una sat in companionable silence in front of the crackling fire. Its shadows danced over the walls, which were filled with colorful books jammed into every possible nook and cranny. Una went over to them and ran her fingers over their lovely covers.

The servant reappeared with a sturdy tray filled with a small pot of hot chocolate, two little mugs, and some food. There was a plate of white cheese and crisp apple wedges, which Indy dug into at once. Una helped herself to a delicious-looking truffle and nearly laughed out loud at the taste of strawberry filling melting in her mouth.

"Her ladyship will be with you presently," the servant said. He looked at Una with his coal-black eyes.

A memory tickled at the back of her mind, and Una peered at the servant's eyes, but there was nothing strange there, nothing strange at all. He winked at her. Then, he left as silently as he had come. Una turned to ask Indy about the boy but lost her train of thought as she tasted the delicious chocolate. How hungry she was, and how delightful it was to eat good food after foraging in the forest!

As they ate, words came easily to Una's tongue, always gentle and kind, but sharp with good humor and fun. The air filled with their laughter, and neither noticed how long they had sat there until the servant reemerged to tend to the fire.

Sometime later, they heard the tinkling sound of the chimes again, and Una knew that something was about to happen. She sat up as straight as she could in her cushioned chair and looked expectantly at the windowed doors set amid the books. The doors opened, once again letting in the warm air and the smell of spring. A woman came into the room, and when she arrived, she possessed every part of it fully. She was not a tall woman but stood as straight as a slim birch tree. Her golden hair shone in the firelight, little curls falling about her ears. Eyes of startling blue were set in an unlined, ageless face. She wore a frilly concoction of creamy pink.

Una, who usually hated pink with a passion, thought it the sweetest dress she could have imagined. The lace overlay was embroidered with flowers, and as the lady came into the room, Una felt the warmth of a summer garden. This was undoubtedly the most beautiful woman she had ever seen. When she smiled, Una couldn't help but stand up and sketch a curtsy.

The lady laughed—a tinkling, joyful sound that Una knew to be the chimes they had heard earlier. "You are such dears," she said. "How welcome you are to my house." Out of nowhere a third chair had appeared, and they all leaned in snugly around the fire. The servant brought a third cup and refilled everyone's hot chocolate, and by the time they were settled in, the three felt like old friends even though no one had uttered another word.

"I am Alethia," the pink-gowned creature said, and Una knew instinctively that it was a fortunate thing they had come to her house. Alethia went on, "I joyfully welcome all those who seek me."

In the firelight, Alethia was bewitching. In one moment, she seemed girlishly pretty, and in the next she intimidated Una with her beauty. In those times, Una was a bit afraid of her, not with the old, clammy, terror-filled fear, but with the sober realization that here was a real Lady.

It seemed Alethia knew this, and she smiled at Una. "You are right to admire me, my dear. It is not arrogant for me to say so, you know. It is the truth. I am as I am, and many years have I guided the people of Story. My heart's desire is that they would live in truth and freedom."

Una wasn't sure what Alethia meant by this, but Indy was speaking now. "Why have you left us then, Milady Alethia?"

"I haven't left," she replied. "I am found by those who seek me. I am everywhere in your world. You see glimpses of me in the beauty of the forest. You meet me in the noble and true actions of a friend. You find me in the hidden places of the heart. I hide myself in many stories, hoping to be discovered and embraced. Yet, in these dark days, so very few seek me," she added sadly. "But you found my book." Her face lit up at this, and she looked like a mischievous child. "However did you come across it, my dears? It has been many years since anyone has come to me through my book, and I thought it had long been lost."

Una was suddenly very glad she had stolen the book from behind Professor Thornhill's musty old tapestry. "It was hidden away," she said. "I don't think anyone knew where it was." As soon as she uttered what could be called a half-truth, Una felt desperately ashamed. Alethia's eyes were kind, but Una couldn't help but think that she knew. "I mean," she faltered, "I found it in a professor's study and took it. I don't know if she missed it, because I didn't see her after that." Immediately, Una felt the weight of a guilty conscience lift, and all was right in the little circle again.

"But some of us have been looking for your books," Indy said earnestly. "Do you know about the Talekeepers, milady? Do you know what some of them have done?"

Alethia shook her head sadly. "Once upon a time I knew all the doings of Story. But I've been bound in my book and unable to leave for a long time now. Tell me how Story fares."

Indy told of the Talekeepers' lies, and Una filled in what she had learned from Archimago's confession.

Alethia's face darkened into a terrible beauty. "The

Enemy," she breathed. "What evil his oath breaking has wrought."

Perhaps it was the air in Alethia's house. Or maybe the food the servant had given them. Whatever it was, Una felt brave for once. She knew that it was her time to do something. They must somehow fight against the schemes of the Enemy. She wanted to try and save Story. "We need your help," Una said.

Alethia looked delighted. "I love it when people ask," she said. "On my oath, I will help you. But you must tell me what it is you seek." She turned her gaze to Indy.

He wasted no time. "Won't you come back with the other Muses?" Indy asked her. "Won't you return to Story?"

Alethia gave him a wistful smile. "Now that someone has found my book, the people of Story are free to come and go as they please. If I can, I will return to Story. But the others?" She stood and moved toward the wall of books behind her. "We must recover their books first." She ran her fingers across the volumes as though she might find the other Muse books hidden among them.

Then she turned around. Her brows were knit together in a little frown. "And, Una. What is the one thing that you seek?"

Una had meant to ask all her questions about what had really happened to the Muses. But she didn't think that was the one thing Alethia meant. What *did* she seek? She wanted to know why she had been Written In, of course. What she was supposed to do in Story. So many questions. And she wanted so many things! She wanted to belong, no longer to be the outcast hiding away in the library or pretending to be someone she wasn't. She wanted to be brave, to stop being so afraid. But she didn't know if Alethia could help her with all of this.

Even on such a short acquaintance, Una felt that she could sit comfortably in silence with this woman. They sat this way while Una sorted through her thoughts. Deep down, buried beneath everything, she wanted to know why she had been left alone. A small voice that she never acknowledged wanted to know why her parents had abandoned her. But she seriously doubted that someone in this world could answer *that* question for her.

Una took a deep breath. "Can you tell me why I've been Written In? Why I'm here in this world?" she finally asked.

Una heard Indy's intake of breath as she said the words and realized too late that he now knew her secret.

But Alethia looked anything but surprised. She

nodded, as though this was exactly what she had been waiting for. "I can answer part of your question, Una," she said. "But first, Endeavor must rest." She waved her hand before Indy, and he slumped into a deep sleep.

"Your Tale is yours to tell," Alethia said calmly. "But only when you will." She sat back in her chair and looked sadly at Una. "You've been Written In, because once upon a time, I Wrote you Out of this world."

"What?"

Alethia's words sounded heavy, as though she was unwilling to say them. "I have often wondered if it was a wise decision. Some of my sisters counseled against it, but the others agreed with me." She turned to face Una and looked her straight in the eyes.

"Una, you are the daughter of the Enemy."

Chapter 32

Peter first stopped off at the Healer's house. The Healer wanted to know how Sam had been wounded.

"Beast," Peter said, edging toward the door. "Wild beast." He thrust enough gold marks at the woman to stop her questions. "Take good care of him." He left the Healer's house quickly. He had lost a lot of time when he blacked out, and now it was nearly dusk. He needed to find Professor Edenberry. If Elton had gotten into the exam, Edenberry would know how.

Edenberry wasn't in the classroom, and Peter thought to try his cabin next. He knew that the professor lived in the forest on the other side of Birchwood's gardens. The sky was clouding over as he raced down the twisting garden paths. It looked like a thunderstorm was moving in. Sure enough, as he reached the cabin door, Peter felt the first drops of rain. Pushing his way inside, he found Professor Edenberry waiting for him.

"Well, boy?" Edenberry asked. "Where's Elton?"

"How did you——?" Peter began.

"I saw you leave. Let's quit pretending, Peter. I know Una's a WI, and you've got to believe that I intend to protect her. I also know Elton's after her. Where is he?"

Peter told him about the beasts and the fight on the dais.

Professor Edenberry tugged at his poof of white hair. "This is worse than I thought." He turned and called to the back of the cabin. "Griselda. Elton's in the exam."

The dryad emerged from behind a curtained-off doorway. "But won't the examiners see if he takes her from there? It will be read by everyone."

The wiry old man shook his head. "If he can break into the exam, he can change it. No one will know what he's done. Or where he's taken Una." He placed his palms together as though he was praying. "What I want to know is, why now? He could have taken her at any time with much less fuss."

Peter felt like he had been punched in the gut. He

hadn't thought about Una being kidnapped. "She has Alethia's book." He licked his lips. "And Elton wants it. I think he's the one who's been destroying them."

Edenberry didn't ask him how he knew about the burned books. Or how he knew about Elton. Instead, he turned to Griselda. "Get the tray," he said.

Griselda disappeared and returned with a silver tray, a little mound resting in the center of it. She held it in front of Peter. "You mean like this?"

Peter peered closer. It was a burned book. He poked a tentative finger at it and sharply withdrew his finger. "Ouch!"

"Don't touch it!" Professor Edenberry came over and roughly grabbed Peter's singed finger. "Serves you right, you fool boy!"

Peter sat down on a wooden stool and sucked on his sore finger. He pulled it out of his mouth long enough to ask, "It was one of the Muse books, wasn't it?"

Edenberry tugged on a worn pair of gardening gloves and gingerly examined the little pile. "We believe so."

Griselda set the tray down. "I went to the Hollow yesterday to search for my tree." She stared at the tray. "I found this instead. This is bad. Very bad."

At that moment, Peter didn't care what Edenberry

and his parents were up to. Or that it had been a secret for so long. Edenberry and Griselda were his only hope for rescuing Una. And every second counted. He slowly pulled the scroll from his pocket and placed it on the table. "Whatever you're thinking, it's worse than that."

It only took them a few minutes to read Archimago's confession, but to Peter it felt like hours. Had Elton found Una? No doubt Horace would wrap Una up as a present and give her to Elton if it would save his own skin. Peter was counting on the Truepenny kid to protect her.

Griselda was weeping, tears running down her cheeks. "The Muses," she breathed.

When Edenberry looked up, his face was gray. He reached a hand behind him to steady himself and then sat on a low table. He set the paper down and stared at it as though it might attack him. "The Muses aren't gone after all."

Griselda wiped her eyes. "I've been telling you that for years, Jack," she said matter-of-factly. "Some of us never believed the Talekeeper lies. The Muses kept their oaths."

"All but one," Peter said with a shiver. "Do you know anything about Fidelus? The Enemy?"

"No." Griselda's green eyes almost looked like they glowed. "But from this account, it sounds like he's imprisoned somewhere."

"For now," Peter said grimly. He told them about the Red Enchantress and how intent she was on finding the rest of the Muse books. Peter didn't know how they meant to do it, but he was sure now about what she and Elton were up to. He felt like he couldn't breathe. He heard with crystal clarity the conversation from Elton's office. *When* he *returns . . .* His heart did a triple somersault. He swallowed, but his mouth was completely dry. "The Red Enchantress . . ."

Peter thought he knew what was coming. He thought he was prepared for the news. But still, his heart froze in his chest when he heard Griselda finish the sentence.

". . . is about to bring the Enemy back to Story."

Chapter 33

The Enemy. The words echoed in Una's head. Chills danced along her spine, and her hands began to shake. She set her mug of chocolate down and willed herself to be calm, willed herself back to five minutes ago, when she'd felt so happy and peaceful. "The Enemy?" she said, staring at the puddle of now-melted cheese on the plate before her. She was afraid of what she might see on Alethia's face. Probably the same horror she felt on her own. *Daughter of the horrible Oathbreaker who did all those awful things?* "But . . ." Her voice broke.

Alethia came over and sat on the arm of Una's chair. "Una, I know the truth is hard to hear, but the only way I know how to tell it is clearly and directly."

The huge lump in Una's throat hurt too much to talk.

Alethia laid her hand gently on Una's arm. "There is so much to tell you, so much you don't know, and much of it has long been forgotten—a fruit of the Enemy's plans. But, you see, I have not forgotten," Alethia went on. "I was there."

Una looked up at the ageless face before her. How old was Alethia? "I don't understand," Una replied. "I thought this all happened a long time ago. I'm only twelve years old."

Indy's chin dropped to his chest, and he gave a loud snore.

Alethia smiled and said in a whisper, "It would seem that way to you, I know. Time passes differently in this world when you have been Written Out of it." Alethia stood and smoothed her skirts. "He wasn't always the Enemy, you know. He once was a faithful servant." Her voice grew soft. "My brother. Fidelus, he was called then. 'Loyal one.' He wrote many Tales and was famous for his trustworthiness and his service to Story."

Just then, a terrible screeching sound came from outside. Alethia dashed through a side door, and Una followed her out to the back garden. It must have once been a place of blossoming beauty, tended with care. Now, everywhere Una looked seemed like winter. A wrought iron gate led to gravel paths that made a maze through untamed shrubbery and bare trees. Alethia ran over to a windswept hill and scanned the abandoned paths. After a few moments, she gave a little cry of alarm, and Una peered through the climbing ivy of the wrought iron. Off in the distance she could see flashes of light, and Una pushed open the reluctant gate and stepped through.

"Too late," a woman's sultry voice said from behind her. "Milady Alethia." The last sounded like a curse.

Una ducked behind the nearest bush and peeked back. It looked like Alethia had tried to run into the house, but a Lady cloaked in scarlet was at the door, a sheaf of papers held aloft in her hands. Una knew at once it was the Red Enchantress, and, from inside her red cloak, she was laughing maniacally.

"At last!" she screamed, and pulled a book out from under her cloak.

"Duessa! Do not do this," Alethia commanded, one pale hand extended in warning.

Una crouched lower. This was not the kindly Lady who had served them cocoa. Alethia's anger made her look as hard as stone. The icy claw of fear gripped Una's heart, and she tried to steady her breathing.

But Duessa only laughed. "You think to sway me?" She shoved the papers she was holding into the book and cast a flaming ball of light toward Alethia.

Alethia deflected it with a flick of her fingers and took a step toward her foe.

Duessa opened her arms wide. "Much has changed since you left, Alethia." More fireballs, faster than the first, shot toward the Muse. "I am not so easily cowed."

Small snowflakes began to fall, covering the air between the women. Alethia stood, frozen like some beautiful statue, the Enchantress's missiles quenched before they even reached her.

Una swallowed, but her mouth was dry. In between fireballs, the Enchantress worked the loose pages into the Muse book. Alethia began to walk steadily toward her, extinguishing the flames as fast as they came. Why wasn't Alethia fighting back?

"You are the last Muse," the Enchantress was saying triumphantly to Alethia. "You've given me the final piece." She held the book high with both hands, a crazed look on her face. "Now we will see him!"

A blaze of red light shot into the air around the Red Enchantress, and the heat of it blasted Una off her feet and jolted her back to her senses. She had to find somewhere to hide. She didn't know what the Enchantress would do if she found her there, but it couldn't be good. She crept down the nearest path, bending low behind the skeletons of dying bushes. Already the sound of the Enchantress's mocking voice was fainter.

But Alethia's clear tones cut across the air. "You are not of his blood," she said. "You cannot free him." And then Una heard Alethia's laughter, hard and merciless, and Duessa's scream of fury. Una moved faster, running aimlessly through the maze of deserted gardens. Every turn she took led her farther away from Alethia's battle and deeper into the desolate foliage.

The snow was falling harder now, and Una's toes were numb. Her mind felt nearly as dull. She couldn't make sense of Alethia's words, couldn't piece together what the Red Enchantress was doing with the Muse book. Was she trying to destroy it like the one in the Merriweathers' potting shed? But every thought led to what Alethia had told her back in the house. *Daughter of the Enemy* kept echoing through her head. Could it really be possible that she was born in this world? That her whole childhood had taken place in a strange and foreign land? She thought of all the foster homes she had lived in, all the years spent wondering about her parents, only to find out the unwelcome truth. Una stumbled and fell onto the gravel path. The strain of the past hours had finally caught up with her, and she wanted nothing more than a place to rest.

She struggled up and somehow kept walking. She saw a stone bench across the way. A few more steps and she could stop. But before she reached it, a figure jumped out in front of her on the path.

"Fancy meeting you here, Una!" Elton said in a syrupy-sweet voice, but she could see the malice in his eyes.

Adrenaline coursed through Una. She sprang forward, but Elton was faster.

He grabbed her arm. "Yes, my pet," he said, "you led us straight to Alethia's house. Once you opened her book, it was a small thing for the Red Enchantress to follow your trail." He jerked her closer. "You're all alone, so let's just quit pretending. Be a good girl and come with me."

"Let go of me!" Una cried. She twisted her arm, but it was no use.

Elton cuffed her hard across the face. "You'll come with me if it's the last thing you do." His eyes shone wickedly. "We can't have you running around Story spreading your little lies, now, can we?"

The metallic taste of blood filled Una's mouth, and her ears were ringing. She felt like she was floating above everything, that she was on the outside looking in on an unhappy scene. "Manners, manners, Mr. Elton. What *will* the other Talekeepers say?" Her voice sounded like it was very far away.

Elton sneered at her. "You think any of the Talekeepers will hear of this? That anyone's reading this exam? Stupid girl! The Talekeepers are nothing. By the time we're finished here, it will be too late for them to do anything, no matter what some little brat says. *He* will be back in Story."

The garden snapped back into focus. *The Enemy.* That was who Elton meant. She pushed back hard against Elton, and he scrambled to hold on to her. One hand was free. She could almost reach her dagger. Elton's grasp was weakening. She lifted her knee and aimed a well-placed blow at Elton's middle.

He groaned and let go of her. She was free. She turned around and ran straight into Horace Wotton.

He trapped her with his arms, more tightly than Elton had. "I don't think so, little Una." Horace's voice was close to her ear. Una felt like she was suffocating. Her arms were pinned to her side, and her face mashed into Horace's chest. No matter how she struggled, his viselike grip pinched tighter.

"Very good, my boy." Elton's voice came up behind her. "Very good."

"Horace. Please," Una managed.

"Shut up," he said. Elton was tying her hands roughly behind her with a piece of coarse rope. Horace stuffed a filthy handkerchief into her mouth.

Una gagged as the foul taste of it pressed against her tongue. Her eyes watered as she glared back at Horace's leering face. His mouth was twisted into an ugly little smile. She kicked him hard in the shins, and he swore.

He pushed her hard, down to the ground. "Stay!" he said, pointing at her as if she were a dog.

"Well done, Horace," Elton said, brushing at his rumpled suit. "Now we need to find the boy."

Chapter 34

The rain pounded on Edenberry's cabin. It was storming in earnest now, and every so often Peter could hear rumbles of muffled thunder. The room was cold, and it felt like they had been talking for hours.

"We need to *do* something," Peter said. "Talking isn't going to help Una."

"Una's not the only one to worry about," Edenberry said. His tone was harsh, and he looked worried. "Professor Thornhill has been missing all day. And I don't like that Snow never showed up for her exam. Something's not right."

Peter made a fist with one hand and punched it into the other palm. *Now Snow's in danger?* It was like his Heroics practical all over again. Two girls for the Hero to save, and he didn't have a clue how to get to either of them. Only this time he couldn't fail.

"Indy will protect Una," Mr. Truepenny said.

Peter clenched his fists tighter. That's what he was worried about. Who was to say any of them could trust Indy? Or Indy's father, for that matter?

Mr. Truepenny had shown up several hours before, a tall bundle of crackling energy, dressed in rich blue robes. Peter knew him at once to be the mysterious man Thornhill had secretly met at the cathedral.

What Peter didn't understand was why they didn't do anything. Well, much of anything. Professor Edenberry had sent messages, and they talked around in circles a lot. Mr. Truepenny had ranted about the corruption of the Talekeepers and the oppression of the masses. Everyone had whispered about the Enemy in hushed tones. Peter scowled. *But what good is all that when Elton might be kidnapping Una right now?*

At that moment, Griselda slipped through the door, letting in a cold sliver of air and the whiff of damp earth. She had gone out earlier to see what she could learn. Now her clothes hung on her wetly, drops of water puddling off them onto the floor. "The other examiners said they never saw Thornhill this morning." She looked at Edenberry. "No one was happy about having to call you in at the last minute. They went on and on about revoking Thornhill's exam privileges, and I just now got away." She stood over a potted plant and wrung the water out of her braids. "No one else has seen a trace of her."

"And Elton's quarters?" Edenberry asked.

"Empty," Griselda said.

"What we need is a plan," Peter said. *Snow or Una. Which one to save first?* Snow could have just skipped her exam that morning. He didn't know for sure that she was in trouble. But Una definitely was. "Are you sure we can't get into Una's exam?" he asked Edenberry.

Edenberry rubbed his eyes with his fists. "We've been over all that before. Only the Tale Master has the authority to interrupt an examination."

"Adelaide would know how to do it," Mr. Truepenny said. "She has studied the old ways. If only—"

"Well, Professor Thornhill isn't here, is she?" Peter snapped. "We need a plan where we actually *do something.*"

"I agree with Peter," Griselda said. "If Alethia is in danger, we must come to her aid." She moved about the room gracefully, dripping water over a flat of

Edenberry's seedlings as she talked. "Elton needs to be watched. We have to know the moment he's back from the exam."

She barely got the sentence out before Mr. Truepenny stood and thrust his red turban back on his head. "I'll go right now. Just wait till I get my hands on his lying Tale Master neck, I'll—"

"Sit down." Griselda patted a tiny shoot. "We need to discuss the whole plan."

Peter leaned forward, hands on his knees. *Now we're getting somewhere.*

Griselda continued. "If he has Una, we can assume they'll come out of the exam together."

Peter stood. "I'll be there. Elton will need a grand welcome after all he's done." He started toward the door.

"Sit *down*," Griselda said, louder this time. "It's no good racing off half-done. Patience—the two of you."

Peter plopped down next to Mr. Truepenny, who looked like he had very little patience left.

"That leaves Snow and Professor Thornhill." Griselda looked at Professor Edenberry. "I stopped by her apartment, and I found some interesting things. The good professor is not entirely what she seems. I think we might find some clues in Horror Hollow." Griselda pulled out a wet piece of paper that hung limply in her spindly fingers. "Apparently, she had an errand there today. A potion she had requested was ready."

Edenberry stood up at this. "Impossible. Adelaide has given up those ways. She told me so herself."

"Sit down," Griselda said gently. "I didn't say she meant the potion for evil. Perhaps she meant it to help Una. Either way, it seems likely that she meant to go there. If we're lucky, the potion master may be able to tell us something more." Edenberry nodded grudgingly, and Griselda looked satisfied. "It's settled. We each have our tasks. The messages we sent earlier should have reached the other Resistance members by now. They travel to Bramble Cottage as we speak, and we meet together tomorrow. Everyone ready?"

Mr. Truepenny stood up first and was halfway to the door before Peter could follow. "Be careful, you fools," Griselda called after them. "Say nothing to anyone else about this. . . ." The dryad's voice grew fainter and was soon lost in the noise of the storm as Peter raced after Indy's father. His fists pumped the air as he ran, as though his speed could somehow keep everyone safe. With each pounding step, he thought of his friends. He hoped that the Healer was taking good care of Sam. That Snow was okay. That he and Indy's father wouldn't be too late to catch Elton. That it wasn't already too late to help Una.

Chapter 35

Horace was barely out of sight when Una heard Indy's voice calling her name. She tried to cry out through the gag, but Elton wrapped a thick arm around her neck and covered her mouth. "I told you to shut up," he said.

She and Elton were crouched behind a thin veil of empty branches, which hid them from view. Indy wouldn't see her until he was right upon them. Elton smelled foul, and Una felt a sour taste burn the back of her throat.

Finally, Indy's tall form moved into sight. He was stooped over, one arm cradled protectively close, his cloak torn and muddied. Even through the branches, Una could see his face was cut, a dark gash running from the corner of one eye to his jaw, the blood glistening against his skin. Una wondered what had happened. The last she had seen Indy, he had been sleeping by Alethia's fireplace. He stopped in surprise when Horace met him on the path.

"Why, hello there, Indy," Horace said.

Indy's eyes grew hooded. "Horace." He said it like he was formally greeting him. "What are you doing here?"

"Looking for you, my friend, looking for you." Una winced as Horace clapped Indy on his hurt shoulder.

Una knew that calling Indy *friend* was Horace's first mistake. His second mistake was to look over to where Una and Elton were hidden. Una saw Indy's gaze dart to their hiding place. One minute was all it took.

Una had never seen someone move so quickly. Out came Indy's sword. He shoved Horace backward, one hand tight around his throat, and pushed him up against a tree. Horace cried out in pain, and Una thought she heard something crack. In a flash, Indy's blade was beneath Horace's chin.

"You lie!" Indy hissed.

"I wouldn't do that if I were you." Elton dragged Una into the clearing. The sharp tip of his knife pressed into her throat. Una didn't dare swallow. "It looks like we're at a standstill, eh, boy?" Elton laughed. "Drop the sword."

Indy looked at Una, who tried to shake her head no.

"Stop moving, little girl," Elton said, nicking her skin.

Indy let his weapon drop to the ground. He still held Horace tightly by his neck. Indy slowly pulled out Alethia's book. "Aren't you forgetting something? You can't defeat Alethia without this."

Una heard Elton sigh greedily. "Give it to me."

"Not until you let Una go."

Elton tightened his grip. "Don't play with me, boy!"

Una's heart pounded loud in her chest. She could feel the blood course through the place where Elton's dagger was aimed.

Indy wrapped his arm around Horace's neck and dragged him along behind. They were very close now, and Una could see his face. He looked tired. How had he gotten past the Red Enchantress? He held the book out to Elton, who had to let go of her to reach for it. As he stretched forward, the knifepoint faltered. In that moment, Una moved. She threw all her weight back against Elton and twisted away from the knife. His arms spread wide as he fell back onto the ground. Indy struck Horace on the head and tossed him to one side, where he lay like a limp bundle of rags.

Una rolled off Elton and writhed against the ropes that still bound her wrists. In a flash, Indy was there. He pulled her to her feet, and in one fluid motion threw the book as far as he could. In the stillness of the garden, they could hear it land with a soft splash.

Elton gasped. "You fool!" He flipped over and began to crawl on all fours. Then, he was on his feet, running down a path.

"Are you okay?" Indy asked, gently untying the rag from her mouth and loosing her hands. Una coughed, her throat raw from the handkerchief. She rubbed her sore wrists and tried to swallow.

"You're hurt!" she croaked, and touched his wounded shoulder lightly.

Indy winced. "Worry about me later," he said. "We've got to get out of here before the beasts find us."

"The beasts?" Una managed.

"In Alethia's house. I was sleeping, and the next thing I knew, two beasts were gnawing me awake."

Una swung her arm around Indy's waist and helped him limp up the path toward Alethia's house. "What about Alethia? Did you see her fighting the Red Enchantress?"

Indy coughed. "Is that what happened? The ground's

all scorched up by the hill. But no one's there." They had only gone a short way when they found the answer.

The red cloak draped across an abandoned fountain like a river of blood. The Enchantress was moaning in pain as she curled her body around a little black book.

Una looked around. Alethia was nowhere in sight. Indy tugged on her arm. She could tell he wanted her to sneak back the way they had come. But Una's eyes were fixed on the Red Enchantress. Almost without thinking, she took three steps toward the woman, and then the decision was made. The Enchantress heard her, looked up, and their eyes met.

Una wasn't sure what she had expected to see. An old hag, perhaps. Not the beautiful face in front of her. Not the mouth curved in a little O of surprise.

"Come here," the Enchantress said. The world swirled in on itself, and everything narrowed to a point as if to mark that moment in time. Indy's voice calling her name was cut short. The numbness in her fingers disappeared. The wet snow stopped falling. The sound that might have been someone crying out was silenced.

It was as though Una and the Enchantress were alone in the world.

"Come here," she said again, and Una found herself

unable to object. The voice drew her on, and Una wanted nothing more than to be near her.

Una went up next to her, close enough to touch, and then she stopped. "Are you wounded?" The words felt strange in her mouth.

The Enchantress's eyes shone wetly and her voice was soft. "Una." She held Una's gaze for what felt like a long time; then she set her mouth in a thin line and looked away. She held up the battered black book. "Take it," she whispered. "It belongs to you as well. I must rest."

Una took the book, and despite her longing to obey the woman immediately, she didn't open it right away. Instead she stared at the woman's face. She had the inexplicable desire to lie down next to her, but the weight of the book in her hands drew her away. The cover was battered, as though someone had bent the pages back. One moment she was studying the book, and the next her fingers had opened it.

There was no spinning sensation, no queasiness like before. Instead the cream pages of the book shimmered like cut glass. For a minute she saw the outline of her own reflection. Then she was looking at a great forest. Everything was crystal clear, as real as life, as though she could reach out and touch the leaves on the nearest branch. A figure dressed all in black knelt before a redwood. The broad trunk stretched up out of sight, its uppermost branches green against a very blue sky. Flowing from the tree was a midnight river, and it was this which occupied the kneeling man. He glanced over one shoulder and bent back to his task. His hands were outstretched, and the dark water coiled up out of its stream into thick bands that looked like inky rope. The man deftly wove them into a long cord, and with each twist, less flowed from the tree. Before long, all that remained was a bed of smudged rocks.

He set the ink-rope down on a nearby stone, calling into the forest, "Duessa. They will come now. Weave your protections."

The woman who emerged from the trees had pulled her dark hair back from her face. Even though her lovely form was clad all in white, Una recognized her as the Red Enchantress.

She stood before the man, murmuring words Una didn't recognize, and spiderwebs of flame appeared in the air around him. His face glowed for a moment before they faded into his skin.

"Call the others," the man said. "It is time."

Duessa had barely disappeared into the trees, when a bright light filled the clearing. When the light melted away, the forest was crowded with people. An army clad all in silver stretched into the trees' shadows, and the tallest warriors stepped forward. Each was robed in an iridescent cloak, and they stood shoulder to shoulder, forming a line in front of the others.

"Fidelus," one of them said. The voice was not loud, but it echoed throughout the woods.

The man in black spun around and drew his sword. Una knew in that instant who she was seeing. That man who had woven the ink was her father. The Enemy. She peered hungrily at his face, looking for any resemblance. His chin, perhaps, was the same as hers. The shape of his ears, the way they fit so snug against his head.

"Father?" she whispered, but the man didn't even flinch. She said it louder, and the word filled her mouth, but none of the figures in the clearing looked in her direction. It was as she thought: they couldn't hear her.

"Fidelus. Do not do this." The figure drew back her hood, and Una saw that it was Alethia, although she looked different, younger somehow, and softer.

"Don't call me that," Una's father hissed. "That is no longer my name."

"Fidelus," Alethia said, "the legend must be fulfilled. The Age of the Muses has come to an end. The Age of the King will begin. Do not be afraid."

One of the other Muses, for Una knew that it must be all the Muses who had come to confront her father, took a step toward Fidelus. Her voice was soft and full of pity. "Brother, this is not the way. Join us. Celebrate the good of our reign and let us pass into a new Tale in peace. You—"

One of the men interrupted her. "It is true, Fidelus," he said excitedly. "We are to have our own Tales written for us. And the King himself will do it when he returns."

"Spero, you are a fool." Fidelus spat on the ground in front of the others. "The *good of our reign*, Clementia? Our reign doesn't have to end! Why should we be characters within a Tale when we can be gods and goddesses over Story itself?" He whipped the cord of ink high above his head. "The ink is here. It is ours for the taking."

"Fidelus, no!" One of his brothers unsheathed his sword. "What you say is untruth! We are only servants.

And our charge is to wait for the King's return. This is not the way to fulfill our oaths. This is not the way to serve."

"I am done with serving." Fidelus leaped up onto the stone and held his sword high, and Duessa appeared behind him, leading a host of warriors. They charged toward the line of Muses with a triumphant war cry. "Kill the WIs first," Fidelus commanded.

Then he gave Alethia a mocking smile. "Will you still keep your Servant's Oath? Will you protect the characters even if it means they slay your own WIs?"

"Yours is a black heart, brother," she hissed. "That you would turn them against us." To the others she called, "Remember our oaths. Do them no harm!"

A great shout rose up from the army who had come with the Muses, but it had scarcely left their lips when a web of lightning flew from Fidelus's fingers, and they all fell down dead. Fidelus laughed as the smoke from his spell hovered over their bodies. "I am tired of writing happy endings for foolish characters. These chose unwisely."

The Muses' cries of horror turned into shouts for justice.

"Oathbreaker!" Spero drew his sword and pointed it

at Fidelus. "You have killed innocents."

But before he could do more, Duessa's forces
surrounded him. Everywhere Una looked, the Enemy's
army was attacking the Muses. The air was filled with
clanging metal and the cries of angry characters. But
the Muses were not fighting back. They deflected the
blows and deftly wove glimmering bonds that wrapped
around their attackers. And none of their opponents
were harmed.

But they had sworn no such oath of protection
toward their treacherous brother. The clearing was
filled with light as balls of fire in every shade launched
toward Fidelus. Yet he remained untouched. With an
awful laugh, he clutched the cord he had made in both
hands and began to suck the ink out of it like some
great serpent gulping its prey.

There was a moment when one of his brothers
almost reached him, but Duessa blocked the way, her
sword moving faster than Una could see. The battle
raged around the fallen corpses of those Fidelus had
killed, and Una's heart grew heavy with the weight
of it. She watched in horror as the cord of ink grew
lighter and lighter. It didn't matter that the Muses
were making headway, that most of their opponents
were now bound in the harmless shining ropes and lay

snoring on the forest floor. It was too late. Fidelus had consumed all the ink, and an unearthly gong echoed through the woods.

Una could sense the change in the air, the wind when there shouldn't have been wind. Duessa dropped her sword, fear written plainly on her face. The rest of her warriors saw this and froze. It was as though the whole world was watching as a blast of dust and ashes rushed into the clearing. Una couldn't see anything after that, and the screams from within the cloud turned her blood cold. Finally, she could make out shapes again, and, when the air cleared enough to see, Duessa and her army were gone. The corpses had vanished. The warriors the Muses had bound lay sleeping on the forest floor. The Muses themselves were untouched, but a pillar of black fire whirled unceasingly where Fidelus had been standing.

The unnatural inferno swept around and around, whipping the flames in wide circles with a loud, rushing wind. The column grew higher and then shot up out of sight with a deafening roar. The stone was empty. Una's father was gone.

"Farewell, Fidelus," Alethia said as she led the other Muses over to the stone.

One of his brothers, the one who had first drawn his

sword, bent down and picked up the small black book that lay there. "He has broken his oaths, and his own words have come to bind him." He smoothed the black cover. "A prison of his own making."

Two of the Muses were crying, but the others stood with unreadable faces and said nothing.

"Sophia," Alethia finally said as she touched the book gingerly. "How long will he be bound?"

Sophia's ageless face turned toward the slumberers. "First, we must tend to the characters." She bent over the nearest one. "It is as I thought," she murmured. "They are under the spell of evil, and do not know what they've done." Gently, the Muses undid the shimmering ropes. One by one they disarmed the characters, who cried out in confusion and fear once they were freed from Duessa's enchantments. The Muses spoke gently to them as if they were young children and told them not to be afraid. "Let this be but a dream to you," Alethia said, making a strange symbol on the forehead of each character before she sent them back to their homes to live in peace.

When the Muses were alone, Sophia took the book from her brother. "Fidelus's prison. His oaths bound him even when his will failed him. One of us could open the book and free him." She eyed the others. "But I fear his heart is filled with evil."

One of the Muses who had been crying wiped her eyes and said in a hard voice, "He killed our WIs. They had no chance."

"*You* are condemning him, Clementia?" another asked. He sounded surprised. "You will not plead on his behalf?"

Clementia set her mouth in a grim line. "I plead on behalf of the innocents he killed, Virtus. Their blood cries out for justice."

Virtus strode over to Sophia. He took the book from her hands. "Then we are agreed. We will keep him bound and, when the King returns, we will deliver Fidelus over to him for judgment." With a tremendous cry, he ripped a fistful of pages from the binding and then another. A cloud of smoke glimmered with each tear. Soon, the volume was rent into six small books, and Virtus gave one to each of the other Muses. "There. If our wills weaken, and we long to free him, none of us can do it without the agreement of the others. Only when his book is whole can one of his blood free him."

The solemn moment was broken by a sound like a whimpering kitten. Clementia shot out of the clearing and returned in an instant, cradling a tiny babe.

One of the Muses took the baby in his arms and held it close. "Duessa loved Fidelus." The baby's cries turned to soft mewls. "And he her. Another promise Fidelus could not keep."

As Una watched, the Muses passed the baby around, each one greeting it in a different way. Virtus bowed low and spoke an indecipherable blessing. Clementia crooned a soft lullaby. Alethia whispered into the infant's ear. Spero tickled the dimpled chin and laughed with delight. Sophia studied the infant's face with such an expression of goodwill that Una's heart trembled.

"A daughter," Sophia finally said. "Fidelus has a daughter."

Una felt warmth steal over her, from her head to her toes, and her eyes filled. She reached out a hand, but her fingers only met the surface of the book. The horror of the battle she had just witnessed melted at the scene of her family. She wanted time to stand still, wanted to replay the moments that were speeding by on the page in front of her. It was as though the thorn in her heart, left there from all her past hurts, had finally been removed. The image in front of her blurred with her tears. *Alethia told the truth. I am from this world.*

The joy she had felt the moment before froze back into solid ice. *Alethia told the truth.* Fidelus was her father. The ruthless Enemy who had killed so many without mercy. The Oathbreaker with the heart full of evil. And her mother? Duessa. *The Red Enchantress.*

The Muses seemed to realize the same thing. "She cannot stay in Story," Virtus said.

"But if she lived with one of us?" Clementia held the swaddled baby close. "There would be no danger in that."

"For one such as her? Half Muse, half character? Even so, would you force another's will and make her choices for her? Then you would become like Fidelus," Alethia said firmly. "I want her to stay, too. She is our own flesh and blood. But it's not safe. For her or for Story. What if she became like her mother?"

Sophia sounded unwilling. "Hasty decisions are not the best ones. But you speak the truth, Alethia. And we must think of her happiness. What would it be like to grow up in Story, the daughter of the Enemy and the Enchantress?"

"We must Write her Out," the Muse who had been silent said. "She has his blood. When one of his blood opens the book, Fidelus will be free." For a moment, it seemed as though he looked straight through the pages at Una. She couldn't be sure, because the scene around her wavered, and then Una found herself staring into her own horrified violet eyes. The Muse's words echoed in her head. *When one of his blood opens the book.* She dropped the book as though burned, and it lay in the abandoned fountain of Alethia's garden. The winter air came back with a vengeance, and Una sat shivering in her snow-soaked cloak. The Red Enchantress was gone.

The next instant Alethia came around the garden corner. She looked older than she had in the book, though her skin was still smooth and fair. Her forehead creased with concern. "Una! Are you hurt?"

Una felt a strange mixture of delight and anger at the sight of Alethia. The happy thought of Alethia whispering gentle secrets to her as a baby mixed in with her own anger at all the unanswered questions. "You didn't want me to stay in Story," Una blurted. Perhaps the Tale she had seen was wrong. Maybe the Enemy wasn't really escaping. She felt a small stirring of hope. Or maybe they didn't share the same blood after all.

Alethia took Una's hand in her own, and feeling

returned to Una's fingertips. "I am the one who wrote the words that put you into another land, another place and another time. It was an old enchantment, one we ought not to have done, that Wrote you Out. We did it to keep you safe." Alethia stopped and looked at Una. There was sadness in her eyes. And regret. "But it was at great cost. To Write someone Out of Story goes against all the magic of the land. Our enchantment turned on us, and the moment you were Written Out, we became trapped in our own Muse books, imprisoned until someone could find our books and release us. We thought someone would come. . . ." She trailed off, a furrow creasing her white brow.

Una barked a laugh, and her mouth twisted around the words. "Fidelus hid your books. Long before." She told Alethia what Archimago had said about hiding Virtus's book. "That's why no one has come to you." She thought of Elton and his beasts. "Though some are desperate to find your book, even now, but I can't think why they'd want to release you."

"If he can destroy my book," Alethia said after she heard Una's account of her fight with Elton in the garden, "he will have power over me. It's what Duessa has done with my brothers and sisters. I am the last."

Alethia shook her head. "I'm sorry we have failed you." A tear slowly trickled down her flawless skin. "We have failed you all."

Una's whole body felt numb. With each new revelation, her heart despaired. There was no hope for her. *There never had been.* "Then why did you bring me here? Why didn't you just leave me back there?" Back where she was safe.

Alethia turned to face her. "Una, I didn't Write you back In to Story," she said simply.

Una let this sink in. Then she forced the words out, sounding braver than she felt. "Then who did? The Enemy?"

Alethia's voice grew grave. "Oh no, my dear. Oh no. You would definitely know if he had Written you In." She gave a bitter laugh.

Una chewed her lip. The truth was very close now. "But who Wrote me In? And Why?" Her voice felt very small as she said, "And now that I'm here, what am I to do?"

Alethia stood, straight and beautiful before Una, all traces of tears gone. She looked more like a warrior than a woman. "Fight. Stand against the purposes of the Enemy. Someone Wrote you In, and you will find out who in the fullness of time. For now, it is enough to know that you have been Written In during Story's darkest hour. You and I alone stand between Duessa and the Enemy's return. She means for one of us to open his book." She adjusted her cloak about her shoulders and looked Una straight in the eye. "A great battle is coming, Una. A battle between good and evil. A battle for Story. But will you be ready to fight?"

At her words Una's courage failed. She looked with shame-filled eyes at Fidelus's book.

"Duessa already gave it to you!" Alethia gasped. "She is more clever than I thought." The sky around them was turning gray mixed with an eerie yellow, and a horrible screeching sound filled the air. "We have no time." Alethia yanked Una to her feet. "You must leave. He has found us."

Una tore her gaze away from the book. "What?"

"The Enemy is here."

Una felt like throwing up. "The Red Enchantress—" she began.

"Will go to him." Alethia pulled hard on Una's arm. "We must fly."

"I saw what happened," Una said in a small voice. "I saw what my father did. What he was."

Alethia looked at Una with compassionate eyes. "My poor child. How this will grieve you."

But the moment didn't last long, and soon Una found herself propelled back inside Alethia's house.

"Endeavor!" Alethia called sharply. "Where are you?" Indy appeared from the next room, Horace leaning against him and sleeping soundly. Alethia swirled the air over his head. "When he is out of the exam, he will wake," she said to Indy. "This will be as a dream to him. Perhaps his heart can yet be turned away from Duessa's schemes." Then she turned to Una. "Our time is short. The Enemy draws near. The servant will take you as far as the entrance to my home. Return to your academy. You will be safe there for a while."

A bolt of lightning exploded somewhere nearby, and the glaring light hurt Una's eyes. Loud thunder followed almost instantly.

"There is no time!" Alethia spoke in a harsh whisper. "You must hurry. Go! Now! We will meet again." She pushed Una and Indy before her down the narrow hallway. At the front door, the servant waited, his brown cloak pulled close around him.

Una turned to thank Alethia, but she was gone. All the lights in the lower level were out, the homey cottage empty and lifeless.

"This way," the servant whispered, hoisting Horace up onto his back as though he weighed nothing. "Be silent."

Indy and Una followed the brown-cloaked form out of the cottage and across the clearing. She wanted to ask the servant about the Enemy. But Indy was with them. And there was no way she wanted Indy to know that she had freed her father, the Enemy.

The storm was upon them. Bolts of lightning tore the sky, and peals of thunder echoed in her ears. Una ducked instinctively, clutching Indy's hand tightly in her own, eyes wide with fear. Never had she seen a storm like this. The thunder rolled on, deep and threatening, and above it all Una could hear the terrible sound of a man laughing. She clapped her hands over her ears, darting wild-eyed looks at Indy. He was staring straight ahead, mouth set firmly, gaze fixed on Horace's lumpy form, but he flinched at the sound of the otherworldly laughter.

They were in the woods now. The shelter of the trees gave Una courage, and she stopped cowering. She stood straighter and squinted her eyes against the powerful wind.

The wildflowers they had seen earlier tossed about, and some tore from their stalks, their delicate blossoms whipping through the stormy air. The petals mixed with a driving hail, giving Una the surreal feeling that she was on some unearthly planet that hailed buttercups and stormed hyacinths. The thunder was softer now, and Una couldn't hear the wild laughing anymore. Was Alethia safe? Where had she gone? The hail stopped, and only the fragrance of crushed flowers filled the air. The servant in front of them paused. "This is the place," he said, setting Horace on the ground. He gave Indy a new book and said, "This will take you back." Then he turned to go.

"You're leaving?" Una reached out for his cloak. "Don't leave me. Please." The last came out in a desperate whisper. She still had so many questions.

"I must return to Lady Alethia." He stepped quickly away, out of her reach, and disappeared back the way they had come.

Una gave a little cry of loss and started to follow him.

Indy grabbed her elbow and pulled her back. "Una!" he said. "We must leave!" He tucked her arm inside his own. Una wondered if he had talked to Alethia. *Does he know I'm the Enemy's daughter?* She was afraid to meet his gaze. She was afraid of what she might find there. When she finally braved a peek, she saw that he wasn't even looking at her. His eyebrows were drawn close in concentration as he traced the cover of the book.

Suddenly, Una felt nauseous and knew that, in the next moment, she was going to vomit all over Indy, all over Horace, all over the book. She tugged her arm fruitlessly, trying to break free from Indy, and looked back over her shoulder. A lightning bolt shot down from the sky not ten paces away. Her stomach was rolling. Everything was a shower of bright lights and pain. Her vision cleared, and she saw the form of a man standing in the smoking crater left by the lightning. She couldn't make out his features. His face was covered in shadow. His black cloak sat unnaturally still in the wind. All of Una's breath went out of her. Her mouth was dry, and she couldn't speak, couldn't run, couldn't breathe.

The man was moving toward them. She pulled weakly at Indy's sleeve, but he didn't even notice. He was still working away at the little book. Una tried to speak. Tried to form the words. Tried to call for help. Her feet were rooted to the ground. The shadow came steadily onward, a low, terrible laugh growing as he drew near.

"How long I've waited." His voice was gravelly, like it hadn't often been used, and Una felt all her will to run melt away. "So long," he said, and stretched out his arm. Closer and closer he moved.

It was as though there was a rope around her waist, drawing her toward the man. *To my father.* Somehow, she loosed her arm from Indy's. Somehow she was stumbling toward the shadow. Her hands were outstretched. Then, a flash of lightning, another blinding moment, another second of mind-numbing pain. Lady Alethia was there, a terrible thing in her beauty, arrayed for battle and standing between Una and her father.

Go back, her eyes of blue ice commanded Una. Una froze, looking beyond Alethia to the man of shadows. She couldn't see him, but she felt him there, wordlessly calling her to himself. She took one more step, and Alethia drew her sword.

"Una. Go back," she said, and Una stopped. She turned and saw Indy standing behind her, face cast down, fingers tracing the pattern, the air around him shivering oddly. Una felt torn, like a shred of fabric that was frayed on every edge. In the next moment, Alethia's servant was at her side. He grabbed her arm and roughly pushed her into Indy. She clutched Indy's cloak as the world wavered. Beyond, in a great clash of

color, Lady Alethia was fighting, bright light battling
with shifting shadow. Then everything disappeared,
the scene in front of them dissolving into blackness,
the familiar whirling at her stomach, the soft thud of
their bodies hitting the forest floor.

Chapter 36

Una and Indy lay on the Tale station floor, enveloped in the quiet of the place. They didn't talk about Alethia's house. Or the dreadful storm. They had come to in a heap, limbs tangled together, both exhausted from their flight. The only sound was Horace's snores, drifting across the stone platform.

It was a long time before Indy sat up. "We should go, Una," he said.

"Where?"

"To the examiners. They will have read what happened. Professor Edenberry. Thornhill. There are others who will help us."

Una stayed on her back and looked over at him. "Our exam isn't being read," she said hollowly. "Elton told me." She began to laugh, a dry mirthless sound that echoed throughout the chamber. "Who is going to believe us, anyway? What are we going to tell them— that we saw the Muse Alethia? That the Enemy they've never heard of has returned?"

Indy looked defeated for a moment as he registered this information. "It doesn't matter about the examiners. We'll go to the Resistance. Find Peter and his parents." He swallowed. "My father."

"You're right," Una said. Hope rose within her and raised her to her feet. "We're not altogether alone, are we?"

"Not alone at all." Indy clasped her hand. Una felt braver with her hand in his, braver to know that she wasn't by herself, that there were others who would help her. She took a deep breath, gathered her courage, and together they stepped out into the light.

TO BE CONTINUED . . .

ACKNOWLEDGMENTS

Laura Langlie, for graciously guiding me through every step of the process, for never giving up on Una, and for being such a kind and available lifeline for a first-time author. My deepest appreciation. I am so glad to be working with you.

Erica Sussman, for your unfailing investment in Una, for your fabulous insight into the story, and for your willingness to help me revise, brainstorm, and revise some more. Many thanks. I couldn't have dreamed up an editor like you.

Tyler Infinger and all the others at HarperCollins Children's whom I know only by the fruit of your hard work, for the gorgeous art design, the brilliant copy editing, and all the other behind-the-scenes work that sent this project out into the hands of readers. Thank you. Thank you. Thank you.

The brave souls who read very early drafts of this book and offered encouragement and input: Emerson, Greg and Victoria, Meg, the entire Gentry crew, Theodore, Beth, Anne Tyler, Ashleigh, and Kate. Bless you! Your kind words energized and challenged me.

To Casey, for sharing every step of the process with us, for cheerfully enduring many rambling writing-related rants, and for everything else, so glad we're friends. And to Christy, for the marathon brainstorming sessions, the speed-reading of drafts, and the writerly encouragement. I owe you an unending supply of pumpkin spice lattes.

The Hopefuls, for your companionship in the writing world, for sharing your stories, and for all the virtual empathy. Cheers! A toast for all our books.

Mr. Hazel and Ms. Baker, for your tireless commitment to high school English students. I've often thought of your instructions to make every sentence count and your advice to keep writing. Thank you.

My mom, dad, and Ben, for the immeasurable love and support you've given me over the years, for fostering a love of reading and writing in our family, and for the countless words of encouragement and babysitting hours. Words are not enough. And to Jon and Kim, for your enthusiasm for anything writing-related and your belief that this book is a rock star. A thousand thanks.

My boys, for loving stories and for loving me. I'm so glad you're ours!

Aaron, for everything. I love you.

STORY'S END

Una Fairchild rolled the freshly printed broadside into a tight scroll, tied a piece of twine around the center, and added it to the growing stack of parchment that was the result of an afternoon's hard work. They needed to grow the Resistance. Fast.

Una and Peter were preparing the broadsides for delivery, while the grown-ups worked a giant old-fashioned printing press on the other side of the Merriweathers' barn. Una had amassed quite a stack of notices. Peter, on the other hand, had barely touched the pile of parchment in front of him. He was busy recounting yet again his battle with the beasts Gog and Magog. Una was sick of hearing how brave Peter had been, but she didn't tell him to stop, mostly because if Peter's brothers were busy listening to him, they wouldn't pester her with unwanted questions.

The previous days had been filled with many heated conversations. The Sacred Order of the Servants of the King thought that the broadside should be all about the long-lost King, whereas the Resistance members were sure that they should focus on overthrowing the Talekeeper regime. They might have argued about it forever, but the imminence of the Enemy's return forced the two groups into a prickly truce, and the one conclusion the now-united Resistance had agreed upon was that they needed to share the true Backstory with the rest of Story's characters and motivate them to fight against Fidelus.

Una laid another stack of papers flat on the bale of hay next to her and winced at Peter's unpleasantly authentic description of the way his blade cut through the dying beast.

"You're a hero," Bastian said breathlessly. "My own brother, the hero."

Peter shook his head. "Sam's the hero," he said, without any of the bluster of his storytelling. "You should have seen him."

Una looked down at the cat, asleep in her lap. *Poor, brave Sam.* Una had tried to hide her shock when she had first seen him at the Healer's. One silken ear was now torn, and his beautiful coat was spotted with holes where chunks of fur had been ripped out. Una cuddled him closer. *He did this to save me.*

Sam's whiskers twitched, and Una scratched the spot under his chin, coaxing forth a deep, throaty purr. Everything had seemed like the continuation of some awful nightmare since she and Indy had returned. Their breathless escape out of the examination. The chaos in the Tale station. The man who stood on a bench and kept saying, over and over, "Crisis Code. Please proceed to the exits in an orderly fashion," until the masses surged around him, and his warning was drowned by the flow of people.

The Resistance wanted to know every detail about the Red Enchantress and what she had said to Alethia. The Sacred Order of the Servants of the King kept making Una retell the bit where the Enemy gulped down the ink. And the kids wanted to know about the fight with Tale Master Elton. Una was tired of trying to keep her story straight. She had the distinct impression that if anyone questioned her too much, she might crack like an egg, spilling her secret all over the place.

What would they all say if they knew that the Enemy was Una's father? And Duessa her mother? *No one can know.*